Julie Kramer is a freelance television news producer for NBC's *Today show*, *Nightly News* and *Dateline*. Prior to that, she was a national award-winning investigative producer for WCCO-TV in Minneapolis. She lives in White Bear Lake, Minnesota, with her husband and sons.

For more information about Julie visit www.juliekramerbooks.com

Also by Julie Kramer:

Stalking Susan

Missing Mark

Julie Kramer

piatkus

PIATKUS

First published in the US in 2009 by Doubleday,
An imprint of The Doubleday Publishing Group,
A division of Random House, Inc., New York
First published in Great Britain as a paperback original in 2010 by Piatkus

A CIP catalogue record for this book
is available from the British Library.

ISBN 978-0-7499-4248-9

Typeset in Sabon MT by Palimpsest Book Production Limited,
Grangemouth, Stirlingshire
Printed and bound in Great Britain by Clays Ltd, St Ives plc

Papers used by Piatkus are natural, renewable and recyclable
products sourced from well-managed forests and certified
in accordance with the rules of the Forest Stewardship Council.

Mixed Sources
Product group from well-managed
forests and other controlled sources
www.fsc.org Cert no. SGS-COC-004081
© 1996 Forest Stewardship Council
FSC

Piatkus
An imprint of
Little, Brown Book Group
100 Victoria Embankment
London EC4Y 0DY

An Hachette UK Company
www.hachette.co.uk

www.piatkus.co.uk

TO JOE,
LOVE OF MY LIFE

# PRELUDE

The bride wept—not from happiness.

She threw her bouquet—in the garbage. The bridesmaids looked helpless. The groomsmen looked sheepish. The mother of the groom looked like she'd rather be anywhere else. Finally, the minister made the announcement to the three hundred waiting guests.

Then the mother of the bride unzipped her daughter's gown and drove her home.

CHAPTER 1

My past sold quickly, despite the down market.

Of course, no one actually died under my roof. Just a couple of near-miss murders that my real estate agent assured me didn't need to be disclosed to potential buyers.

But now I needed to move fast and she promised me this was the place. "I have a feeling about you and this remodeled bungalow," Jan Meyer said. "The owner is anxious to leave town and just dropped the price twenty grand."

Jan enjoyed playing matchmaker between buyer and seller. Especially since she knew I'd made a killing on my own real estate deal and had plenty of cash to put down. So she took the key out of the lockbox and prepared to give me the tour.

"You might just fall in love with the kitchen," she said.

Not love at first smell. The house had a definite odor. And it didn't seem to be coming from the kitchen.

While Jan went to open some windows, I followed my nose to a closed door where the smell seemed strongest.

Journalists prefer open doors. So I turned the knob and peeked inside. Then quickly slammed it shut before any flies could escape.

"What is that horrible smell?" Jan asked.

"I think it might be the owner."

"Is he dead?" she gasped.

I nodded as I headed back outside to call the police from my cell phone.

"Did he have a heart attack?" Jan followed behind, anxious for details.

"In a manner of speaking."

I hadn't gotten close to the man on the floor. But I could see the congealed pool of blood around his body and the knife sticking out of his chest.

That's when I decided to keep renting.

CHAPTER 2

Some days I wish I could just write about sweaters. After all, sweaters never hurt anyone. And no reporter ever got kidnapped, blindfolded, and paraded in front of Al Jazeera's audience for writing for *Vogue*. Of course, no sweater ever got a gold-medal 40 share in TV ratings either. Except perhaps Kathleen Sullivan's figure-hugging crew necks during the Winter Olympics in Sarajevo.

Sweaters are the mashed potatoes and gravy of a woman's wardrobe—the ultimate comfort clothing—unless gravy accidentally drips onto a pricey cashmere. But I was nowhere near the kitchen, so I could safely curl up in a hand-knit sweater of scratchy wool looking out an upstairs window at a narrow view of White Bear Lake. I don't actually live on the lake, but if I angle my chair and crane my neck just right, I can watch the whitecaps and fishermen on the legendary water.

I'm Riley Spartz, an investigative reporter for Channel 3 in Minneapolis. Close to five months ago I fled my highly sought-after urban neighborhood for a fresh start after a TV sweeps story went bad. Lakeshore homes in this northern Twin Cities suburb go for a million bucks plus, but the rest of the town is quite affordable.

My landlord recently moved out, listing this place for rent because his next-door neighbor held perpetual yard sales that attracted traffic at annoying times. Always looking for a bargain, I'd even checked out the inventory myself, but found only overpriced junk.

Today I paged through the weekly *White Bear Press*, delighted by irksome crimes that wouldn't merit a mention on a major-market TV newscast. Nothing makes a woman living alone feel safer than reading police reports about teens caught smoking behind the school and bicycles stolen from open garages.

A want ad for an item I definitely wasn't looking to buy caught my eye and my imagination.

FOR SALE: WEDDING DRESS. NEVER WORN

Mystery and emotion, all in one line.

Forget sweaters. A wedding dress is much more likely to garner a 40 share. Viewers love weddings. The research proves it.

In the world of television ratings, two weddings stand out. And both brides would probably have been happier if their wedding dresses had never been worn.

In 1969, when Miss Vicki married Tiny Tim on *The Tonight Show Starring Johnny Carson*, 45 million viewers made that episode the highest rated in talk-show history.

That was nothing compared to the wedding of the century. A dozen years later 750 million viewers worldwide watched as Prince Charles and Lady Diana promised to forsake all others. That royal wedding delivered royal ratings, but ultimately royal scandal. The bride and groom learned (as I reluctantly learned from my own brief marriage) no "I do" guarantees happily ever after.

When it comes to TV weddings, happiness and ratings may be mutually exclusive. While Prince Charles's sequel ceremony to Camilla Parker Bowles tanked in the ratings department, the marriage seems to be thriving in the happiness arena.

Now TV weddings are typically interactive events, like the *Today* show where viewers choose gowns, cakes, rings and honeymoon destinations for the happy couple, or reality shows, like *The Bachelor*, in which grooms propose marriage before our voyeuristic eyes.

I circled the "Never Worn" want ad with a red pen and pondered whether the story behind the wedding dress might be worth a television news story.

Perhaps a lesson about love and loss, if I could sort through the he said/she said of a broken engagement. Was the big day called off because of a tragic parachuting accident? A philandering groom caught with a bridesmaid after the rehearsal dinner? Or perhaps a wedding guest revealed a juicy secret when the minister inquired whether anyone knew any reason why this man and this woman should not be joined in holy matrimony.

Doubtful that the truth would prove as irresistible as the scenarios in my mind, but maybe the story could be a lesson about second chances if the gown made it successfully down the aisle on the back of a new bride.

As an investigative reporter, I seldom get a chance to tell love stories.

The May ratings book loomed, just on the fringe of the June wedding season. A tantalizing tale of doomed courtship might spike the overnight news numbers. The Channel 3 bosses were always anxious this time of year because the May sweeps were arguably the most important—Christmas holiday ad rates are based on those figures. Jingle all the way.

I had no blockbuster investigation up my sweater sleeve this sweeps. I'd sat out the February ratings book because I was a mess personally and the November book remained an unpleasant reminder of my blood, sweat, and tears.

My hypothetical wedding-dress chronicle was unlikely to require a major investment of time or money, so if the back-story was compelling, Channel 3's news director, Noreen Banks, would probably give me a green light. Another reason: we had a mandate from the suits upstairs to attract more women viewers because advertisers think they control the household cash.

In May, Minnesota ladies also control the TV remote, because fishing season opens and their menfolk flock to boats like ducks to water. Noreen might certainly seize this wedding-dress opportunity to throw the big bosses upstairs a bouquet . . . I mean a bone.

So I reached for the phone to dial the number in the "Never Worn" newspaper ad to find out who dumped who.

"YOU LOOK BEAUTIFUL," Madeline Post said as I twirled this way and that in front of a full-length mirror in her little-girl-pink bedroom.

I hadn't intended to try on the gown. But when she insisted, it did occur to me that it would be harder for Madeline to kick me out the door when she learned I was a reporter if the garment was literally on my back.

The dress looked even better up close than on the e-mail fashion photo she'd sent me the previous night. The kind of dress a fairy-tale princess might wear. Satin. White. Strapless. Fitted at the waist with a ball-gown skirt that

8

flared at my hips. Interesting sparkles around the bustline. The dress accentuated my figure, decent but not voluptuous. And it contrasted nicely with my brown shoulder-skimming hair. I'd checked the designer's reputation online and knew this almost bride had spent nearly fifteen grand on her dream dress.

Not exactly. Her mother had actually written the check. Because, according to Madeline, it was her mother's dream dress.

"She wanted me to look like Cinderella," Madeline explained. "But I wanted an outdoor wedding and would have been happy wearing a sundress or even jeans."

"Why didn't you tell her?"

"The big wedding meant the world to her. Because she compromised on having the ceremony outside, I compromised on the dress. And she's done so much to raise me and my brother after our dad died."

Because I was trying to pose as someone other than a reporter—a self-absorbed bride, in fact—I didn't follow up on that nugget, though I was quite curious to learn more about her father's death.

Besides checking out Madeline's dress, I'd also checked out Madeline and her fiancé, Mark Lefevre. Or rather, I had Lee Xiong, our newsroom computer geek, check them out with a crime database he'd assembled from several law enforcement and court agencies. Xiong came to the United States as a toddler refugee from Laos. He flourished in Minnesota, despite his parents' poverty and the state's winters, and became a respected producer at Channel 3.

His cyber report showed the bride had a clean record here in the state, while the groom had been picked up on a minor marijuana possession charge a decade earlier that netted nothing more serious than a small fine and the requirement that he attend drug-education classes.

Madeline's place was not far from mine. I'd left her name, phone number, and address with Xiong along with instructions for him to call the cops if he didn't hear from me in three hours.

Normally I wouldn't have hesitated answering her ad alone, but the recent Craigslist nanny murder—in which a disturbed young man posed as a local mother in need of child care before killing the coed who answered the ad—did cross my mind and made me more cautious than usual about meeting strangers in nonpublic places.

Those precautions might not save my life, but they'd make it easier to find my body if things got ugly. And this way my parents could console themselves with the knowledge that at least they were able to give me a Decent Christian Burial. And I could console myself that at least my murder would lead the late news although I wouldn't put it past Channel 3 to bump me down to the second section just so the station had something lurid to tease at the top of the show and again at the first break to hold viewers into the second quarter hour of the newscast.

I'd found Madeline and Mark's engagement announcement and photo online. At twenty-four, she was ten years younger than her fiancé. Her face pretty, not stunning. Her most noticeable feature, her splendid golden hair, long and flowing.

The first thing I observed about Mark was an odd, diagonal scar across his forehead. Not a lightning bolt like Harry Potter's, yet still mysterious in this age in which plastic surgery can fix most facial flaws. Mark's hair was dark, frizzy, and shoulder-length, and he had black Groucho Marx eyebrows and mustache.

She was beauty to his beast.

I read that he was a comedian and I wondered if that was supposed to be a joke or a euphemism for unemployed. Especially when I saw that Madeline came from M-O-N-E-Y. Big money. Old money. Trust-fund money. Her great-great-grandfather on her mother's side had been a founding partner of one of Minnesota's Fortune 500 companies—a maker of countless useful office products and industrial items most folks take for granted. Her mother was sitting on an impressive pile of family money and company stock. So when Madeline spoke of all her mother had done to raise her, well, she wasn't describing working a shift job and stretching a baked chicken over an extra meal.

Which made me mildly curious just why she was selling her never-worn wedding gown. And extremely curious why it was never worn to begin with.

"So what do you think?" Madeline asked, startling me out of my internal dialogue. "How about two thousand dollars?"

It was a steal at that price. But my bridal days were over and it was time to level with her.

"You see, Madeline," I began.

"Okay, fifteen hundred."

While she came from money, it was quite possible the young Miss Post might not have actual access to it yet, or might even have run through her share already. But she clearly wanted the dress gone. And a minute later, after I explained who I was, she wanted me gone, too.

I'm generally considered among the best-known TV reporters in the Minneapolis–St. Paul market, so I was surprised, yet pleased, when Madeline didn't recognize me right away at the door. Not everyone watches the news, I reminded myself, as she now fumed visibly.

"You're a reporter?" Madeline's voice trembled with outrage and her wide blue eyes got wider. "I thought you were interested in the dress."

"I am interested," I assured her. "I think the dress might make a great story."

"A *story*?" She threw open the door and waved me out of her condo with all the gusto I had anticipated. I turned and asked if she minded unzipping me first.

"Think of it as a free television ad," I said. "Soon as we get that dress on the late news, you'll have a bidding war."

That image stopped her. She shut the door.

"Do you think I care about the money?"

Madeline buried her face in her hands and started to cry. Tears made her engagement ring sparkle like the diamond it was—a real big one, at least two carats. Between sobs, she grabbed me like the sister I wasn't and dripped wet splotches all over the expensive satin dress that still clung to my figure.

I generally don't like people I don't know touching me. But I didn't say anything because I sensed Madeline's embrace meant she would soon share her deepest secret.

CHAPTER 3

I was meandering my car through a spaghetti of freeway construction on my way back to the station when the assignment desk called to direct me toward University Avenue near the state Capitol. Just a mile away, I got the word, "Officer down, shots fired."

Officer down.

I pushed a flashback from my mind of a cop and husband—mine—who didn't get out alive when a building exploded. I no longer wore Hugh Boyer's ring on my finger, but he remained in my heart and on my mind, especially when I heard news of any cop in danger on the job.

I wasn't the first reporter at this crime scene, but I also wasn't the last. A middle-aged gawker across the street from the yellow police tape told me an ambulance had left less than ten minutes ago.

"Lights? Siren?" I asked.

"Full speed," he said. "Flashing and screaming."

That was good news. If no ambulance was called, that was a bad sign. If the ambulance left the scene with no commotion, that was also a bad sign. Both scenarios would suggest that the victim was already dead and everyone was waiting for the medical examiner. That the ambulance seemed to be racing death suggested the officer was still alive, the race still winnable.

Three television cameras were on sticks, photographers shooting the aftermath of the crime. Luckily, one of the cameras was ours. At least I'd have video to go with my live shot. Now I needed facts.

I hadn't worked with this particular cameraman before. Adam Treguboff had joined the Channel 3 news team a couple of months ago, just before I rejoined the newsroom. I'd been fired for insubordination last fall (according to my personnel file) but then wooed back (according to my paycheck). He once offered to buy me a drink, just because we were both new. I knew a line when I heard one, so I corrected him on two levels: I wasn't new and I wasn't inter-ested, even though he had nice shoulders—a physical trait mandatory for hoisting a broadcast camera to eye level at short notice.

According to the calendar, as well as my body clock, I'd slept alone 674 nights. Yes, I wanted to end my no-sex dry spell, but when I did, it wasn't going to be with a source or a news colleague. I knew better.

Tonight, at the scene of breaking news, Treguboff help-fully pointed to a St. Paul K-9 vehicle surrounded by other cop cars.

"Probably trying to pick up a suspect trail," I said.

"I don't think so, Riley," he answered. "Most of the action seemed to center on the K-9 car. And I have yet to see any dog."

The St. Paul police media guy indicated he'd make a statement in twenty minutes—a gift to the TV crews so we could take him live at the top of our newscast. The live trucks had their microwave dishes in the air, searching for a signal in the sky. I ducked inside the front seat to check my hair and makeup in the rearview mirror. Blush, powder, lipstick. Not perfect, but a good enough touch-up until the station switches to high-definition next year, revealing every facial flaw.

A second Channel 3 crew had been dispatched to Regions Medical Center for updates on the officer's condition. But so far the doctors weren't talking, and the victim's family was sheltered in a back waiting room off-limits to the public and the media.

Our police reporter had just learned the identity of the injured officer even though the name had not been officially released. Cop buzz described the victim as a female K-9 officer who'd been honored recently for a major drug bust. That crew headed for her home to interview neighbors and try to obtain a photograph.

Because of intense public interest, cop shootings automatically become team reports for news organizations. The rest of the newscast is typically abandoned. Weather and sports cut short. That day's timeless feature story held for a weekend newscast.

Through my earpiece I heard our lead anchor, Tom McHale, setting up the news of the day. I picked up his toss, and from the field I filled time with details about tension in the neighborhood as we waited for the St. Paul police public information officer to step to the microphone.

((RILEY/LIVE))
A ST. PAUL POLICE OFFICER
WAS SHOT ABOUT AN HOUR
AGO . . . FOUR BLOCKS FROM

THE STATE CAPITOL.
NO SUSPECTS ARE IN
CUSTODY . . . NO MOTIVE
HAS BEEN DETERMINED . . .
WE JOIN POLICE AT A LIVE
BRIEFING FOR THE
LATEST . . .

The cop explained that officer Emily Flying Cloud was currently undergoing surgery. She'd apparently been leaving a restaurant with her K-9 partner when she was shot from a distance. A bystander dialed 911 from his cell phone. According to a witness, her dog had snarled around the officer's fallen body and kept everyone else back until the first squad arrived.

A newspaper reporter inquired whether her dog's actions might have delayed medical attention. The public information officer dismissed that by saying first responders were on the scene in just over a minute and none of the gathering crowd was trained to render assistance anyway.

As he continued his briefing, out of the corner of my eye I noticed a large black-and-tan German shepherd straining his leash, held by a pudgy cop with a receding hairline.

Police were asking for help from the public—perhaps someone noticed something unusual prior to the shooting, perhaps a description of the assailant or a suspicious vehicle. The PIO was running out of steam and content so the producer in news control gave me a wrap in my ear, then instructed me to toss to our reporter standing by at the hospital, so he could also regurgitate what had been said minutes earlier.

I didn't hear the stunned scream from the control booth because my own scream drowned it out. When I watched the air check later, the scene would have been funny if it were happening to another reporter. Just as the camera switched from the PIO to me, and I opened my mouth to speak, I flew out of frame.

My photographer panned down to me on the ground, flat on my back, a big dog sitting on my chest, licking my face.

CHAPTER 4

I n TV news, they love ya till they don't love ya anymore. They can be the bosses. They can be the viewers. They can be the advertisers. Occasionally that love can last an entire career, but more likely by the end of a contract, a ratings book, a newscast, or even a live shot, the love is gone.

Noreen clearly loved me less at the end of tonight's newscast than at the beginning. With her jet-black hair, luminous skin, and business-chic wardrobe, she looked prettier, as well as younger, than me. I hate that combination in a boss.

She muttered something about me being "amateurish on air" a couple of hours later when I walked into her fishbowl office in the middle of the newsroom. Only glass walls separated her from her subjects. This office design cut into her privacy, but also ours.

"Another way to look at it," I responded, "is that I landed an exclusive with the partner of the wounded cop."

The big dog was Shep: a German shepherd who had been my roommate and bodyguard last fall when a serial killer

18

was tracking my investigation into dead women named Susan. Shep's attitude and performance made it clear that he was better suited to being a public servant than a household pet. He even had the scars to prove it, including a torn ear. He'd since become a legend in the police K-9 world—Minnesota's top drug-sniffing dog.

With his police partner felled by a bullet, Shep latched on to me like old times. The St. Paul cops reluctantly gave me temporary custody since he refused to go home with anyone else. Police departments don't house their K-9 troops in kennels. They live with their human partners and are trained to work only with them.

Noreen didn't actually mind Shep being in the newsroom: she was a big animal lover, and even had a dalmatian of her own named Freckles. She was the kind of news tyrant who wouldn't take shit from anybody but would pick up her pup's poop unflinchingly.

"Shep better not distract you from May," she said.

"No, he'll be a ratings attraction," I countered. "He can sit beside me for my set piece tonight at ten."

"Well, Riley," Noreen considered, "I guess there's some promotional value in that."

"Absolutely," I used my best suck-up-to-the-boss voice. "You're always telling us how viewers love animals and children."

"That is true." She nodded as if there was no disputing facts. "But your hours are so unpredictable, this can't be a long-term arrangement."

I couldn't tell if her concern was for Shep or me. Probably Shep.

"It won't be. I'll put in a call to Toby Elness. Shep likes him best."

Toby was Shep's previous owner. He had a big heart, but

19

a small house filled with an eclectic mix of dogs, cats, birds, and fish. He had noticed Shep's potential for law enforcement and had donated him to the K-9 unit. Turns out, Shep was a natural-born police dog.

"Toby's very proud of what Shep has accomplished," I continued. "I'm sure he'd enjoy a reunion with him until Officer Flying Cloud recovers."

The latest word from the hospital: she'd survived surgery. Doctors removed a nasty bullet from her lung.

The latest word from the cops: no leads on the investigation. They theorized a sniper shot her from the top of a parking garage down the block.

"As long as you're here, Riley," Noreen said, "let's talk about May sweeps."

The problem with being a television investigative reporter is sweeps. February, May, and November are major ratings months in which viewership is measured and careers made and lost. These months carry a different pressure than daily news. General-assignment reporters can knock off a story a day and count down to the weekend. For investigative reporters, each day of researching for the next blockbuster usually brings them another day closer to deadline, but still no story.

"I'd like to turn a piece on the meth cartel, Noreen. Remember?"

"I thought we already canned that."

She was referring to the dead body I'd found while house hunting. Ends up, the murder victim was a drug dealer. His buddies stopped trusting him. And in those circles, when the trust is gone, so is your life.

Channel 3 aired twenty seconds about the homicide on the early news, but Noreen had nixed my suggestion we delve deeper, calling the corpse an unsympathetic character.

20

"Viewers don't relate to murder victims with lengthy rap sheets. Bring me a dead drug dealer people will care about," she said, "then we'll talk."

Now that cold medicine containing pseudoephedrine is no longer available over the counter without identification, dealers are bringing crystal meth up from Mexico instead of making it themselves in rural Minnesota farmhouses. Crank, glass, speed, ice, zip, by whatever name it's called, the potency of methamphetamine makes it America's most addictive drug.

Visually the harm is easy to demonstrate. Addicts lose their teeth and sometimes their minds. I wanted to show meth flourishing in unexpected neighborhoods. Like the one I almost bought into.

"If I could just get some additional resources to help me on stakeout," I said, "I think it would lead somewhere."

"Not in time for May it won't," Noreen responded. "Besides surveillance-intensive investigations are hugely expensive. You don't have enough evidence to merit that kind of expenditure."

We'd be aiming to track people with eyes in the back of their heads. That meant three chase vehicles, always trading position, sometimes following in front of the target car, sometimes on parallel streets. Noreen was right about the resources required for successful surveillance.

Money stood on the front line of most story discussions these days. Across the country, television stations were losing news viewers to the Internet and still hadn't figured out how to fight back beyond cutting staff.

Channel 3's February viewership fell double digits from the previous year, but the drop couldn't be blamed on the network's leading prime-time lineup. Noreen recently balanced the newsroom budget by axing a beloved million-dollar meteorologist whose contract was up. The audience reacted by boycotting his replacement, furthering the ratings slump.

Bosses usually prefer canning off-air personnel to on-air personalities, but they can only slash so deep in that direction. Keeping newscasts on the air requires a legion of producers, directors, photographers, video editors, tape-room engineers, and others. Rumors were circulating that unless the May numbers were good, our network owners would demand our budget be trimmed another 10 percent.

And while I wistfully contemplated the days of a 40 share—the equivalent of a TV grand slam out of the ball-park—industry consultants proclaimed those news numbers gone. Only the Olympics and perhaps an *American Idol* scandal stood a chance of scoring a 40.

Under the current media meltdown, 30 was the new 40.

Newspapers were sinking even faster. The Minneapolis *Star-Tribune* and *St. Paul Pioneer Press* had cut staff with buyouts and layoffs. Both papers now seemed to be putting their energies into suburban stories they'd normally reject as too soft or too local.

"We need to turn investigations faster and cheaper." Noreen's voice had an "or else" tone. "I need more face time from you, Riley." That meant she wanted me to turn more stories—to get my face on the news more often.

"I understand," I answered, not exactly agreeing but not wanting to argue, either.

Sometimes a reporter's value is judged not just by rating points but by the quality of their work. Whether their stories create community buzz; whether they land major journalism awards.

More recently, reporter worth comes down to a basic math formula—story count. Because newsrooms are computerized, those numbers are easy to run. Simply type in a reporter's name and search through the last year's story archives . . . then call them in for a job review.

Noreen had done her math.

"Here's your story count for last year," she said, handing me a piece of paper.

I didn't need to see the number in black-and-white. I already knew I'd had a bad year by that measure. But I also knew that I had a strong finish in terms of ratings. Channel 3 had won November on my back. But I knew better than to bring that up. The previous sweeps are old news.

"I'll crash on May, Noreen," I said. "I promise."

She looked skeptical.

Large-market TV newsrooms from Miami to Phoenix to Los Angeles were slashing expensive investigative units to improve their bottom line. And just because viewership is in decline doesn't mean station owners are willing to sacrifice profits. A TV station aims for a 40 percent profit margin; a grocery store survives on 1 percent.

"Okay, Riley, I'll bite, what else do you have for May?" Noreen demanded.

Our conversation was not going well for me. Shep rubbed against my leg and gave me an idea about how to curtail the discussion.

"It's complicated, Noreen," I stalled. "And Shep needs to go outside. How about if we sit down tomorrow when we have more time?"

Noreen glanced at the clock. "How about if you just talk real fast."

So I threw out the wedding-dress story because I really didn't have much else beyond a rehashed consumer investigation about food manufacturers reducing package sizes to avoid raising prices and hoping consumers wouldn't notice.

"Let me get this straight." Noreen leaned over her desk so she could look me in the eye. "The groom vanished more than six months ago, and no one ever filed a police report?"

Hard to believe. And harder to explain.

"That's how it looks so far. I need to do more research. Everybody seemed to figure he got cold feet and would show up eventually."

"It's odd, Riley," Noreen continued, "but I'm not sure it's a news story."

"You're just saying that because the victim is a man instead of a young woman."

"I think it's a little premature to call him a victim." Noreen paused, weighing the possibility, as unpleasant as it might be, that I could be right.

"If a bride disappeared the night before her wedding, we'd be tripping over network crews," I said. "The story would be so 24-7, there'd be wall-to-wall satellite trucks."

It's a media fact. Missing women get much bigger news play than missing men. And missing white women get the biggest play of all. I knew better than to bring that up with Noreen because it's a statistic that newsroom managers are quite sensitive about. According to the FBI, more than 50,000 American adults are missing. Almost none get the household-name status of Natalee Holloway, Laci Peterson, and Chandra Levy.

"Even if something did happen to this guy," Noreen said, "we're a little late in the game."

The media, particularly 24-hour cable news networks, like to jump in early on missing person cases and ride them to their happy or unhappy endings.

Crimes that are solved immediately don't garner the ratings that an ongoing mystery does. Anytime there's a fresh tip on missing Iowa anchorwoman Jodi Huisentruit, the cameras swarm. And it's been nearly fifteen years since Jodi's red pumps were found scattered near her car after she failed to show up for her early-morning news shift.

"Any evidence of foul play with this missing groom?" Noreen pressed.

"Not so far," I answered honestly, "but I haven't looked yet. It does feel suspicious that this much time has passed."

"What does your gut tell you about the bride?"

"My gut tells me the bride thinks something real bad happened."

Madeline had sobbed, telling me her story. The dress actually had been worn, just not down the aisle. She'd waited for her betrothed, along with three hundred guests, until it became clear the nuptials were off. Because she hadn't been married in the gown, Madeline still considered it a virgin, even if she wasn't. She was selling the dress because she couldn't bear to see it hanging in her closet anymore and feared her mother would explode if she simply threw it out.

"And she'll go on camera?" Noreen asked.

"Oh yeah," I bluffed. Actually the going-on-camera part of my discussion with Madeline remained unresolved.

By that I meant that I figured there was still a fair chance of me talking her into a television interview even though she'd already rejected the idea. She wasn't opposed to Channel 3 investigating her fiancé's disappearance; she just didn't want to be included in all the lights, cameras, and action.

"Madeline wants to know what happened to Mark," I said. "She also needs to know she did everything she could to find him. Even though you're right, Noreen, it is a little late in the game."

Time is everything in a missing person case. The exception being a kidnapping for ransom. Otherwise, it's pretty much a no-brainer that the victim's family goes public right away. The more time that passes before a break, the less likely the mystery will be solved. Of course in this case, we couldn't even be sure we had a case.

"She better cry," Noreen warned.

I knew she meant the bride.

I'd done enough missing person stories to know viewers need to connect with the victim and the best way to make that happen is to show a family in pain from the limbo each new day of uncertainty brings. A single tear falling down a cheek can be more visually powerful than uncontrolled sobbing. Easier to watch, too. The former can mesmerize viewers while the latter can make an audience squirm.

Some viewers cry exploitation when an interview subject breaks down on camera. What they don't understand is that sometimes interviewees need to cry and no one else can bear to listen. Their circle of friends and family might feel uncomfortable if they get emotional and might admonish them to keep their feelings inside. Yet I've seen tears bring catharsis, even gratitude.

Journalists are allowed to reassure interviewees that it's okay if they cry; we're not allowed to tell them it's actually *better* if they cry. Because if viewers care enough about the missing person, they might call in with tips that can help the investigation.

Noreen also maintains that tears spike the overnights.

"She'll cry," I assured my boss, knowing it would be tough to get a five-minute-plus block in a May newscast otherwise.

"Hmmmm."

Noreen touched a pen to her upper lip as she contemplated a desk-calendar version of the large May strategy board—which stories were running what nights—hanging in the closed-door conference room around the corner. The board was one of the most closely guarded secrets in the newsroom; only key employees had access. This made Channel 3 less likely to be scooped by our rivals on enterprise stories.

The journalistic quality of a television news station can be judged two ways. The most obvious is how it handles the Big Story of the Day. The story everybody in town leads with. And it's pretty easy to stack up the competition and see who landed an exclusive interview or who got the money shot or who simply beat the pants off everyone else.

Less obvious, but perhaps more telling of a station's personality, is how it handles discretionary news. Those are stories it's not obligated to cover but chooses to make time for anyway.

Many nights it's insipid drivel, but occasionally a station breaks a story that brings acclaim *and* leaves viewers breathless. What's difficult for die-hard newshounds to accept, is that either option—drivel or critical acclaim—can be ratings magic.

And drivel is definitely cheaper to produce.

So Noreen waved her pen like a magic wand over the half-dozen still-empty slots in May as she silently debated whether to write down NEVER WORN, the inconclusive story of a wedding dress, a reminder of heartbreak.

She tapped a Sunday in May, always an important night because the network's blockbuster lineup leads into our newscast, giving us prime-time promotional opportunities to hold that massive audience and translate it into ratings, which translate into ad revenue.

I smiled in anticipation, welcoming the pressure, wanting to prove myself—until Noreen slammed her pen down and

27

leaned back in her chair, her arms crossed. And just like the fabled Wicked Queen ordered the huntsman to bring back the heart of Snow White, Noreen gave me my assignment.

"Show me her tears. Then we'll talk."

CHAPTER 5

had just learned another reason for pushing the wedding-dress story: Shep.

Toby was on his way out of town to an animal rights conference in California. He'd always been a sucker for a furry face, but lately he'd grown interested in the politics of animal rights. He'd only be gone two days, but we decided it would be less disruptive for Shep if he just stayed in one place, my place, until his K-9 trainer recovered enough to care for him.

So I'd stopped at a pet store and stocked up on Shep's favorite dog food, some dried pig ears, and a tennis-ball squeaky toy. Since the missing-groom story was centered in my White Bear Lake neighborhood, letting the big dog in and out of the house was easier if I was chasing clues closer to home than if I was chasing news in downtown Minneapolis or beyond.

I grabbed Malik Rahman, my favorite photographer, as well as good friend, and we drove to Madeline's place to put her on camera before she could change her mind.

Madeline lived in a waterfront condo near White Bear Beach. Several of her neighbors, mostly rich retirees, watched from their porches and patios as we followed her inside, carrying the camera gear. They may have been curious, but they were also raised to mind their own business. So no one questioned us about what we were doing or which station we were with or when this was going to run.

Madeline had debated whether or not to be interviewed. In her social circle, appearing on the news was as gauche as waving one's arms in a crowd shot at the Minnesota State Fair.

She finally agreed after I pointed out no one was looking for her missing fiancé. Not family. Not law enforcement. And frankly, the trail was cold. Years from now, if he was never found, she might wrestle with guilt and regret unless she was able to assure herself she did what she could when it mattered.

Malik lit the room to add some dramatic shadows. He draped Madeline's wedding gown over the couch, artistically panning the camera from hem to neckline. Then he hung it from a doorway and shot front to back while I tilted the dress. Photographing their engagement picture, he started tight on the couple's faces and pulled wide. For the invitation to witness the marriage he used a rack focus, first shooting blurry before bringing the image into focus with a stylish camera move.

Finally he dubbed home video from the rehearsal dinner so we'd have a copy of Madeline and Mark gazing into each others' eyes as the whole room applauded. Warm-ups to get Madeline used to us and the camera. Also, if the interview went bad and she threw us out, at least we'd have sound and pictures.

These were the last pictures ever taken of Mark. He wasn't

your cliché tall, dark, and handsome groom, but he was presentable. He wore a black shirt, gray pants, and a narrow silver tie with dark stripes. He moved comfortably through the crowd, meeting and greeting guests. His face looked a bit peculiar with his bushy eyebrows, mustache, and hair, but his manner seemed pleasant.

Again, my eyes were drawn to his scar. I wanted to ask about its origin but kept quiet, fearing I might upset the bride. Despite his odd appearance, Mark seemed a class act until he wove a mother-in-law joke into his toast to his bride, which he read off a blue note card.

It occurred to me that comedians often have distinctive physical characteristics. Fat-boy Louie Anderson. Jay Leno with his big chin and two-tone hair. David Brenner's nose. Mae West and her impressive . . . talent. The best of them use their looks to make us laugh at our own flaws, physical or not. For all I knew, Groucho Marx was Mark's professional idol.

Later I watched him wrap his hands around Madeline's waist and drop a kiss on her neck. Knowing that this might have been the final time they touched made the casual buss erotic and made me feel like an intruder.

She seemed a different Madeline on tape than the person in front of me now. I couldn't quite tell how until she flashed a smile for the camera and I recognized it as the kind of smile that could launch a toothpaste commercial. TV reporters are very cognizant of smiles and I knew Madeline had never smiled that way for me. These pictures might be the last pictures ever taken of a joyous Madeline. And Madeline's face, which I once thought was merely pretty, now looked stunning.

During the interview, I pressed her about that night, the last time she saw Mark, whether anything seemed unusual.

"With him?" she asked.

"Yes, or anybody else in the wedding party."

"No. Everybody seemed happy for us. So very excited."

"How about Mark? Is it possible he was having second thoughts?"

"No." She was adamant, closer to indignation than tears.

"How can you be so sure?" I tried coaxing some on-camera emotion. I didn't use the word "jilted" because I didn't want her to clobber me with the tape rolling.

"Because he loved me." She looked at me, unwavering confidence in her gaze and tone. "I could see it in his eyes. I could hear it in his voice. I could taste it on his lips."

That was some lyrical sound bite she laid on us. And the way she said it was almost vampirish.

As she leaned forward, I leaned back to give her space. Her fists were clenched. Her delivery flawless. "That was supposed to be our beginning, not our ending. Something's wrong."

I tried to lighten the mood by asking her how Mark proposed. She struggled to answer before emotionally describing a magical night of romance on bended knee in the moonlight.

But to my surprise, Madeline Post was too tough to cry on camera.

WHEN IT COMES to a missing person, it's often an inside job.

Sometimes the culprit is even the missing person themselves. Like the runaway bride from Georgia. Or the missing coed in Wisconsin. Both women staged their own disappearances for reasons that were never very well explained.

When a child vanishes, it's frequently a parent. Sometimes a custody dispute. Sometimes a cover-up when an abusive relationship goes too far. Occasionally an accidental death the parent can't face.

When a woman goes missing, her man moves to the head of the class of suspects. But the reverse is seldom true; girl-friends rarely become suspects. And Madeline didn't fit that category for several reasons.

First, she was allowing media scrutiny. And guilty girls don't usually do that. If she had anything to do with her fiancé's disappearance, all she had to do was keep her mouth shut and she'd be home free.

Second, as the bride, she was under almost constant observation following the rehearsal dinner. She stayed up late at her mother's house, giggling with the maid of honor. And while the groom isn't supposed to see the bride before the wedding, that tradition doesn't include the wedding party, the hair and makeup guy, the manicurist, and the photographer. Plenty of witnesses could vouch for Madeline's whereabouts. No one could vouch for Mark's.

Third, Madeline had no clear motive. Public humiliation is not on any bridal registry. She lost face when she lost her fiancé. And her mother was shelling out enormous sums of money to marry her only daughter to Mark Lefevre. So if he *wasn't* dead, Madeline probably *would* kill him.

CHAPTER 6

Without Madeline's tears on tape, my NEVER WORN story was probably dead for May. At least in Noreen's mind. But until my boss came right out and asked me how the bride's interview went, I intended to explore the case from a couple of other directions.

I left Madeline's house armed with a guest list from the wedding. As we'd gone over the names, I'd made who's who notes in the margin. Most were friends and relatives from the Post side of the family. Madeline didn't know the specifics behind all the guests on the groom's side. But she circled the names of the two people who presumably knew the bride and groom best.

THE BEST MAN was traveling on business for the Minnesota Department of Transportation so I listened to him on the speakerphone in my house while Shep explored his new surroundings. The telephone interview was a trade-off. Face-to-face I'd get a better sense of Gabriel Murray and his story. But this way, my taking notes

34

wouldn't make him nervous and I'd get answers faster.

Normally, I'd wait to meet in person, but Gabe wouldn't be back from St. Louis for a few days. He was attending a conference on concrete bridges. His state agency had been through a rough stretch ever since one of Minnesota's main bridges had collapsed during rush hour.

I knew what Gabe looked like because Mark had introduced him as his best man on the home video of the rehearsal dinner. Corporate suit and haircut. A contrast to the groom's cartoonish but affable appearance.

Gabe knew what I looked like because he watched television news. He claimed Channel 3 was his favorite, but probably just said that to all the TV stations. He agreed to discuss Mark Lefevre as long as I agreed not to bring up the bridge fiasco or press him about when the new one would be completed.

First, we chitchatted about his wife and kids and life in the suburbs. Then he recounted how, when Mark failed to show up for the wedding and didn't answer either his home or cell phone, Gabe—in his role of best man—drove the most likely route from the park in White Bear Lake, where the ceremony was supposed to take place, back to his friend's Minneapolis apartment.

During the half-hour trip, he watched for Mark's black Jeep. He didn't see it flipped over in a ditch or stalled on the side of the road. He didn't see it wedged against a tree or wrapped around a light pole. And he didn't see it parked anywhere near Mark's apartment building though he circled several blocks in each direction.

Gabe banged on Mark's door anyway, but no one answered. Finally he convinced the landlord to open the small apartment.

Empty.

"Was the bed slept in?" I asked.

"Hard to tell, what guy living alone makes his bed?" he answered. "But his tuxedo was hanging on the closet door. So if he was heading to the altar, he was underdressed."

"Did you notice the clothes he wore at the rehearsal dinner lying anywhere?" I asked.

That might prove whether Mark made it home after the party.

"I don't remember what he was wearing."

"Black shirt, gray pants, silver tie with dark stripes."

As I watched Madeline's home video, I paid close attention to Mark's attire in case we needed an official description of what her fiancé was last seen wearing, or in case we needed to help identify a decomposing body. I wasn't trying to be negative; I just like being prepared.

"Honestly, I don't remember much about the apartment," Gabe said. "When I saw he wasn't there, I left."

Then, with an anxious feeling in his stomach, Gabe drove what he deemed the second most likely route back to the waiting wedding party. Again, no sign of his buddy.

By now Shep had sniffed enough corners in my house to verify not only that he was the alpha dog but that the place was cat-free. He nudged me to play, but I tossed him a dried pig ear to chew on because I needed to concentrate on taking notes.

"What was it like when you got back to the wedding party?" I asked Gabe.

"Confusion. Madeline was upset. Her brother was trying to comfort her. Her mom livid. His mom mortified."

He described how Mark's mother fussed nervously with the flowers, just for something to do. She was a florist and had designed the wedding bouquets and floral arrangements for her son's big day. Burnt-orange roses and brick-red berries with dried wheat. Just as I was wondering how Gabe could possibly remember such a specific autumn mix yet couldn't recall what his pal was wearing at the rehearsal dinner, he explained that he and Mark used to work in her flower shop after school to earn spending money.

In fact, Gabe said mother and son had been at odds recently because she wanted him to take over her floral business and he wanted to pursue a comedy career. He only helped out at her shop if he was short on money. Marriage to Madeline meant Mark would never have to make another prom corsage.

"Was he funny?" I asked. "As a comedian?"

"I laughed."

Gabe wasn't an objective critic. They'd met in grade school when Mark's mom moved into the neighborhood with her then little boy. After high school, they'd drifted apart, but reconnected five years ago at another dude's wedding. The laughs felt just like old times.

"I was honored when he asked me to stand up for him."

I believed Gabe. Even though I couldn't see his face, his voice, just then, had the quiver of a guy trying not to let on that he was scared.

One thing never changed during their friendship: Mark was the class clown. Always pulling pranks. Gabe chuckled on the other end of the speakerphone as he relived how his buddy took their sixth-grade teacher's dress out of a Laundromat dryer and wore it to school as a Halloween costume.

"So I wasn't too worried when he was late to the wedding," he said. "I figured he'd show up in a gorilla suit or something."

When the ceremony didn't start on time, the guests began to pick up on the drama. First they whispered. Then they pointed. Then they snickered. It was a relief when the minister finally told everyone to take their wedding gifts and go home.

"I halfway expected Mark to be waiting at my house or at least show up when all the commotion died down," Gabe said. "But I never heard a word from him again. Even if he decided he wasn't ready to get married, why would he write off his friends?"

The situation made no sense. But neither had the engagement. Mark was his buddy, but even Gabe couldn't see what Madeline saw in him.

I questioned him about his take on the couple's relationship. Solid? Steamy? Stormy?

"That's the funny thing," he said, "they didn't really have a relationship. They lacked history."

The pair had met in a downtown Minneapolis bar near a comedy club where Mark and other wannabes did stand-up routines. She'd seen his act that night and raved about it to him. Strange, according to Gabe, because while Mark's humor made men laugh, snort, and hoot, most women considered his antics stupid.

But the joke was on them because exactly two months after they first met, Madeline Post, the only daughter of one of Minnesota's wealthiest families, was engaged to Mark Lefevre and due to be married the following month. The pair picked a Saturday afternoon in early October to forsake all others. Not bad for a guy whose day job was working in a downtown parking garage.

"How did Madeline's family like him?" I asked.

"Well enough. Her brother was friendly. Madeline's mother started off a little aloof, but Madeline told him she's like that with everyone. Takes a little while to warm up."

All Gabe could figure was something happened to his

friend after he left the rehearsal dinner. The party was held at Rudy's Redeye Grill, a popular upscale restaurant known for its steaks and coconut shrimp. It was connected to the White Bear Country Inn where many of the wedding guests were staying. The party videotape showed dark wood, red walls, rich atmosphere.

"Did you guys do anything later?" I asked. "One last night on the town, perhaps? Throw back a few drinks? Check out some babes?"

"Actually my wife and I were among the first to leave," Gabe answered stiffly. I wasn't sure whether he felt sheepish that he cut out early or offended by my suggestion that he might be a party boy.

Gabe mentioned that he lost his coat that night, a distinctive black leather jacket with a loon stitched on the back. He hoped he'd left it in his car. Nope. He returned to look at the restaurant. No luck. Please let it be at home, he thought. Not there. He concluded that someone had stolen it, not a huge problem except his wallet was in the inside pocket.

"I was rushed the next morning because I had to call my bank and cancel all my credit cards. Otherwise I probably would have checked in on Mark, razzed him about his last hours of freedom and given him shit about paying me back."

"He owed you money?" I asked.

"Two thousand dollars. Not enough to disappear with and not enough to disappear over. He was going to pay it back right after the wedding."

"Did he say what the money was for?"

"He didn't have to. I trusted him. We had a don't ask, don't tell policy. Later he mentioned wanting to wow a girl."

"A courting allowance?"

"Who knows? It started out just a couple of hundred bucks, but before long it was adding up to a couple of thousand."

"Are you sore at him?" After all, two grand is two grand.

"I'm worried about him, not the cash."

Gabe said it like the subject was now closed, and because I didn't want him hanging up on me, I respected that.

So what kind of person was Mark? The kind of guy who'd walk away from his life and not look back? Welsh on a debt? Publicly spurn and mortify a woman who loved him?

"If he wanted to end things with Madeline, wouldn't he just dump her?" I asked. "How did he call it quits with other girlfriends?"

That question brought a long pause on the speakerphone. Suddenly I wished we were face-to-face so I could read him better, because I must have hit on something he didn't want to discuss.

"You know what I mean," I pushed. "Normal it's-not-working breakups or crazy business?"

Still no answer.

"Gabe, what aren't you telling me?"

I explained that I needed to know the truth about Mark if I was to have any chance of finding out what happened. Now was not the time to hold back facts, or even suspicions, for fear of embarrassing anyone.

"This is tough on Madeline, Gabe, but she's cooperating. I need your cooperation, too."

With clear reluctance, he told me that Mark had been engaged to someone else when he met Madeline. But it wasn't serious.

"How can being engaged not be serious?" I asked.

"They hadn't picked out a ring, much less a wedding date," Gabe answered. "It was more like an understanding."

"So how understanding was she about Mark's new fiancée?"

Another pause. "Not very," he finally admitted.

40

"And Madeline was okay with it?"

"I'm not sure she knew."

When the two men got together it was typically a boys' night out, so Gabe had only met Mark's old flame a few times. Her name was Sigourney. He couldn't recall her last name. They'd dated on and off for a couple of years. A few days before Madeline and Mark's wedding, Gabe was visiting his old pal when the phone rang. Mark let the machine pick it up. Sigourney started leaving a we-need-to-talk message. Mark disconnected the call without saying a word.

"A WHIRLWIND COURTSHIP?" I smiled at the maid of honor, trying to put the best possible spin on the engagement.

"A quickie wedding," Libby Melrose corrected me.

The first thing I noticed was her hair. Cropped short and carrot red. She wore a leather beret like a crown, but a few curls escaped to frame her face. Unlike Madeline, who wore very little makeup, Libby was a cover-girl combo of lip gloss, blush, and mascara.

She and Madeline had attended the same exclusive prep school. Then Madeline went to college on the East Coast, Libby on the West. Both returned to Minnesota and still saw each other socially at places like the elite White Bear Yacht Club, where the wedding reception was supposed to be held.

Once I assured Libby that I just wanted to talk for background, not on camera, she was fine with meeting with me. So I continued that approach. "You must have been touched when Madeline asked you to be her maid of honor."

"Surprised was more like it."

I liked Libby's blunt style. Sure, she and Madeline were friends, though she'd never considered theirs the bosom

41

buddy—best woman type of friendship of which maids of honor are made.

"Let's just say I'm not planning on reciprocating when I get married," she said. "Frankly, I have friends I'm tighter with, but I held up my end of the deal for Madeline. Same can't be said for the groom."

"What was Mark like? What were they like together?"

We were sitting outside and people were walking by, so she lowered her voice. "They'd only known each other a couple of months. I suspected she was pregnant. When he skipped out just before the ceremony, I was certain. Guess I was wrong." Libby held her hands palms up in a playful but non-apologetic gesture.

Like many reporters, I had a knack for making people comfortable and getting them to open up. It transcended age, sex, or occupation. Most of the time people want to talk, otherwise the media wouldn't exist. It's a question of approaching them the right way and helping them understand how they benefit.

Sometimes they agree to an interview because they want to control the legacy of a loved one. Sometimes they talk to celebrate an accomplishment. Sometimes they need the public's help to solve a crime. Often they talk because in the course of an interview they also gain information.

And of course, there are those who talk because they've always wanted to be on TV.

Right now Libby and I were slumming outside Cup 'n' Cone, a local ice-cream shack that had reopened after being closed for the winter. The sun was warm, the sherbet cool. Small children chased each other in a circle around a fallen kiddie cone.

But best of all, the maid of honor was full of delicious gossip.

42

Like how some of the wedding guests were miffed to have been cheated out of the celebratory feast, especially when they heard that Madeline's mother had directed the caterers to box up the steak and scallops and wedding cake for a St. Paul homeless shelter where the clientele was unlikely to appreciate such a spread.

And how others were perturbed that they couldn't return the wedding presents because Madeline and Mark's gift registry specified that the linen, crystal, and silver all be engraved with their initials: MM.

And how Libby figured Mark must really be something in bed, because otherwise what could Madeline see in him?

"I'm not saying she was as gorgeous as Julia Roberts or he was as homely as Lyle Lovett, but it was a mismatch on a lot of levels."

She did concede that the two might have felt a bond because they both lost their fathers as children. She didn't know what happened to Mark's dad, but Madeline's had been struck by lightning while playing golf at the Dellwood Country Club, a mile from their home.

Libby had never met him, but from a picture in Madeline's bedroom of herself as a toddler holding hands with her father, he resembled Madeline's older brother. Tall, dark, handsome.

"She doesn't talk about her dad much. Hardly at all even. He died when she was four. Her brother was going to walk her down the aisle."

We sat there a minute, not speaking, both of us likely visualizing the same image: a feminine white figure with a male companion who was much too young for the situation.

Probably to change the subject, Libby also said Mark made Madeline laugh.

"I went with her to that comedy club one night. I didn't find his humor all that funny, but she couldn't take her eyes off him."

She told me that Madeline and Mark wrote their own wedding vows but Madeline's mother had to insist he not include any jokes.

"That was where Mrs. Post drew the line," Libby said. "That and the prenup, of course."

"And Mark was okay with that?"

"It was nothing personal. All Post spouses sign prenups. The joke ban he took a little harder."

She also confided that the big rock on Madeline's ring finger was a family heirloom.

"So Madeline was fine becoming Mrs. Mark Lefevre?"

"It doesn't have quite the same social ring, does it?" Libby said. "According to the marriage license, she was going to use the name Madeline Post Lefevre. I never got to sign it as a witness."

No point in trying to get a copy. Since the wedding never took place, the license wouldn't have been filed with the county.

"Did her family raise any objections to him or his career path?" I asked.

Libby explained that before Madeline introduced Mark to her mother and brother, she reminded them that the Post family has always supported the arts and she expected no less for her betrothed.

"Of course the kind of art they had in mind was highbrow, like the Saint Paul Chamber Orchestra or the Guthrie Theater or the Ordway Center," Libby said. "Not some guy who, at best, belittles politicians they hold dear or, at worst, finds farts amusing."

"Maybe you should be the comedian," I said, laughing.

She shook her head and smiled. "Not my world. Good comedians have to make fun of themselves. I just like making fun of other people."

At least she was honest about herself. I hoped she was honest about the rest of her information.

"But once Madeline and Mark announced their engagement," she continued, "Mrs. Post seemed fond of him. Madeline getting married didn't seem nearly as big a deal as Madeline moving out of the family compound the year before."

"Say again?"

"The estate had plenty of room and Mrs. Post enjoyed having both her children living there. Roderick didn't seem to mind, but Madeline felt isolated."

"Did Madeline have any old beaux waiting on the sidelines?" I wondered if an old flame might have sought revenge.

Libby shrugged. "Nobody special."

"That's sort of hard to believe." At least it was for me. "I mean, she's a woman with a lot going for her."

"You mean looks and money?"

"Well, yeah." Again, I appreciated Libby's candor.

"Madeline never had long-term boyfriends," she said. "Oh, she had prom dates. She had suitors. Certainly. She was a Post. But she seemed indifferent to them."

"No raging hormones?" I asked.

"Not until Mark."

We chatted some more about what magic he had that others lacked. In my experience, the rich tend to date the rich. The pretty tend to date the handsome. The plain tend to date the ordinary. As a comedian, Mark might have been funny, but as a romantic partner, he was simply funny-looking. And Libby knew nothing about his puzzling scar.

45

She never asked about the facial mark; Madeline never mentioned it.

"For a while, I wondered if Madeline might be gay," Libby said, "but she didn't seem remotely attracted to women, either."

We were covering so much intimate ground, I wished I was taking notes. But I knew Libby would clam up the minute I reached for a pen and paper.

"It was like she wanted a relationship," Libby continued. "She went through the motions, but never seemed to get past the second or third date."

"Until Mark," I added.

She nodded. "Until Mark."

"Did she ever mention if Mark had any old girlfriends who might be trouble?"

"Not to me, but you can ask her yourself. There she is." Libby pointed to the parking lot where Madeline was approaching us.

I hoped this wasn't going to be awkward. But then, Madeline must have known I'd want to talk to Libby; she'd given me her name. To my surprise, she walked right past us and into a coffee shop, with no second glance.

"What's the matter?" I asked Libby. "She acted like we weren't even here. Is she mad at us?"

"No," Libby said. "This happens a lot. She's not the most observant person. Always has her head in the clouds. Unless we speak up, she won't even notice us."

I expressed my doubt about that. But then Madeline walked past us again, this time carrying a coffee cup. She unlocked her car, got in while balancing her drink, and drove away—oblivious to our presence.

CHAPTER 7

When I let Shep out for his morning business, my next-door neighbor was opening his garage for yard sale business.

As predictable as a standby call ten seconds before air, every Thursday, Friday, and Saturday, George (I didn't know his last name) would set up a card table in his driveway next to a YARD SALE sign and display assorted junk in hopes of unloading it. In bad weather, he simply moved his car to the street and his operation indoors. After-hours, visitors rang the doorbell, conducted their affairs, and left—usually minutes later.

Shep wanted to visit. George wasn't the most neighborly neighbor, but I decided to get the introductions over with.

"Anything good this week?" I asked.

George wasn't nearly old enough to be retired but didn't seem to have a real job, either. "Depends on what you're looking for." George didn't bother to look up. He seemed intent on arranging an eclectic collection of ceramic salt-and-pepper shakers shaped like woodland creatures.

Shep headed past an old exercise bike to a corner of the garage and began sniffing and pawing on a wooden sewing cabinet marked NOT FOR SALE.

"I'm allergic to dogs," George said.

I apologized, explaining that Shep was living with me temporarily, and wouldn't it be nice to have a watchdog in the neighborhood?

"I don't like barking."

"He's very quiet," I said, "unless he smells trouble."

Shep continued pawing at the cabinet. It didn't look the least bit fragile, but George appeared nervous just the same.

"Better get him out of here," he said. "Don't want him breaking anything."

Like we were surrounded by valuable inventory. A plastic bench held a collection of VHS action movies from the nineties. A cardboard box overflowed with stuffed animals that looked overloved and underwashed. And a dusty aquarium, now empty except for a few plastic plants and a fish cave, sat next to a box of faded *National Geographic*s.

No price tags. George preferred to wheel and deal depending, I suspected, on the type of vehicle the shopper drove. Owners of rusted-out clunkers seemed to get better prices than carpool moms with Lincoln Navigators.

That was the mystery. Regular foot traffic paraded up and down his yard and he didn't even advertise beyond the homemade sign. I attributed it to location, location, location and wondered if George might sell some of my castoffs for me on consignment. But now seemed a bad time to ask since Shep had made such a poor first impression. So I pushed the big dog back over to my side of the property line and told him to stay while I grabbed the morning newspapers.

Without Shep, I'd still be sleeping in, though not for long.

Spring wasn't a season to be cherishing Saturdays for those of us who work in television news. May loomed like a vulture. Not that I was comparing journalists to scavengers, but I enjoy thinking both play a crucial role in cleaning up the world.

Speaking of which, like a good dog owner, I cleaned up after Shep, making an earthly deposit in the garbage can by my garage. Then the two of us played newspaper tug-of-war for a minute before going inside. Both daily papers were thin, evidence of the cut in manpower and newsprint. And since I don't read sports, I finished them quickly.

As I boiled some water for instant oatmeal, I pulled out a notebook to chart clues in the missing-groom story.

One angle I deliberately didn't bring up with Noreen (because I didn't want my boss thinking I see serial killers behind every corner) was the fact that several young men have been reported missing in Minnesota and Wisconsin over the last few years. A map of the missing eerily follows a path along Interstate 94. La Crosse. Eau Claire. The Twin Cities. St. Cloud. Conspiracy theorists even include cases from Illinois, Indiana, and Michigan to raise the tally of the missing to dozens.

Some of the men have never been found, including one whose abandoned car was discovered four years ago on the side of a freeway three miles from where Mark was last seen.

Others were found drowned. Their bodies recovered weeks or months later not far from where they disappeared in water that had seemingly been well searched. Rumors of a serial killer targeting drunken college men in La Crosse, Wisconsin, became so frenzied that an FBI task force reviewed the cases and concluded the victims became intoxicated at bars or campus parties and stumbled drunkenly into the Mississippi River.

Their families don't accept that explanation: they believe the men were pushed or thrown while incapacitated. Mainstream media, including Channel 3, has generally discounted these cases as coincidence. An Internet blog disagreed, saying coincidence phooey—drowning in coincidence, maybe. One of our broadcast competitors floated a theory that an organized pack of roving murderers killed the men, leaving smiley-face graffiti behind to taunt police.

During a news conference, authorities pronounced the conjecture unfounded and announced they'd found the real killers long ago—Jack Daniels, Jim Beam, and Bud Weiser.

Mark didn't fit the key element of the victim profile. When I watched the video of the rehearsal dinner, he didn't seem the least bit drunk. The best man, maid of honor, and bride all confirmed that conclusion.

Also, theirs was a private party. Hard for a roaming serial killer to crash. The guest list was known. And none of the invited had an obvious motive to harm the groom.

He was also a decade older than most of the other victims. And his car remained missing. I was weighing the significance of that clue when I dozed off on the couch to the rhythmic crunch of Shep chewing his pig ear.

CHAPTER 8

"It was late Saturday afternoon when I raced past the emergency vehicles parked outside the northeast corner of the Mall of America. The flashing lights reminded me of the test drills held there to prepare Minnesota for terrorist attacks. If terrorists were responsible for today's news event, they'd picked a curious target: Underwater Adventures—a large walk-through aquarium, popular with tourists and school groups.

"I expected media. I just didn't expect you." Nick Garnett stood in a shallow puddle, a small sunfish flopping clumsily around his ankles.

I felt a brief flash of awkwardness. Garnett was head of corporate security at the Mall of America. A former cop, a former source, and I hoped, not a former friend.

"I was on call," I answered, "so I'm who you got."

Channel 3 rotates reporters through a weekend on-call list so if news breaks and the scheduled staff are already committed to other stories or too far away to respond, the list is activated.

51

Garnett and I hadn't seen each other much since last fall when he almost bled out in my front yard protecting me from a pit bull after being wrongfully accused of murder because of my serial-killer investigation into dead Susans.

"Over here, Riley." He waved me in ahead of a bunch of other reporters, so I clearly had read too much into his silence.

After all, Garnett was a busy man. He'd successfully recuperated from his injuries, but failed at a reconciliation with an ex-wife. Both tasks required a certain amount of privacy, so he evidently accepted that we each needed time and space to heal.

Physically, he had healed nicely and looked in prime shape. He wore a more elegant cut of suit than when he lived on a homicide detective's salary. With a hint of gray in his hair, he looked hunky in an older-man sort of way.

Emotionally, I couldn't tell where he was in the healing department, but I knew I wasn't finished. Journeying back from the abyss can be complicated.

He and I shared an intimacy that came from trust, not sex—trading news scoops during our careers and never once burning each other. Surviving last fall's bedlam should have brought us even closer; instead it left our relationship feeling undefined.

Many of life's lessons I learn from fictional characters in books and films, but I often grasp their significance too late to implement them.

Like the end of the 1994 bus/extortion movie *Speed*, when Keanu Reeves and Sandra Bullock, locked in each other's arms, open their eyes to discover they've survived Dennis Hopper's madness. Reeves reminds Bullock of her theory that relationships based on intense experiences never work. Looking back, I realized my liaison with Garnett echoed that movie moment. I wished I'd had the guts to blurt out the heroine's line and say, "Okay, we'll have to base it on sex then."

But clever dialogue eluded me, and so did passion. I wasn't ready then. And I wasn't sure I was any more ready now. As a practical matter, television sweeps have no room for amour.

So I kept the conversation work-related, asking, "What happened, Nick?"

"You wouldn't believe it," he answered.

As he turned his head to look at me, his shirt collar fell short of covering the still-pink scars on his neck from the dog bites. On the skin of another man, I might have fantasized about undoing a button or two to inspect the marks closer, but on Garnett, guilt outweighed curiosity. That kept any unprofessional yearning under control.

"Couple of crazies came through and hammered the hell out of the glass with baseball bats," he said. "We've been picking up fish for the last half hour."

"Can I get a camera in here?" I was all business.

"Pool camera only. This is too big and public to let you go exclusive. Besides, Riley, your station wasn't even the first one here." He shook his head in admonishment.

Not that I wanted to make excuses, but one of my TV competitors is geographically closer, another is simply better at reacting to breaking news. Pooling tape meant one station, in this case ours, would be allowed to shoot crime-scene video, but was required to share it with everyone else.

"Fine, Nick," I agreed, "if I can't have it alone, just make sure no one else does."

"Deal. The photographers are going through security and getting credentials. They should be down in a couple of minutes. Then you can have your photo op."

I watched as a middle-aged bald man with a buff body

wrapped a wet towel around what looked like a small shark with a long nose and placed it in a cooler of water with a whiskered exotic fish.

"Will they be okay?" I asked.

The man wore an Underwater Adventures name tag that read "Ahab." If he'd been a mad sea captain in a former life, he hid it well that day. No wasted energy shaking a fist at the sea or sky.

"Some we can put in other tanks," he said. "These we'll transport over to the Minnesota Zoo, along with other survivors. The lucky ones."

He put a cover on the cooler and motioned toward the back of the room at a small pile of glassy-eyed fish that, if they weren't lying on a cement floor, would clearly be floating belly up.

"We had to prioritize," Ahab explained. "Luckily, the scoundrels spared the saltwater creatures."

He and a skinny woman with a Pisces tattoo on one arm loaded the cooler onto a cart and pushed it down the hall. Just before disappearing around a corner, he brushed his hand over his eyes and blinked, as if wiping a tear. I've seen people mourn the loss of money, career, spouse, and child. Fish grief, that's a new one.

"He's the aquarium director," Garnett said. "Doesn't want to do any media interviews right now. You guys can shoot for three minutes behind the crime-scene tape, then I'll give a brief statement to everyone. After that, we're kicking you all outside."

Not a problem, we had just over an hour before the evening news. We'd need to be setting up for our live shots, plus this way I didn't have to worry about the competition getting better shots than me, since all the stories would use mostly the same video.

"Any surveillance tape?" I asked, searching for some way to make my piece stand out from the pack. The Mall of America has one of the most comprehensive video-camera systems in the retail world. Very little happens on its turf that's not watched by someone.

Garnett ignored my question.

"Maybe somebody'll recognize the suspects," I pressed. "They could call in an ID."

It happens. Look at *America's Most Wanted*. Happens all the time.

"I don't think anyone will recognize these guys," Garnett replied cryptically.

"How can you be so sure, Nick? Come on, TV can be a tool for law enforcement. Use us."

"Television? A *tool* for law enforcement?" His voice carried more than a hint of incredulity. "Now, Riley, we both know full well . . . television is . . . is a godless abomination."

"And we both know that that must be from Peter Finch, *Network*, 1976," I guessed.

Garnett was also a film buff and we enjoyed playing Name That Movie Quote during normal conversation. The tradition dated back ten years to our earliest days as rookie reporter and veteran cop. He didn't stump me too often. But now, stationed at the Mall of America, with fourteen movie screens within a hundred yards of his security office, he had an advantage. Especially since my rental wasn't wired for cable TV.

"Actually, I think I made that line up," he said.

"Really? Television is a godless abomination? It's very profound. Maybe even catchy enough for T-shirts. You're sure it's not from *Network*?"

"Pretty sure," he nodded. "But we could rent it sometime to double check."

"Let's do that. My place. Loser buys the pizza."

And with that exchange, we both knew we were okay.

Of course, the real reason I wanted the surveillance tape was because this was a slow-news Saturday. If not for this fish shtick, Channel 3 would be leading tonight's newscast with obvious tips on lawn-mower safety after a south Minneapolis man got his foot caught in one. Actual video of thugs crashing tanks of fish would probably go national.

"So how about it? Release the tape? We both know it exists."

"Bloomington cops will have to make the call on that," he said. "They're handling the investigation. Go bother them."

Bloomington police have a substation in that corner of the Mall of America, just up the escalator from the aquarium. Most of their mall calls deal with petty crimes like shoplifting or kids violating curfew. When the fish-in-crisis call came, officers responded, but just missed the perpetrators racing out the skyway to the parking garage. It wasn't the kind of crime they'd ever trained for. Right now they were taking witness statements and dealing with crowd control.

One of Channel 3's photographers waved at me and Garnett motioned him through the confusion. Luis Fernandez was another fairly new photog, that's why he worked the weekend late shift. I wished I had one of our veteran shooters. Not that they were more skilled behind a camera, but a couple were fishing fanatics and would have been helpful in identifying the victims.

"Wow." Luis focused his camera on a pile of carp, still breathing, slow to die. Low priority for rescue. "This is some crazy business."

Garnett led us down a fake jungle path with artificial

tropical plants and trees. Various plastic and stuffed animals decorated the route unconvincingly. We arrived at a glass-walled tunnel, usually the highlight of the aquarium tour. On a good day, visitors were surrounded overhead and on each side with a million gallons of water and an extensive school of fish as well as turtles, sharks, and stingrays.

Today wasn't a good day.

The power had been turned off to avoid electrocution. The tunnel was dark; the conveyer belt stalled. Aquarium employees waved flashlights. Luis activated his portable camera light and we all gasped at the large hole in one side of the freshwater tunnel. Water above that line, along with many of the inhabitants, had been sucked out onto the floor. Most of the water spread outward so it was now only ankle deep. On both sides of the tunnel, below the damaged tank wall, desperate fish moved slowly in cramped space.

They were the fortunate ones. Others lay on the floor, gasping for air, their gills quivering as staff members worked to rescue them.

I better understood Ahab's tears. And while fish aren't among the most huggable or emotional of earth's creatures, these survivors certainly looked despondent.

"Time's up," Garnett said. "You newsies go back upstairs."

We didn't argue because I didn't want him to regret allowing us access. And I hoped he'd share new information as it came in—with me, not the rest of the pack.

"Nick, you're sure to get tip calls once viewers see this," I said. "And if we get anything on our end, we'll let you know."

Slamming fish tanks was just the kind of prank vandals would brag about over a few beers. Garnett promised to finalize reward information before airtime.

Reporters from four TV channels, both daily newspapers, and one radio station all played the Minnesota Nice version of paparazzi and waited patiently outside the Bloomington cop shop until a communications flack stuck his head out to sneer "No comment!" before slamming the door in our faces.

> ((RILEY/LIVE))
> POLICE ARE STUMPED BY A
> FISH FRENZY AT THE MALL
> OF AMERICA TODAY.

I had just fed the aquarium tape back to the station from Channel 3's live truck and was scripting my story. For television news each line is typed about two inches wide, making for easy reading, and timing out to about a second a line. This helps the newscast producer estimate the length of any story quickly. Instead of punctuation, I generally put a series of dots to indicate a pause point during my read.

> ((RILEY/NAT))
> TWO ARMED INTRUDERS
> BROKE INTO UNDERWATER
> ADVENTURES AND
> SMASHED AQUARIUMS . . .
> LEAVING FISH
> FLOUNDERING . . . NO
> MOTIVE HAS YET BEEN
> DETERMINED . . .

The weekend news anchor, Erin Jackson, followed up with a planned question about an Underwater Adventure story a few months earlier in which a large tiger shark named Jesse tried to eat a smaller shark. The little shark survived only because a rescue team wrenched it, literally, from the jaws of death. Because a visitor's cell-phone camera captured the drama, the shark exhibit broke attendance records by using the gripping photo in all their publicity.

Channel 3 was always anxious for any chance to rerun that particular image.

((ANCHOR Q&A))
AND HOW ABOUT THOSE
TWO SHARKS, RILEY . . .
WERE THEY AMONG THE
SURVIVORS?
((RILEY SOT/FILE TAPE))
YES, ERIN,
THEY'RE JUST FINE . . . NO
SHARKS OR OTHER
SALTWATER CREATURES
PERISHED IN TODAY'S
ATTACK . . . BUT MANY OF
THE MORE FRAGILE
FRESHWATER FISH WERE
NOT SO FORTUNATE . . . AND
THE FINAL DEATH
TALLY HAS YET TO BE
RELEASED.

I did my early newscast as a live shot without a hitch or glitch, filling a solid two and a half minutes about the tragic loss of fish life. But instead of letting me do the late news back on set at the station, like we'd agreed on earlier, the producer insisted I again go live in front of the Mall of

America. Even though it was now dark outside. Even though it was now raining. And most insulting, even though the action was long over.

But that's TV news.

CHAPTER 9

Noreen called me into her office the following Monday morning to admire a spike in the Saturday overnights and attribute it to my coverage of the fish story. Saturday usually has fewer news viewers than any other night of the week, but I declined the compliment because my coverage was really no different than my competitors'.

Then her motive became clear.

"You've been doing such a great job on spot news lately," she continued, "with the police shooting and the fish attack, I'm wondering if that's a better place for you this May."

She smiled like she was offering me a promotion. But her smile was insincere.

In the world of TV news, on-air talent succeeds by projecting warmth. That trait didn't come naturally to Noreen, which probably explained why, even with her beauteous looks, she gravitated to management instead of anchoring. Viewers can sense a false performer. For bosses, a cool demeanor counts more and what subordinates think counts for nothing.

"No," I answered, wasting no words on subtlety.

There's nothing subtle about spot, or breaking, news. It's News of the Obvious. Fire. Plane crash. Bank robbery. High on adrenaline and low on brains. Reporting live for a minute-thirty on whatever the latest news development is or was hours earlier, often fed to you by the newscast producer off the wire. It's usually an entry-level job for rookies with lots of energy and little experience.

I'd been there, done that.

"No," I repeated. "I have a job. I'm an investigative reporter."

"I see. Well then, Riley, show me your investigation."

Just then we heard an overhead page calling, "Riley Spartz, you have a guest in the front lobby."

Normally I'd roll my eyes because I wasn't expecting anyone and I have a theory, proven numerous times over the course of my career, that nothing good ever walks through the front door. Exclusives don't come that easily. Mystery guests are usually viewers who are so angry that they're determined to yell at you in person. Or those who can't understand why their story idea has been rejected by every news outlet in the market. But instead of rolling my eyes, I decided to embrace this mystery guest as my lucky break.

"Can we please talk later, Noreen? I really need to meet with this source. It's important."

She waved me off, but reminded me that we weren't finished.

VIVIAN POST, THE mother of the almost-bride, declined an offer to come into the Channel 3 newsroom and sit down, preferring to conduct matters in the station lobby where she informed me that she only had a minute to spare because her car was out front waiting to take her shopping.

Her wide blue eyes matched her daughter's, but Mrs. Post looked young to have a child Madeline's age. And fit. In a fight she could probably take me. And she had to be mid-forties. At least ten years older than me. Not a sign of gray in her dark hair. She smelled good in an expensive sort of way.

"I'm sorry for your pain—" I started out expressing sorrow for all she and her family had been through these many months, but she dismissed me as one might dismiss a servant, if one had a servant.

"Whatever Madeline's told you, I'm here to tell you our family doesn't care to be featured on your program. So thank you for your time and good day." She turned to leave.

"Excuse me, Mrs. Post."

Working in television, I've developed a high tolerance for bitchiness. Give or take. But her manner was so high and mighty that I made a mental note to tell the security desk to post her picture and not buzz her into the station again without an appointment.

"It doesn't work that way," I said. "I don't need your permission to broadcast this story."

No need to tell her that NEVER WORN hadn't even been slated on the May board. But I'd already shot tape, done research, and one way or another, I intended the missing-groom story to see air.

"Well," she answered, "I'm sure my lawyers won't have any trouble getting a court order preventing you."

"I think they just might."

I tried explaining the concept of the First Amendment. But just as I got to *Near vs. Minnesota* (1931), the most significant Supreme Court decision involving prior restraint

63

and establishing that the government cannot prohibit publication, Vivian was climbing into a black Mercedes, the door held open by a young man in a dark suit.

"The ruling was upheld again in the Pentagon Papers case!" I yelled as the vehicle pulled away.

So bottom line, we'd win in court. If we got to court. But Noreen would be loath to spend legal fees on a story she didn't believe in. Especially facing the current newsroom economics. So I needed to make her a believer before she ordained me Channel 3's spot-news machine.

I walked around the outside of the station and went in the back door by the guard desk so Noreen wouldn't see me sneaking past her office.

Back at my desk, I started to map out the missing-groom story to see what still needed to be done. I wrote Madeline's and Mark's names on a wall board along with data I'd collected. I'd not been able to run their names and dates of birth through the national crime records because I needed a cooperative police source to do that check. Since Nick Garnett had traded his police badge for corporate life, that proved elusive.

WEDDING/October 6	MADELINE POST	MARK LEFEVRE
ENGAGED/1 month	No criminal record	Minor drug charge
KNOWN EACH OTHER/	$$$$$$$$	comedian
3 months	cooperative w/media	old girlfriend?
	mother from hell	

As soon as I wrote "hell," I felt I probably was a bit harsh regarding Madeline's mother. Her formidable style might have come more from being a single parent than from being filthy rich. Checking the newspaper archives, I found an obituary and brief story about Madeline's father's death.

He died on the eleventh hole, seeking shelter under a tree during a sudden thunderstorm.

Mr. Post had owned several car dealerships in the Twin Cities, so his marriage to Vivian blended old money with new.

Examining my lists on the board, I realized I needed to learn more about Mark. He was still a mystery. I pulled his and Madeline's engagement announcement from my file and noted that his mother lived just outside of Hudson, Wisconsin.

Getting no answer at her home, I checked for florists in the area and soon located her at work. Surprised by my call, she welcomed a visit to discuss her missing son. So twenty minutes later, Malik and I were on our way to the cheesehead state.

By the time we got to the YOU ARE LEAVING MINNESOTA sign, he was dozing in the passenger seat while I drove over the St. Croix River. Malik preferred that division of travel duties—him sleeping, me driving. He claimed it kept him sharp when it came time to shoot video. He'd learned to sleep on command in the army and practiced that skill anytime he could. I didn't really mind because it gave me time to brainstorm without having to listen to chatter about his home life. And his soft, pleasant snore soothed my racing mind.

The trees along the riverbank were turning green and the wind was brisk enough for whitecaps on the water. No boats in either direction. I turned north just after the WELCOME TO WISCONSIN sign.

I dialed Madeline because I wanted to fill her in on my meeting with her mother before her mother brainwashed her against me.

"I probably shouldn't have told Mother about the story,"

Madeline said. "But we're very close. In some ways, she's more like a big sister than a mom. 'A big, bossy sister,' I like to tease her. But she feels it's not healthy for families to keep secrets. They only cause heartache."

"She's so right," I said.

I often use a similar tactic to get reluctant interviewees to open up. And how could I argue that Madeline should keep secrets from her mother but share them with me?

So I decided to keep my current destination secret from her. The last thing I needed was Mrs. Post contacting Mrs. Lefevre and shutting her down before I even reached the front door.

"It sounds like you and your mother don't necessarily have to agree on everything, as long as you're upfront about it." I was testing to see if Madeline was still on board with my investigation into her fiancé's disappearance.

"Absolutely, Riley," she said. "I love her dearly, but if it was up to Mother I'd still be living at home."

That didn't sound like much of a life to me. After all, I'd met Mother. And while I didn't need the mother of the bride's cooperation for my story, the bride herself was essential.

"So we're still cool then, right, Madeline?"

"Right. I've thought about this a lot over the last couple of days, Riley, and whatever reason Mark vanished, knowing can't be worse than not knowing."

That philosophy certainly made sense then. But at that moment, I had no clue how this story might unfold. So when I assured Madeline that her decision was sound and promised to tell her the truth, no matter what I discovered, I sincerely believed it was the best course.

CHAPTER 10

I nudged Malik awake as I pulled in front of Jean Lefevre's small-town-cute floral shop, painted a variety of pastel hues. We left the camera gear inside the van so as not to spook her. Mrs. Lefevre bore no physical resemblance to her frizzy-haired missing son. With pink cheeks and white hair, everything about her was adorable.

I loosened her up by placing an order for a spring bouquet to be sent to Shep's K-9 partner, who was still in the hospital. Rarely can you ingratiate yourself with two sources in two stories in one swoop.

Mark hadn't lived at home for years, but as his mom explained while expertly arranging tulips, daffodils, and other early blooms in a glass vase, they had never been out of touch for more than a few weeks.

"He was a good boy," she said.

I immediately noted she used the past tense.

"You're speaking like you think he's dead," I pointed out.

"I do think he's dead."

No other theory made sense to her. Long past the point

67

of worrying about embarrassing her son, she'd gone to the police a couple of weeks after the wedding fiasco, filed a missing person report, and gotten the runaround.

"They told me adults are entitled to privacy and big boys don't need to check in with mommy if they want to take off."

I must have smiled at her characterization of the police response because she felt compelled to defend it.

"Basically, that's what they said," she insisted as she tied a blue lace ribbon around the neck of the vase. "I tried calling the media, even your station, but nobody cared."

I didn't doubt her. Missing men don't trigger immediate searches unless they're vulnerable adults or there's evidence of foul play. Neither existed in Mark's case. And frankly, past experience tells cops that when men go missing, they're often in Vegas.

I asked whether Mark might have taken his comedy act on the road. Maybe tested his talent on the Strip.

She shook her head. Only death would have kept him from his wedding. And besides, if he had an act going somewhere, he'd have called her to come and watch.

"He always said a friendly audience can spread laughter like the plague."

She'd given the police a picture of him and a description of his Jeep. They told her they'd put out a license plate alert, so if the vehicle was stopped, the officer on the scene could make inquiries. If Mark was still missing after a month, they'd enter his name in a national register of missing persons. She called each month to check, but the police never had anything new to report. And she doubted they were doing any actual investigating.

"What did you think of him wanting to be a comedian?" I asked.

"I didn't have a lot of patience for his dream," she admitted.

Much of his life, she had to go around apologizing to people and telling them he didn't mean it. Or make him go around apologizing to people and telling them he didn't mean it. The problem was, in most cases, Mark did mean it. Reducing a target to tears seemed almost as fulfilling as garnering a belly laugh. Like the time the lunchroom cook cried after he climbed on a cafeteria table and read a list of top-ten Secrets About Hot Lunches.

While his early start seemed to indicate an attack comedian in the making, as he matured, his humor became less cruel and more sophisticated. But he could still crush a mother's feelings.

Mrs. Lefevre stuck a card in the flowers and wrapped them in yellow tissue paper while explaining that her son had been a bright student, but dropped out of college after a year because he claimed it didn't offer what he needed. He also wanted nothing more to do with the flower shop because he said girls would think he was gay. He could tell that remark hurt her, so he claimed to be joking. But that was another problem with Mark, it was hard to tell when he was serious and when he was joking.

What's a mother to do with an aging, aspiring comic?

Then Mark met Madeline and she believed in his talent and he called her his muse and she asked him to marry her.

"Wait a minute," I interrupted. "She proposed to Mark?" That scenario was very different from Madeline's.

"Yes, that's what he told me. He seemed elated, even relieved. Like he had wanted to pop the question, but didn't quite dare."

"And you were happy for him?"

She paused while wrapping plastic over the floral arrangement. I enjoyed watching her work and breathing the fragrant air inside her shop.

"Well, it was all very sudden and their worlds were quite different," she said, "but maybe opposites do attract."

She told us she needed to deliver these flowers and another bouquet to an assisted-living center on her way home after she closed up. I asked if we could follow behind her and stop in at her house and shoot some photographs of Mark. If she said yes, I planned on asking if we could also videotape an interview.

As I helped her carry one of the vases into the lobby of the assisted-living center, I asked about her son's fiancée. She said she was fond of the girl, but didn't really feel she knew her all that well.

Did Madeline love Mark?

"Desperately," she said as we set the flowers on the front counter.

Desperately. I pondered the implications of that word as we walked back outside.

"Did Mark love Madeline?"

"I'm sure he did." That sounded less definitive.

"You don't sound so sure," I responded.

"Mark loved opportunities." She paused in front of her car as she searched her purse for the keys. "If an opportunity presented itself, he'd grab it and figure out the consequences later."

That candid observation, from his mother no less, made me ponder Mark's character and wonder if the consequences of marriage had only just occurred to him hours before the wedding.

Malik and I followed her car until she pulled into the driveway of a small white rambler with black shutters. Not surprisingly, her front yard was colored with crocuses and other spring blooms.

Somehow wedding talk turned to the mother of the bride and I got an earful of how snooty Mark's mom considered Madeline's mom. Her pet peeve: Vivian Post couldn't be bothered to remember Jean Lefevre's name.

"Whenever we met, I always had to remind her who I was," she said. "Also she kept checking to make sure I knew to wear light gray, not dark, for the ceremony."

She shrugged like whatever, and got out some photo albums for me to page through while she made coffee. I already had pictures of Mark and Madeline together, but needed some of him solo. I found one showing him swinging a golf club. In another he wore a high-school graduation cap and gown. In both cases, his forehead was covered so I couldn't see whether his scar was recent or old. Most of the album was filled with boring shots of visiting relatives sitting on couches or at the table trying to eat while some family shutterbug insisted on using up the end of a roll of film no matter who was still chewing.

In one of the more recent ones, Mark had his arm around a goth girl who certainly wasn't Madeline. Black hair, pale face, uncertain smile. But Mark beamed at the camera.

Mrs. Lefevre identified her as Mark's old girlfriend, and bingo, now I had a name and face for the other woman. Sigourney Nelson. Mrs. Lefevre even had a phone number.

I didn't want to flat-out accuse her son of being a heel, so I casually inquired how serious things had been with Sigourney.

"Actually," she explained, "I had expected them to get married."

"Really," I said. Now we were getting somewhere. Had

Sigourney presented an opportunity to be grabbed? "Do you think there's any chance he ran off with her?"

"I don't think so. She was very grouchy when I called a few days later to ask if she'd seen Mark. She didn't seem to believe me when I said he was gone. I left another message the following week, but she never returned my call."

During much of our conversation, Mrs. Lefevre sounded as hardy as a perennial, but Malik and I soon learned she was actually soft as a pansy. Maybe it was because we had just looked at Mark's baby pictures. Maybe it was because someone was finally taking her son's disappearance seriously. Maybe it was because she had something to feel guilty about. Whatever the reason, when Malik brought the gear inside we discovered that, unlike the bride, the mother of the groom was not too tough to cry on camera.

"He would not go months without contacting me, his mama."

We used the natural light from the window so she wouldn't be distracted by too much television equipment and so we could get started while she was still emotional.

"I need to find him. Dead or alive. I need to find him." I paused to admire her sound bite and replay it in my mind. Definitely a keeper.

"Do you think he might have killed himself?" The question bordered on insensitive, but still had to be asked.

"No, he had everything to live for. He was getting married. If he killed himself, where's his body?"

Her point was valid. Suicides typically want to be found. That's why so many do their dying deed in a familiar place like at home or in a garage, or a public place like a high bridge or tall building. Yet some suicides do go off into a wooded area for their final moments and aren't found until months or years later when a hunter stumbles across their bones.

"Besides," she said, holding up a gold cross dangling from a chain around her neck, "suicide is a sin."

News organizations typically don't cover suicides, unless the deceased is a celebrity like Kurt Cobain or takes others with him before turning the gun on himself like the Virginia Tech shooter. I did not want Mark to be a suicide or it would mean I did a whole lot of work for nothing.

"Was he involved in anything that might have caused him some trouble?" I continued. "Drugs perhaps?"

That was a firm no. But mamas might be the last to know if their little boys are using or dealing.

Then I thought of Mark's scar and recalled another missing person case from the year before. A Minnesota man, gone for two weeks, found sleeping in a hail-damaged pickup at a Wisconsin truck stop. He had no idea who he was or how he got there. Months earlier, according to his family, he'd slipped in a bathtub, hit his head, and began to suffer periodic bouts of amnesia.

"When did Mark get his scar?" I asked. "Could his memory have been affected by a head injury?"

The question made his mother fidget, but she debunked my amnesia theory by telling me Mark got the scar in a childhood accident and never appeared to have any lasting effects.

I had another question that I knew would make her even more uncomfortable, which was why I saved it for last.

I asked her why she waited so long before going to the police.

She mumbled something about following the advice of the Post family.

"But this was your only son."

"I know." A tear dripped down her check. She made no move to wipe it. "But everyone said I would just embarrass Mark more."

I didn't have any trouble believing that Mrs. Post pushed to keep things quiet, though I figured her true motive was to avoid embarrassing her daughter, not her daughter's fiancé. But right now, my reporter's instinct told me that Mrs. Lefevre, if not lying, was definitely holding something back. I'd spent enough time with her in her flower shop that I had a good baseline on her normal behavior. Right now, her voice was high, her gaze evasive and she was tapping the floor nervously with her foot.

I repeated my original question. "Why did you wait so long before calling the police, Mrs. Lefevre?"

No answer. More tears.

"Time is everything in a missing person case, Mrs. Lefevre. Why did you wait so long?"

I stayed silent. Mrs. Lefevre hung her head like a wilted orchid. Finally she looked up and told me she didn't go to the police right away because she had thousands of dollars in unpaid parking tickets.

CHAPTER 11

"**Y**ou were kind of hard on her," Malik observed on the ride back. "At least she went to the police. That's more than bridezilla did."

"I pushed her because I felt there was something to push for," I said. "I still think there's more she's holding back."

"We all have stuff we hold back." He was punchy because I was making him drive while I made notes about our meeting.

"You too, Malik? You holding back on me?" My cameraman had seemed a little distant the past couple of days.

He didn't answer as we passed the WELCOME TO MINNESOTA sign on the freeway. I didn't say anything, either, because over the years I've learned that sometimes the best way to get a person to talk is to keep my own mouth shut.

We were approaching downtown St. Paul when he told me that he was disappointed I was suddenly so gung ho on the missing groom and didn't seem to care much anymore about investigating meth.

"Meth?" I said. "I care plenty. It's Noreen who put the kibosh on that project."

"But if *you* really cared, Riley, you wouldn't care what she thought. You'd do it anyway. Like with the wedding dress."

"I guess I didn't know you cared so much about the meth problem, Malik." He started paying extra-close attention to the traffic just then. "Do you want to tell me why?"

He didn't look like he wanted to, but finally, while keeping his eyes straight ahead on the car in front of us, he started to speak softly.

"My sister was an addict."

"Your sister? Which one?" I recalled him having three. No brothers, though.

"Hafsa. The youngest. She put our parents through hell."

I didn't have to ask for details. I'd covered addicts and their families enough to know what he meant. Crystal meth is the most addictive, most accessible drug on the planet and can turn good kids into trash. "You said she *was* an addict. Is she recovered now?"

"She's dead."

Now I was the quiet one. Fatal meth overdoses are rare. But addiction can lead into a dangerous world of violence, prostitution, suicide.

"She crashed her car while high," he said.

"I'm so sorry."

Sometimes "sorry" is all I can say. I was surprised that Malik had kept his pain to himself. The reporter-photographer dynamic can be the closest of all TV news relationships. We spend so much time together in a van, we see the best and the worst in each other and develop an us versus them alliance. One reporter I know calls her photographer the Husband She Doesn't Sleep With.

76

"I'm so sorry." I repeated my regret because saying it once didn't seem enough. Twice didn't do the job either. "I'm so very sorry."

"Happened a year ago," Malik said. "I didn't feel like talking. But lately, when you made noise about doing a meth investigation, I began thinking maybe that would help me get some perspective."

"It would," I agreed. "I'll put it on my Stories Noreen Doesn't Know About list and keep plugging away. We'll find something to hang it on, Malik. I promise."

For the first time since we began this conversation he took his eyes off the road, looked at me, and nodded. Once again, we had an us versus them alliance.

Then he went back to concentrating on the drive and I went back to making notes about our meeting with Mark's mom. One detail I circled was the discrepancy over who proposed to who. I didn't have enough information to confront Madeline. Yet. And if I pushed too hard, too soon, I might push her away.

Remarkably, that didn't happen with Jean Lefevre, even though I bullied her to tears during the interview. I stopped writing and thought back to an hour earlier, on the other side of the river, while we were packing up the gear in the back of the van and she came outside.

I'd thanked her again and assured her I'd keep her posted on anything we might find about her missing son. I expected she had followed us to ask that we not air her tape or that we never set foot on her property again. Instead, she was apparently one of those people who feel freed by a good cry, and asked if we'd like to return another day and see any of Mark's things.

Malik and I looked at each other. "What kind of things?" I asked.

She explained that Mark had one month left on his lease when he disappeared. The apartment came furnished. When the rent went unpaid, the landlord packed everything in boxes and put them in storage. She'd paid a considerable fee to retrieve the items. Now everything her son owned was stored in her garage. She hadn't been able to bring herself to sort through the boxes.

All she could imagine were the memories; all I could imagine were the clues.

Mrs. Lefevre led us to the garage where she opened a squeaky door, fumbling for the light. Malik and I took a quick peak inside. She showed us a wall of boxes stacked neatly against one end. I opened the closest one labeled "Desk" and struck gold in the form of a laptop computer.

"Have you looked at this?" I asked her.

She shook her head.

"Do you mind if I try?"

I didn't mean personally. Until recently I didn't have even the cyber savvy to know how to put that sideways smiley face on the end of my e-mails like everyone else does. I hoped to hand off Mark's laptop to Xiong and see what computer secrets he could mine.

"I never even turned it on." She explained that it seemed too much like snooping.

"We're past snooping," I said. "If your son cared about his computer, he'd have taken it with him."

So Mark's mother let me take the laptop. I wanted to comb through more boxes then, but she had a church meeting so we made plans to come back another day. And despite how we'd ended her interview, she actually did seem to be looking forward to seeing us again.

"But we have to schedule it around the *Amorphophallus titanum*," she said.

"The what?" I asked.

"The corpse flower, it's on the verge of blooming."

I wondered if her son got his sense of humor from his mom, but she picked up on my confusion.

"It's a rare jungle plant that smells like rotting flesh when it blooms. It's expected to unfold sometime this week."

She explained that flower aficionados were awaiting the botanical wonder at the Marjorie McNeely Conservatory in St. Paul's Como Park. Apparently, only 122 such pungent events have been documented worldwide since the plant was first discovered in the Indonesian rain forests in the 1870s.

"Minnesota will have a place in floral history." She clasped her hands together and smiled in anticipation.

THAT AN OFFICIAL missing person report had been filed by his mother gave me a reason to hound the cops about Mark Lefevre the next day.

"We got nothing," said Captain Walt Shuda as he opened Mark's file. He wouldn't let me read the reports because the case was still classified as an open investigation, even though months had apparently passed since anyone in law enforcement had peeked inside.

"Why does TV care?" He seemed more curious about that development than about Mark's fate.

"A bit odd is all," I answered. "He had a lot to walk away from. And he's been gone a long time."

"You'd be surprised," Captain Shuda said. "Sometimes the longer they're gone, the harder it is for them to come back."

Because Captain Shuda was head of the Minneapolis Missing Persons Unit, I had to put some stock in what he was saying. Even though Mark was last seen in White Bear Lake, and even though the person making the report, his mother, lived in Wisconsin, Minneapolis police actually had jurisdiction. Unless foul play is suspected, like with missing spring-break coed Natalee Holloway in Aruba, law enforcement where the missing person lives typically has charge of the case.

"I got a stack of missing person cases I can't get the media interested in." The captain gestured to a pile of files stacked in the back of his office. The top one looked dusty. "Think it's because they're not young, blond, or pretty?"

"It's more complicated than that," I responded.

But actually it wasn't. I knew it. And Captain Shuda knew it. TV gloms on to a few high-profile cases, usually involving attractive women, and the rest are left to sort themselves out. Or not. Without foul play or Mark being a vulnerable adult, his missing person file would sit with the pile unless I stirred something loose.

But I couldn't be that candid with Captain Shuda. Instead I expressed regret we couldn't cover all the missing person cases out there. "Not even John Walsh is that good."

It comes down to practicality, I explained. Space is limited in a newscast. So is staff. I stayed away from the specifics of how newsworthiness is determined. Down that path, in debate with non-newsies, lies madness.

Then the captain reminded me about the time I followed the police chief on a law enforcement conference to Florida and filmed him playing golf while a session on "Keeping Your City Safe from Terrorism" was under way. "You found time to put that in your news."

It's no secret that the chief and I have issues. But that particular incident happened nearly four years ago. And the chief survived the political fallout nicely by explaining that his golfing foursome included a high-ranking official from the Department of Homeland Security who was giving them private tutoring on terror avoidance because so many Fortune 500 companies are located in Minnesota.

I suspected the real reason Captain Shuda sought a philosophical discussion on media coverage was to avoid a similar discourse on police handling of missing person cases. He knew victims without vocal families also get less attention from law enforcement.

"By the time we even got the report," he said, "there was a foot of snow on the ground."

I'd already checked the weather that October weekend with Channel 3's meteorologist and confirmed an abrupt climate change. A cold front moved in from Canada and the mercury plunged more than 40 degrees in two days. With the sudden drop came twelve inches of snow. So even if police had received a timely missing person call and had mounted an immediate search, Mark's trail was cold right from the start.

"So what have you learned in the Mark Lefevre case?" I phrased my question in a nonconfrontational manner because I wanted the information straight and because I might need him to go on camera later.

"We got no leads."

Captain Shuda explained that Mark's car hadn't been stopped by any law enforcement officer since his disappearance. He hadn't been arrested anywhere in the United States. No activity on his bank account, either. Without leads, the cops didn't have much to investigate. Which left me another day closer to deadline, and still no story.

SIGOURNEY NELSON ALSO proved a dead end. She'd disconnected her phone. Moved from her apartment. Hadn't updated her driver's license address. Owned no property, not even a car. Didn't appear to have been born in

Minnesota. And didn't have a hunting, fishing, or snowmobiling license, either.

"That is all the databases we have to check," Xiong said. "I will work on the laptop now." Mark's accounts were password protected, but Xiong thought he might find a way past them.

Besides having Xiong run a computer background check, I'd door-knocked on Sigourney's former neighbors who were clueless as to where she'd gone. As for tracking relatives, the name Nelson made that path unpromising. The Minneapolis phone book alone had thirteen pages of Nelsons and I gave up calling after a dozen strikeouts.

Sigourney had vanished as completely as her old boyfriend.

CHAPTER 12

In the past months, Nick Garnett must have picked up some technology tips from his teenage son because a text message from him popped on my phone, reading "Somthin fshy re mal atack."

"Go jmp lak," I texted back.

I figured he was hoping to get some more crime-stopper tips on the fish frenzy, but truthfully, unless they had an arrest, it was bordering on old news.

"Whpper fsh tale," he sent back.

"Anglng fr pblcty?" I countered.

"U dont tke bait, yr cmpetiton wil."

I couldn't chance that, and since it would take forever for him to pony up the details texting, I drove over to the Mall of America to tell him—in person, in a nice way—to knock it off.

There I learned, unofficially, not for attribution, that one of the fish from Underwater Adventures was missing.

A very famous fish: Big Mouth Billy Bass, the Minnesota record largemouth bass.

"What do you mean Big Mouth Billy is gone?" I asked.

"You were there that day, Riley," Garnett said. "Rescuing live fish and counting up dead fish. It was very chaotic. Only later did they realize Billy was AWOL."

To the Minnesota world of bass anglers, he's iconic. Even I had heard of Big Mouth Billy and I'd grown up in a family who considered the only good fish to be a fried fish. Sports led the newscast four years ago when Billy was landed. Eight pounds, fifteen ounces of scrappy, fighting bass. The entire struggle recorded on home video. Not giant by Florida or California standards, but mammoth here in the Midwest.

"Who would kidnap a fish?" I asked. "And why?"

Garnett shrugged.

Unlike Minnesota's state fish, the walleye, lake bass are not particularly good eating. Especially not big ones. They tend to be tough.

"Do you think someone would stuff Billy and hang him as a trophy?" I pressed.

Garnett shrugged again. "Seems unsportsmanlike."

These days it's frowned upon to mount exceptional fish as trophies. Catch and release is considered more courteous to other anglers, not to mention the fish. Following numerous photo ops, Billy's captor donated him to Underwater Adventures so everyone could share the wonder. They even sponsored a public contest to name him and he ended up with the moniker of a robotic singing fish toy.

How could a thief display the real legendary lunker without arousing suspicion? Maybe pure possession, not bragging rights, was the motive. Illicit art collectors hoard stolen masterpieces that can never be shown outside their ultra-private galleries. Perhaps Billy was destined to become a shrine in some fish fanatic's secluded northern Minnesota cabin.

"Even if we had any leads, he'd be hard to ID," Garnett said.

"You mean because all fish look alike?"

"Well, that, and he was last weighed two years ago. Ten pounds, nine ounces. No telling what he's at now. How could we even prove it was Billy if we found him?"

I pondered that dilemma as I headed back to the station to pull file tape from our news archives for what I expected to be the lead story, and also to check if there might be any identifying marks on the missing fish.

Channel 3 had two pieces of tape: home video of the record fish being reeled in and Billy first being displayed at Underwater Adventures. Forty-seven seconds total. I slowed it down, frame by frame, but all I could see was fins, scales, and a tail.

Over the years, Tom McHale, our lead anchor, had turned his private bass-fishing hobby into a public obsession that viewers found endearing and oh so very Minnesotan. When Tom heard the news about Big Mouth Billy he pushed the producer to play the story straight off the top and promo the hell out of it during *Wheel of Fortune* and beyond.

((TEASE/SOT))
TUNE IN AT TEN FOR A
CHANNEL 3 EXCLUSIVE . . .
HOW DID MINNESOTA'S
MOST FAMOUS FISH
BECOME THE ONE THAT
GOT AWAY?

I should have seen it coming.

Noreen, an animal lover, was also hooked on the Billy mystery and was convinced that viewers would be, too. After all, they love animal stories. The research proves it.

So the next morning, after drooling over the overnights, then reviewing a note from Tom about how important this theft case is to all Minnesotans, Noreen wrote BIG MOUTH BILLY and drew a fish-shaped outline around the words on the second Sunday in May, where she had declined to slot my missing-groom story.

Trust her to care more about a missing fish than a missing person.

"There's plenty of foul play in the fish case." She defended her decision. "You have yet to bring me any proof your guy didn't simply take off for places unknown."

I hated to concede that she could be right. I needed to keep in mind, contrary to what viewers see on the news, most of the missing adult cases tracked by the FBI are actually men. And plenty of those missing show up later with a rueful explanation that they just had to get away for a while. But I didn't think Mark Lefevre was going to waltz through the door all sheepish and apologetic.

"And the leads are much fresher in the fish case," Noreen continued. "So we need to put our resources where they have the best chance of success. Rent a boat. Buy some hip waders. Do whatever it takes."

Noreen seemed to be giving me a blank check—unheard of in a television news investigation these days. Especially since she'd just nixed my meth surveillance story because of cost.

"You don't actually expect me to find this missing fish?" Better I know the stakes now than on the air date.

"Not right away. But I want a follow-up story that shows Minnesota how much we care."

"And how much is that?" I was almost afraid to hear her answer.

Just then Noreen and I heard applause and noticed the general manager of the station standing outside her door, clapping vigorously.

"We care plenty," he announced. And because he said it, that made it so.

I've learned not to get too attached to GMs. Our network owners constantly rotate them in and out of the front office searching for a magic formula to hit that elusive profit margin.

The only time GMs usually want to sit in on a story meeting is if the news department is preparing to hose a car dealer. Car dealers are among a station's most lucrative advertisers; car dealers are also the most complained-about businesses on the Channel 3 viewer tip line. Dealers like to flex their money muscles so the station sales department will lean on the GM to lean on the news department to kill such investigations.

"Recovering the state's most beloved bass will build viewer loyalty for generations," the GM stressed.

His eyes got bright and shiny as he imagined all the viewers demonstrating their gratitude by reaching for their television remotes and switching news channels. And just like that, despite Channel 3's tight finances, he announced that the station would offer a $10,000 reward for the safe return of Big Mouth Billy.

Then he winked. "Just think of all the free publicity."

Noreen gushed over the brilliance of the plan. "And if the fish is found, the station gets the inside track on the rescue."

The GM nodded enthusiastically, then threw his hands in the air and shared the best boon of all. "If the fish is never found, it won't cost us a thing!"

I NEEDED SOME air, so I went to the hospital to visit Emily Flying Cloud, the wounded K-9 officer, and assure her that Shep was in good hands—mine—while she recovered.

She thanked me for the flowers, which sat on a corner table by a potted green plant next to a gold-foil box of high-end chocolates. I wondered if any dark-chocolate coconuts remained.

"So Shep's staying at your house?" Emily seemed anxious about his whereabouts. I hoped she didn't have misgivings concerning my ability to care for him.

I nodded, even smiled to reassure her that he was doing just fine.

"That's good." She seemed relieved. "I'm glad he's with you. But keep a close eye on him. Police dogs are never off duty."

Instead of a badge, a bandage covered Emily's shoulder. Another wrapped around her midsection. And an IV line ran from her wrist to a plastic bag hanging on a pole near her bed. She also had a hairline skull fracture from where her head hit the concrete. Hospital staff had shaved off part of her long black hair to clean the wound. Her condition had stabilized, but she remained in the hospital for observation because she'd had some minor bleeding on the brain.

Emily acted grateful for company, even though talking seemed a bit of a strain. Mostly, she wanted to gush about her partner.

"Shep's got more raw talent in his nose than I've got in my entire body."

I laughed. "I'm sure that's not true."

But she insisted otherwise. "Seriously, I could be replaced a whole lot easier than he could. Do you know how many police dogs develop bad hips?"

Her previous shepherd had come from a prized K-9 blood-line in Czechoslovakia and Emily had to learn Czech commands before she could teach her dog English. They'd spent eight years fighting crime together before her pooch partner went to that big doghouse in the sky. When Shep became available, Emily jumped at the chance to partner with him.

There was some debate whether to change his name. Current K-9 policy calls for patrol dogs to respond to formi-dable names like Nitro. Or Chaos. Or Gunner. All the better to intimidate bad guys into surrendering before the dog is unleashed.

Shep's name was tame by those standards. But because his primary duty was drug detection, the K-9 officials decided not to go through retraining, which can be time consuming and might not be successful in an emergency situation.

Emily also explained that law enforcement dogs aren't always German shepherds, but can be golden retrievers, Labradors, or even your basic humane society mutt. "It all comes down to the nose."

I've been told more than once that I have a nose for news, but I don't think that's what she meant.

Drug-sniffing dogs, like Shep, are trained to scratch at a suspicious package. Bomb-sniffing dogs, however, are trained to sit down next to a questionable item.

"Can you guess why?" she asked.

I was just about to when she feebly pantomimed KABOOM with her fingers. "Two different alerts for two different tasks. That's why bomb dogs are single purpose."

Then she explained how scent lineups are popular in Europe, but have been slower to catch on in United States law enforcement. There, the dog takes a whiff of a sock or a crime scene, then is moved past a group of people, including a suspect. If he alerts at the correct one, that's considered probable cause.

"Well, you probably need to get some rest," I told her as I glanced at my watch and got up to say goodbye.

But she started quietly reciting all the special skills K-9s can be trained for and it was sort of like that movie scene when Bubba Blue tells Forrest Gump all the ways to prepare shrimp, so I sat back down and zoned out until I heard her mentioning something about dogs who find missing people.

"Tell me more about those again," I said.

"Search-and-rescue dogs," she explained. "It's a very broad category. They look for people buried alive after natural disasters or terrorist attacks. They can track people who've committed crimes and fled. Children who wander off. Hunters who lose their way."

Mark Lefevre's trail was stone cold. No search dog could possibly get a scent after so much time. Or could it?

"What about dead people?" I asked. "Can these dogs find bodies hidden in clandestine graves?" I wasn't trying to be negative. I just like being prepared.

"Those would be cadaver dogs." Emily explained that they are considered the elite of the K-9 world. Given a whiff from a small bottle containing decomposing human remains, the best can find bodies underwater or underground.

I asked her about a recent police case in Minneapolis in which a young boy was beaten to death by his aunt. A search dog, brought in to sniff out the house, failed to find his body, hidden in a clothes dryer.

"What went wrong?" I wondered.

"That dog probably wasn't a true cadaver dog. Never exposed to a dead body and didn't recognize that it and the missing boy were the same thing. Human bodies are hard to come by for K-9 training."

She told me about recent K-9 success stories in Minnesota that inspire handlers. Last spring one dog discovered the bodies of two young brothers frozen in lake ice on the Red Lake Indian Reservation. The boys disappeared four months earlier and had been feared abducted. The year before, authorities in southern Minnesota found a headless body. A police dog later found the severed head in a distant location.

"I've actually started training Shep to be a cadaver dog." She smiled proudly. "He has enormous potential." She'd been using a decaying human tooth to teach him the elusive scent of death.

"Maybe I can help," I said. "I seem to stumble across more than my share of dead bodies."

She laughed, like I was joking. So I didn't mention I'd actually been up close to three in the last six months, and not by choice, either.

Maybe I'd confide more after we got to know each other better.

I promised to bring Shep along on my next visit and instead of looking pleased, Emily looked panicked. "No, Riley, it's best if you leave Shep home."

"Don't worry, Emily," I said. "K-9s are allowed in hospitals. Just like service dogs for the blind or handicapped." I was surprised she didn't seem to know that. "And just think how excited Shep will be to see you."

She closed her eyes momentarily, then glanced back and forth, like she was checking to make sure no nurse was around. "I'm begging you, Riley. Keep him out of sight and keep him away from me."

"What's going on here?" I asked. "Why are you getting all weird on me?"

Emily paused, as if weighing how far she could trust me. After all, we'd just met. Then she slumped back in her pillow, apparently deciding she had no choice. "Shep was the sniper's target. I accidentally stepped in the way."

That theory made about as much sense to me as roving packs of organized serial killers pushing drunken college men into rivers across the country and leaving smiley-face drawings behind. I wondered if Emily's pain medication was off.

"Why would anyone want to shoot Shep?"

"The usual motive." I shrugged and she rolled her eyes at me. "Riley, which are you? Ignorant or innocent?"

"Neither," I answered. "I'm confused."

"Money," she said. "Money is the usual motive."

She explained that Shep was so successful at detecting drugs that Minnesota's meth confiscation had gone way up and drug dealers were losing big money and doing big time in the big house.

"And they blame him?" I asked.

"Sure they do. You've heard of the war on drugs? Well, he's the state's not-so-secret weapon."

I thought of the periodic news briefs showing Shep being honored for this bust or that bust. He always seemed to be smiling when they put a medal around his neck. The police considered it good public relations. But Emily worried that someone, perhaps with the help of a department traitor, had put a contract out on Shep.

"He's a dog with a price on his head."

CHAPTER 13

Vivian Post's address was only a couple of miles from mine, but millions of dollars separated the property values of our homes. I knew she was loaded, at least on paper, but not until I drove down the narrow curves of Peninsula Road did I grasp the historic cachet that old money can buy.

"Why don't you come out to the house for a drink," she'd said on my voice mail. "I feel like we got off to a bad start."

Her tone sounded patrician, implying perhaps it was my fault that she and I failed to hit it off.

I suspected a call to her family attorney, most likely billed out at around $500 an hour, had advised her of the difficulties in Muzzling the Media and instead suggested a strategy of trying to Shape the Story.

Influence came naturally to their family. For generations, they'd influenced the arts, education, and politics of Minnesota. Wings of hospitals, university buildings, and museum masterpieces exist for the rest of us because of their altruism.

The estate stretched over the tip of a peninsula jutting into White Bear Lake. A stone mansion, built by a corporate mover and shaker and later owned by a U.S. ambassador, sat on a cliff commanding views from all directions.

As I drove up, the windows of the house seemed like eyes watching my arrival. Spring was late coming to the estate compared to the rest of the town. Green flourished on my street; gray still ruled here. A vision of Edgar Allan Poe's crumbling House of Usher reverberated from my college-lit days and, like the narrator of that particular tale of woe, I, too, felt a brief, irrational fear.

Mrs. Post herself answered the door, directing me past a suit of armor in the entryway that lessened my angst by reminding me of an old Scooby-Doo cartoon. We entered a large sitting room with one entire wall of floor-to-ceiling windows and another featuring a stone fireplace. Two bottles of wine—one red, one white—and a few crystal decanters of liquor were spread on a small antique table along with a pot of hot tea and miniature appetizers and desserts. She motioned for me to join her on a weathered leather couch with a scratchy, old polar bear skin draped over it, head, claws, and all.

People in this town take their burly mascot seriously. Many display statues of white bears in front of their houses or fly flags from their porches. One car dealer even has a giant white bear monument sitting on the roof of the dealership. Each summer, he paints swim trunks on it; each fall he paints over them.

"I had no idea we were practically neighbors." Vivian flashed me a professional smile and I saw where Madeline got her dazzling teeth.

"Me, neither." I doubted this neighbor ploy would develop into the kind of relationship where we borrowed sugar or brought in each other's mail, but I smiled back anyway and asked how Madeline was doing.

"She does seem to have her heart set on this story of yours." Mrs. Post offered me a drink. I indicated the hot tea. She poured me a cup and herself a glass of white wine.

"Maybe Madeline needs some answers," I said.

"How likely is it your answers will bring her comfort?"

We both knew no guarantee existed, so I said nothing and instead bit into a small, spicy piece of cheese bread with diced tomatoes.

"I just see more pain ahead and no mother wants that for her child. I would do anything in my power to spare her grief."

Mrs. Post seemed sincere. And I had no doubt she had wielded plenty of power and money in the past to spare Madeline all kinds of grief.

"But Madeline's an adult now." I saw no harm in stating the obvious. "Making adult decisions, like who to marry."

"I had no objection to her marriage. One of the advantages of having family money is that we're free to marry for love. Madeline loved Mark. That's all she had to say to win my blessing. His paycheck never entered the debate."

"That's very understanding, considering they hadn't known each other very long and came from very different backgrounds."

"That's what a prenup is for." Vivian Post smiled graciously and assuredly, as only the truly wealthy can. "Mark signed willingly, knowing that if the marriage failed, he would get very little. Their engagement was brief, but during that time I grew fond of him."

"How come? What did you like about the guy?"

She paused, pressing a finger to her chin, as if searching

for the right word. "I guess you might say he was memorable."

Seemed an unusual adjective for a son-in-law.

"In what way?" I asked.

"Some people, you meet and never give them a second thought," she said. "Mark made an impression on me. I understood what my daughter saw in him."

"You said Madeline loved Mark. Do you think he loved her?"

"Last fall I would have said yes without hesitation. Now I don't know what to think about his motives. My daughter has a kind soul and doesn't deserve this anguish."

Perfect timing to cut to my primary question. "So what's your theory on where Mark is?"

"I have no idea. My first thought was he had a car accident on the way to the ceremony. We waited for some word, but heard nothing. By then Madeline was hysterical so I sent the guests home."

"Did it occur to you to contact the police?" It seemed only fair I give her the same treatment I gave Mark's mother. "Do you wish you had?"

Just then a man walked into the room. For a second I mistook him for my photographer, Malik Rahman. He had the same physical characteristics, height, weight, dark hair, and swarthy complexion. But I'd purposely come alone because I wanted Mrs. Post to relax and feared a camera would make her clam up. She introduced the man as her son, Roderick, who lived in a new wing of the house built over the garage.

"I asked him to join us," she explained.

Mrs. Post and Madeline shared the same facial features and complexion. I remembered Libby, Madeline's maid of honor, remarking that Roderick took after his father in appearance. Malik's father was from Pakistan, but I knew very little about Mr. Post's roots.

Because Mrs. Post was a widow, I didn't feel I should pry too deeply into her husband's background this early in our relationship. I know from personal experience that widows don't like virtual strangers digging for details about their deceased husbands. As for me, Hugh's death was Google-able by anyone who cared to learn how the governor's bodyguard was killed in the line of duty.

After a closer look, I recognized Roderick as the man driving Mrs. Post's car outside the station the other day. Roderick appeared to have overheard the last part of our conversation concerning whether the family had or should have contacted the police when Mark vanished.

"Just tell her the truth, Mother," he said.

"Tell me what?" I asked.

The two of them looked at each other. He nodded, seemingly to encourage her, so she began to speak.

"I thought it best to wait when Mark didn't show up for the ceremony." She looked me directly in the eye like she had nothing to hide. "We didn't know what we were dealing with at first, and I didn't want to risk complicating matters by involving law enforcement or the media."

"How would that complicate matters?"

Roderick shook his head at my apparent naïveté and Mrs. Post paused before giving me a lesson in the disadvantages of being rich.

"We had to consider the possibility that Mark might have been kidnapped for ransom."

That one, I didn't see coming.

Her theory put a whole new spin on his disappearance and the behavior of the Post family. Vivian and Roderick explained how their waiting game unfolded. First they waited for word from Mark. When they heard nothing, they waited for word from kidnappers. When they heard nothing, they just kept waiting.

Ransom kidnappings are rare in this part of the world, though Minnesota's had some whoppers with lasting impact.

Like seventy-five years ago, when the Barker-Karpis Gang snatched the president of Hamm Brewing Company (better known now for its advertising jingle and bear mascot than its foamy refreshment). They held William A. Hamm Jr. prisoner in their gangster hideout until they'd collected a ransom of a cool hundred grand.

A perfect plan—almost.

Except the FBI crime lab used a forensic breakthrough to crack the case. Now called "latent fingerprint identification," scientists painted the ransom notes with a silver nitrate solution to raise the invisible fingerprints and prove the kidnappers' identity.

Four decades later, kidnapping was again on the front pages in Minnesota. Virginia Piper was abducted from her home by two masked men. Her housekeeper was taped to a chair. A note demanded one million bucks in twenty-dollars bills—the largest ransom in U.S. history back then. She was discovered two days later, chained to a tree in a state park, after her retired investment-banker husband paid up. The case was never solved and very little of the ransom—just four grand—was recovered.

Every major anniversary, some journalist or another tries to unlock the mystery. I'd even taken a crack at it myself during a long-ago sweeps month, interviewing a killer behind bars who seemed a reasonable suspect.

"But clearly Mark wasn't kidnapped," I said to the Post family.

"In retrospect, yes," Roderick agreed. "But how were we to know? Waiting seemed prudent. Action seemed rash."

"Even if he had been taken for ransom, wouldn't you still want help from the police?"

He explained, as casually as if discussing health-care coverage or automobile-insurance deductibles, that their family had kidnap insurance on his mother, his younger sister, and himself.

"If we had received a ransom demand for Mark, our insurance carrier would have first contacted a private security team with experience in such matters. They would have made the decision when to coordinate with local law enforcement."

While the Posts didn't typically reveal that kind of information to strangers, preparation for such financial emergencies wasn't unusual in their social circle. Roderick's future brother-in-law would have eventually been added to the family insurance policy. Now that wasn't necessary.

Roderick seemed more comfortable socially than the other members of his family, yet he deferred to Vivian several times during my visit. His conversation was more relaxed, but he also had less personal stake in the outcome of my investigation than did his sister. That might make him a better source to cultivate.

His mother mentioned that he supervised the Family Foundation. I murmured my admiration for the charitable work done by their organization. He was explaining the political challenges of philanthropy when Madeline suddenly entered the room and the conversation.

"What's going on?" She clearly wasn't expecting to find company, particularly not me.

"You remember Riley Spartz from Channel 3," Roderick said.

Of course she does, I almost blurted out. We just met the other day. You don't have to treat her like a child. But I kept my mouth shut, except for hello, and let Roderick spin our meeting however he wished.

"Well, Mother and I wanted to discuss Riley's television story regarding Mark and see if we could lend some assistance."

"It's good to see you again, Madeline," I said.

Madeline seemed confused to find me chatting amiably with her mother and brother. Maybe even a touch peeved. Maybe even a bit suspicious. I stood up on the pretense of stretching, but really stepped aside to give them some personal space.

While Vivian and Roderick, in whispers, assured Madeline they weren't plotting behind her back and only had her best interests at heart, I admired a wall display of antique photographs of their ancestors. The pictures weren't the usual boring family head shots but, rather, adventurous poses on moose hunts, African safaris, and deep-sea fishing expeditions.

A glass case held an odd collection of weapons: old guns that looked like they couldn't fire anymore, knives with feathers on the handles, and ornately carved mallets. Some of the pieces seemed to be from the Old West, others from more exotic locales. I was curious about their history, but before I could inquire, Mrs. Post called for us all to sit down and visit.

It was one of those uncomfortable moments where we all looked at one another but no one said anything. Sort of like a holiday dinner with bothersome in-laws. To help defuse the familial tension, I remarked how nice it was to have both the bride's and groom's sides cooperating with my investigation.

"What do you mean?" Madeline asked.

So I explained about Mark's mother also being on board for the story and how she gave me his laptop and was going to let me dig through his belongings for possible leads into why and how her only son vanished. I remember thinking that bit of news should also ensure the Post family's continued assistance.

All three Posts smiled. Madeline, gratefully. Vivian, nervously. Roderick, skeptically. For a brief flash, they reminded me of the trio of monkeys who saw, spoke, and heard no evil.

AT HOME, I refilled Shep's water dish, gave him a scratch behind the ears and a good-doggy pep talk. Then I walked to the bookshelves which showcased my collection of classical literature. I pulled a slender volume of horror off the top shelf and considered whether Vivian had intentionally named her children after the doomed siblings in "The Fall of the House of Usher."

Probably just a crazy coincidence, but I thought it best not to ask. Especially since Poe had hinted at an incest theme in that particular masterpiece.

I actually felt sorry for Vivian. She seemed like one of those people who are well-meaning but make terrible first impressions. The rich don't have to work at being cordial the way the rest of us do.

But when I crawled under the covers that night and opened my Edgar Allan Poe book, I shuddered as I read of the mysterious sensitivity affliction befalling the Ushers until their entire family line was consumed.

CHAPTER 14

I spent most of the next day transcribing tape interviews, so by late afternoon, my mail slot in the newsroom was crammed full of paper. I carried the stack back to my desk without much enthusiasm because nothing good seems to come by mail these days. Not snail mail anyway. All the good news comes by e-mail.

And my paycheck is deposited straight to my bank. Most of my personal bills are paid online directly through my checking account. So I hardly ever touch money. My remaining bills I route to Channel 3 since I prefer to keep my home address private and wasn't sure how long I'd stay in my new place. I separated nuisance mail from that with news value. Most government agencies even send news releases by e-mail now to save on postage and paper, so there wasn't much from the stack of paper that didn't end up in the trash.

Less news, more junk.

One envelope didn't have a return address, but that wasn't unusual; often tipsters want to remain anonymous.

Sometimes they're blowing the whistle on a crooked employer and fear retribution. Sometimes they're launching political dirty tricks and need to cover their tracks. Sometimes they just want to whine about a news story but don't have the guts to sign their name.

This letter writer's reason was none of the above and became clear the minute I unfolded the note, made up of words cut from newspaper headlines and glued to a sheet of paper. Primitive in a high-tech age.

> FISH SHOULD BE FREE AND NOT ON DISPLAY IN GLASS CELLS. WE WILL RELEASE BIG MOUTH BILLY INTO THE WILD AS A LESSON NOT TO IMPRISON NATURE'S CREATURES.
> THE ANIMAL LIBERATION FRONT

I wasn't sure if the note was genuine or a joke, but I wished my fingerprints weren't on it.

I phoned Malik to bring his camera to my office. He'd left the station five minutes earlier and was not pleased to turn around in rush-hour traffic. His wife, Missy, no doubt had supper ready and the kids were waiting for him to walk through the door so they could yell "Daddy! Daddy!" and rush him with hugs and kisses.

"Do I have to?" he asked. I'd probably understand his reluctance better if I had what he had waiting at home.

"Overtime," I answered. Usually raising Malik's paycheck raised his spirits. But this didn't seem to be one of those times. Missy must be grilling steaks.

"Can you really not do it?" I asked. "Or do you just not want to do it. Honest, it'll be worth it when you see what came in the mail."

"You always say nothing good comes in the mail anymore."

"Well, I was wrong."

So he returned and when he looked beyond my giddy smile and saw the makeshift note, Malik gave me a big thumbs-up.

A mere sheet of paper . . . not only did its cut-and-paste message spell out a fascinating criminal motive; it spelled a turning point in the investigation. And for a television news station in the midst of sweeps, that combination can also be spelled r-a-t-i-n-g-s.

There's a saying in the news biz: When you don't have a lot to shoot, shoot a lot of it. So Malik shot a full tape of the letter from every conceivable angle, in close-ups and wide shots, carefully arranged on a piece of black velvet. To look classy.

First he photographed the pasted words straight on, then with a pan and a zoom, later with some fancy-focus moves. He also videotaped each word individually in case we wanted to edit together a quick-cut montage for variety. The envelope had a Minneapolis postmark with a down-town zip code, so he spent several minutes shooting the hell out of that, too.

When he finished, I called Noreen and told her I had something to show her. She was busy watching the end of the six o'clock news and wanted me to just bring it to her office. I said no. She said this better be good. And she said it in her I'm-the-boss-and-you're-not voice.

She walked into my office, took one look, made a joyful noise, and called our media lawyer, Miles Lewis. His first words after he arrived back at the station were, "Have you called the authorities yet?"

"It could be a fake," I said. "I'd hate to cry wolf over a

fish. Let the cops watch it on the news. If they want it, they can call us."

"But I'd hate airing it if it's a hoax," Noreen said. "Then we'd look stupid."

"The validity of the note is for law enforcement to decide, not us," Miles said. "We have what could be evidence of a crime. We need to turn it over."

His decision didn't surprise me.

That's why I made sure we videotaped it before he arrived. The last thing I needed was the cops arriving with their hands out for the letter while we were still setting up lights. Lately, I'd caught myself thinking like a lawyer. An unpleasant but increasingly necessary part of the job of an investigative reporter.

While I silently congratulated myself for being one step ahead of Miles, he continued laying down the law, or rather, his interpretation of it. "If the police shrug it off, then you can do whatever you want. But they get first crack."

"Can we still air the story?" Noreen asked.

I sure thought so. "If the cops want the note for their investigation, that gives our story credibility." Once a story has legs, it's easier to run.

Miles agreed with my news analysis. "As for airing it, that's an editorial decision, not a legal one. Air it or don't air it. I'm just telling you at some point you need to offer it to law enforcement."

Noreen and I both nodded at the same time. An unusual enough occurrence that we looked at each other with surprise and suspicion.

Miles wanted to count heads. "Right now, do only the four of us know about this letter?"

Malik had been so quiet in the corner, I'd forgotten all

about him. He preferred avoiding legalese debates. "Just the four of us," I repeated.

Miles warned us to try and keep this development quiet in the newsroom until we made a decision about our coverage. That might be difficult, I thought to myself, the other staff already had to be wondering what was going on in my office. Anytime Miles showed up, that usually meant trouble.

Most of his lawyering took place in an upstairs office, poring over the fine print of contracts or negotiating personal-services terms with valued employees. He typically only came down to the newsroom for script review. Playing First Amendment attorney made him proud he went to law school.

Noreen dialed the Bloomington police. I listened as she explained that we had received information that might be related to their missing-fish investigation at the Mall of America.

"It concerns the Animal Liberation Front." She hung up the phone and told us an officer was on his way.

Using two pencils as chopsticks, I carried the note from my office to the conference room, stopping first at the photocopy machine. I didn't want any cop looking longingly at other boxes or files stacked in my office and showing up later with a search warrant.

While we waited, I Googled the Animal Liberation Front, otherwise known as ALF. I already knew this wasn't the first time the international animal rights group had been linked with plots to free animals. But I was surprised at how frequently they'd struck in Minnesota, which indicated a strong following in the state.

The group claimed responsibility for numerous ecoterrorism acts starting a decade ago when they raided a

University of Minnesota lab to free more than a hundred research animals, mostly mice. According to campus officials they caused $2 million in damage, which works out to about $20,000 a mouse. I know freedom isn't free, but to me that price tag seemed steep.

I pulled some news file tape from the incident and saw crime-scene video around a large campus building with police cars parked outside. ALF provided the media with interior shots of cages upturned and broken laboratory equipment. In a sound bite from a news conference, a university researcher contended that the attack set Alzheimer's studies back years.

Looking online for other cases, I noticed that a few years ago a related animal rights group set fire to a genetic research center under construction at the U of M, resulting in more than $600,000 in damage. More file tape for me. And since then, the Animal Liberation Front had freed thousands of minks from local fur farms (Minnesota being the third-largest fur-farming state in the nation).

When the Bloomington detective arrived, he wasn't alone. An FBI agent accompanied him, acting all law and orderly. Neither cracked a smile when I asked if they were fishing for clues or casting for suspects. Both drifted to the note and envelope in the center of the conference table like leeches to blood.

I'd already forgotten the FBI guy's name because his kind are generally uncooperative with the media, though I'd stuck his card in my purse.

"Has anyone touched this?" he asked.

I raised my hand. "It was addressed to me so I opened it."

"We'll be needing to fingerprint you."

"We'll get back to you on that," Miles said in his big-shot attorney voice. The last thing I wanted was for the feds to have my prints on file. I wouldn't put it past them to already have my name on some watch list or another.

The FBI guy scowled and explained that the Animal Liberation Front was the nation's most destructive domestic terrorism group and our country needed the cooperation of all of its citizens to put a halt to their sabotage.

"We're talking about a fish," I said. "Shouldn't you guys be worrying more about Al Qaeda?"

"Terrorism is terrorism," he responded.

Noreen motioned for me to be quiet, which was actually good advice because I was about to inquire where that FBI attitude had been in the weeks leading up to September 11, 2001. Zacarias Moussaoui, considered the twentieth hijacker, was locked up in a Minnesota jail after a flight-school manager tipped the feds that his newest student wasn't interested in learning how to land an airplane. FBI headquarters had messed up big-time in refusing to search his computer. It wasn't a moment they liked being reminded about.

Now the FBI guy was asking us not to air our lead. The Bloomington cop nodded in agreement, although the feds were clearly taking charge of the investigation.

"We're a news organization," Noreen said. Good for her. The late news was still a good two hours away. Plenty of time to make air. "No one's life is in jeopardy. I'm not sure we can comply with your request."

Privately, I suspected animal lover that she was, she might secretly be rooting for the Animal Liberation Front.

Miles backed her up. "Our civic duty was to provide evidence. We've done that."

"If we lose our chance to recover the fish," Mr. FBI said, "it will be your fault."

I suppressed a snicker at the absurdity.

Ever since British media voluntarily blacked out Prince Harry's combat deployment, even government agencies here in America were starting to think they were entitled to secret censorship deals with the media.

Then the FBI guy said something about how Operation Piscis Absenti was highest priority.

"What did you just call it?" I asked.

"Operation Piscis Absenti," he said. "That's the code name for the operation."

I must have looked puzzled, so he explained that Piscis Absenti was Latin for "missing fish."

"What's the matter with calling it the Big Mouth Billy Bass Case in plain old English?" I asked. That's what the media had dubbed the caper. "Or how about Bassgate?"

"It sounds trivial and obvious." He justified the use of Latin by insisting that it lent an aura of seriousness and sophistication to the investigation, thus making it easier to obtain federal resources. "Once the public hears Operation Piscis Absenti, that will become the preferred code name."

Noreen and I gave each other another look that said, Okay just for this story, we're on the same wavelength. But Miles nodded like the FBI guy was making perfect sense. Understandable because the law is full of pretentious Latin phrases.

I'd heard enough about the FBI guy's strategy to make his investigation appear more important than his colleagues' cases. It didn't seem all that different than jockeying for better play in a newscast except tax dollars were involved. I could have pointed out that Piscis Absenti might not go over big with the media because it's hard to pronounce and harder to spell, but I needed to get some real work done. No story ever got written sitting in news meetings all night.

Just then Tom McHale stuck his head in the conference room to see what was going on. Tom was an old-school anchor, who started as a street reporter and became a top investigative journalist before moving to the high-profile, big-bucks job of news reader. That meant he had to leave his tough-guy persona behind—while an investigative reporter's job is to piss people off, a TV anchor's job is to be loved. I understood the conflict. But even if he'd sold out for cash and a cushy schedule, Tom hadn't lost his news instincts. He sensed when something was up in the conference room.

"There's been a development in the Big Mouth Billy Bass Case," Noreen said.

The FBI guy pursed his lips in a pout, probably because she hadn't used the official code name.

"But we're still weighing our options," Noreen continued, filling Tom in on the action as he pulled up a chair.

I handed Tom a copy of the newspaper-cutout letter and all became clear to him. He had that elated look anchors get when they know they're going to cream the competition with a big exclusive right off the top of the newscast.

"What's to decide," he asked, "except whether Riley or I get to hold the letter up on set? I vote for me."

"There are some complicating factors." Noreen tilted her head toward the FBI guy as she explained the situation.

"Let's not forget the fishnappers sent the note to a TV station," I reminded everyone. "They're expecting media coverage. Who knows what they'll do if they don't get it. I better get started on the ten."

"I vote for that," Tom said.

I even ad-libbed a story opening to help build consensus.

POLICE ARE INVESTIGATING
A LEAD IN THE BILLY BASS
CASE IN WHICH A
CONTROVERSIAL ANIMAL
RIGHTS GROUP CLAIMS TO
HAVE KIDNAPPED THE
FAMOUS FISH. THIS
LETTER . . . SENT TO ME
HERE AT CHANNEL 3 . . .
THREATENS TO RELEASE
BILLY INTO THE WILD AS A
LESSON TO US ALL.

I looked around the conference room to gauge reaction.

Predictably, both law enforcement officers shook their heads. They didn't want publicity, and the FBI guy was increasingly sore because no one was saying the code name.

Predictably, Tom argued the presentation would be stronger if he waved the letter, then tossed to me for details. "The content is excellent, though." He looked toward Noreen for approval.

But she and Miles had their heads together, whispering, before announcing, unpredictably, that we'd hold the story for twenty-four hours.

I rolled my eyes at what saps they were until Noreen told the cops she'd be expecting our camera to be allowed at the scene of any arrest. Deal or no deal? Between the $10,000 reward and the kidnapper's note, Channel 3 was trying to corner the market on the fish story.

"We hear you, but we can't promise," FBI guy said.

"Then I can't promise, either," she said.

"*I* hear you," he replied, emphasizing the word *I*.

She seemed to think that meant they had a deal. The

Bloomington cop pulled out a set of tweezers and put the original note and envelope in plastic wrap. I figured they'd have the lab run a fancy fingerprint trick like in the Hamm kidnapping to see how many sets of prints popped.

Tom, shaking his head in disappointment, went back to prepping for his newscast. Malik kept his mouth shut as he had during most of the meeting. At least he'd get home in time to read *Good Night Moon*.

I followed the law enforcement pair down the hall and out of the building. No point in me hanging around the station, either, since my story had been put on hold. Then the FBI guy turned and unexpectedly asked if I'd like to join him for a drink.

I shook my head. "I don't get personally involved with sources." That wasn't necessarily true, but I disliked his attitude.

"This could be a business drink," he suggested.

I paused to consider it and just as I decided I might cultivate some useful information out of him, he must have decided he was getting nowhere with the federal approach and nearly ruined his chances with a tired cliché.

"Maybe I'd just like to get to know you better."

"If you knew me better, you'd like me less." That was my stock reply to that pickup line.

"I don't like you much already," he answered. "So I won't be disappointed."

"Fine. Neither will I."

So we walked across the street to Brit's, a pub known more for its bar than its menu. Since technically we were off duty, he ordered a beer to show me what a regular guy he was. I ordered an iced tea with lemon to show him I wasn't buying it.

"How do you like working for the FBI?" I asked.

"I consider it an honor and a privilege." His chest even puffed out a little when he said it.

Okay, I thought to myself. One of those.

"What's it like working for a TV station?" I don't think he really wanted to know. I think he was just being polite.

"It's a lot like working for a vampire," I replied. "It can suck the life right out of you." That was another one of my stock lines. I have no trouble saying it with a straight face because I know it to be true.

He seemed to be having a hard time deciding whether to respect my honesty or disapprove of my dissing my employer to a complete stranger. So the FBI guy talked about cases he'd handled and I talked about stories I'd covered. And I was starting to think he wasn't such a bad FBI guy after all. I finished the last sip of my drink and was about to ask his name again, when he indicated he needed to leave and picked up my empty glass with a napkin.

"The waitress will clear that," I said.

"I don't mind." He left three twenties on the table. Impressive, because most cops are measly tippers.

"That's too much."

"I don't mind."

Then he turned and walked out the door with my glass and, I suddenly realized, my fingerprints.

CHAPTER 15

I needed to escape all thoughts of fish and cops, so on my way out of downtown I stopped at the Minneapolis Comedy Club where Mark Lefevre used to work. I wanted to see if anyone there had any insight into his disappearance. The bouncer at the door pissed me off right away by not bothering to card me.

I asked about tickets, but he waved me in free. That made me feel special until he explained: "Open-mic night. No charge."

The laughs had already started when I grabbed a seat in the back. The crowd was an eclectic mix of race and dress, mostly under thirty. A waiter knelt beside me in the aisle and took my drink order in a whisper while the comic onstage made a crack about Minnesota's struggling football team and their dreams of a new stadium.

The amateur talent each had a four-minute time limit, enforced by a red flashing lightbulb on the ceiling, to wow us with their stand-up routine. I laughed more in an hour than I'd laughed in a long time. I laughed at things I probably shouldn't have laughed at and wouldn't have laughed at if I hadn't been sitting alone in the dark with a carafe of sweet booze.

I laughed about sex and drugs and roadkill.

A heavyset man in the next section laughed so hard and so continuously, I feared he might collapse. A woman in the front with puffy blond hair kept heckling the comedians and they heckled her back in a war of words. Eventually a tall man in a green polo shirt with the club logo tapped her on the shoulder and motioned her to follow him. Her chair remained empty for the rest of the performances.

I thrived on the people-watching as much as the humor. The comedians were a parade of individuality. One bombed and one was *the* bomb. And the others fell somewhere in between. Some brought friendly cheering sections along, obvious when one portion of the room laughed and applauded a lame one while the rest of the audience seemingly sat on their hands.

When the lights came on and the room emptied, I told a young woman collecting drink menus that I worked for Channel 3 and asked to see the manager.

A minute later the same man who had escorted the heckler outside came over, smiled, and shook my hand. "I'm Jason Hill. What can I do for you?"

I recognized his name from Madeline and Mark's wedding guest list, but hadn't known his connection to the groom until then. A couple of minutes of chatting made it clear he had hoped the club could land some free publicity on the news, and was disappointed that all I came to talk about was Mark Lefevre.

"That washed-up bum?" he said. "I gave him a break and he left me high and dry."

He motioned me over to a corner table away from the cleaning crew where we sat as he explained the economics of comedy. A simple lesson in supply and demand. More comic wannabes existed than were needed. Mark started off on open-mic nights, like the rest of the laugh newbies, doing stand-up for free. Clubs make their money on those nights on drinks, not admission.

"That's why we try to discourage overly vocal audience participation." Jason was alluding to the blond woman he'd evicted. "The open-mic guys aren't getting paid to take abuse."

Like many comic newbies, Mark had raw talent. Despite early hooting, he stuck with his hobby and became a regular.

"He had thick skin," Jason said, "I'll give him that. But he was inconsistent. Sometimes his material was dynamite, but too often it was weak. I told him he needed to be steadier."

Mark showed so much improvement during his last couple of months that Jason offered him a warm-up spot. Coveted in the comedy world, it came with a small stipend, but more important, it offered a chance to perform next to a traveling headliner in front of a paying audience.

"How'd he do?" I asked.

"He didn't embarrass himself or the club. And that's always a possibility with these guys. He'd suddenly developed a real confidence onstage and was exciting to watch. Like he got religion or something. Yet not too good. You don't want your warm-up guy to be funnier than your headliner. That can cause its own problems."

"Artistic jealousy?" I asked, while thinking murder motive.

"No. No," Jason insisted. "It's a brotherhood."

"Really?" I'm afraid my voice held a hint of sarcasm.

"So that feud between Letterman and Leno was just a big misunderstanding."

"Well, there's always a little healthy rivalry," he conceded, "but my guys love each other." Then I wondered why he looked uneasy.

"You know what I think is funny?" I said. "The vocabulary comedians use to describe their work. Laughter seems such a gentle goal, but your terminology is so violent."

He looked puzzled.

"You know what I mean, Jason," I continued. "If a comic does real good stand-up, he says I *killed* that night."

That loosened him up. Jason smiled, laughed, and played along. "And if he does bad, they say, man you *died* out there."

"And don't forget *punch* line," I added. We went back and forth about the significance of *making* someone laugh, when I argued laughter should be voluntary.

"Remember some guys would *kill* for a laugh." Jason delivered the line with just the right amount of inflection. By then he figured I might have enough material for my own monologue about how comedy can be a competitive, cutthroat business.

"I could slot you for next week's open-mic night," he offered. "I'll even let your station bring a camera in if they want to cover it."

I could tell he was still hoping to get the club's name on the news. But I declined, explaining that I was in the middle of sweeps and only had time for work. "Those laughs we shared tonight are the last laughs I'll have for weeks."

Which led me back to the reason I'd stopped by the club in the first place. "Nobody seems to know where Mark is. Any ideas?"

"Zippo. I know he skipped out on his wedding. I was

there with my wife, invited guests. What he does in his personal life is none of my business. I gave him space after that debacle. But the following week he was scheduled to take the stage and he no-showed me. Unacceptable."

The penalty for missing a performance: banned from the club. No exceptions.

"Mark knew the rules," Jason said. "I figure that's why he hasn't been back."

"Could he have hooked up with a club in another state?"

"Comedy is a small world. I think I'd have heard something because clubs use referrals from other clubs. Most of the time, though, we prefer to develop our own stars."

"TV stations are the same way," I said. "Much cheaper to develop your own than to bring in proven talent." Not always better, but definitely cheaper. Then stations can also promote them as hometown, a tactic viewers seem to prefer.

Jason appreciated that I understood business. "I'm just lucky that Chad was here that night to fill in. Cripes, he even had fresh material prepared."

"Who's Chad?"

"He was the guy Mark beat out for the warm-up act. You saw him tonight. He joked about fetishes and national holidays."

I remembered Chad all right. He was *the* bomb.

"He still uses open-mic night to work out the bugs in his monologues. He's probably next door at the bar."

We walked over and found Chad surrounded by groupie chicks with navel rings peeking from under short, tight T-shirts. Jason waved him over, introduced me, and explained my mission before saying good night. Even though we'd shared some laughs, he seemed glad for an excuse to hand me off to someone else to question about Mark Lefevre.

Chad Giswold was fairly good-looking for a comedian, his only physical oddity a gap-toothed grin that was sort of endearing à la Letterman. I didn't feel guilty staring because he was giving me an obvious once-over and his eyes were not on my smile. He didn't believe the part Jason said about me being on TV.

"Really? TV?" Chad asked skeptically. "Well, I suppose you're sexy in a North Dakota kind of way."

"That's not a real effective compliment." I was careful not to laugh. I knew his type and suspected positive feedback would only encourage him. And I was sensitive about the fact that I hadn't checked a mirror in nearly twelve hours. I just hoped nothing was stuck in my teeth.

"Don't worry about how you look," he assured me, placing his hand suggestively on my hip. "In the dark, who can tell?"

Then he offered to prove his sincerity by going home with me. I might not have had sex in nearly two years, but he didn't make me yearn to end my libido's dormancy.

A girlfriend once told me, after her divorce was finalized, that those court papers made her a virgin again—legally if not anatomically. And as tempting as it might have been to prove she was still hot stuff—both to herself and her ex— she needed to choose her first partner carefully, and think about what she wanted from that relationship. Her philosophy seemed just as applicable for widows.

So while Eve had been tempted by the serpent to taste the apple, I told myself I was a virgin again and made of stronger stuff. And Chad was no apple.

I showed him my press pass as proof that I was a legitimate television journalist and explained that, regrettably, in the news department, we have strict rules about sleeping with sources.

"Honest, I could lose my job."

Chad seemed to buy that answer as the only reasonable explanation for my brush-off.

But he had nothing to offer concerning the mysterious disappearance of Mark Lefevre.

"Barely knew the guy."

CHAPTER 16

I f I was infuriated at the FBI guy, that was nothing compared to how I felt after I opened the Minneapolis paper the next morning and saw the banner headline: BIG MOUTH BILLY TO BE FREED?

Scooped on our own story, and not by their hotshot investigative team, either. By their *outdoors* reporter. In the world of news, that's humiliating.

"A controversial animal rights group may have kidnapped a famed record largemouth bass and might be preparing to release it into the wild, sources tell the *Star-Tribune*."

The article didn't name names, not even Channel 3's, but the story regurgitated all the stuff I'd heard the night before about ecoterrorists being America's most destructive domestic enemy.

I was reaching for the phone to scream things at the FBI guy that I couldn't say on television, except I still couldn't remember his name. I fumbled with my purse for his card. Then the phone rang with Noreen on the other end telling me to get in to work pronto and start preparing a story for the noon report. Too late for me to appear on the morning news.

"That jerk!" I felt on the verge of hyperventilating.

"We'll deal with him later." She hung up.

I didn't bother to take a shower. I was too busy trying to rewrite the story in my head so I could take rightful credit for the break in the case. The newspaper didn't appear to have a copy of the actual letter, which gave me an edge in terms of props. True, I wouldn't able to sit on the news set and wave the original. I'd have to settle for a high-quality photocopy and the video Malik shot. But our promotion department would make certain viewers knew which television station turned the original note over to authorities like a good corporate citizen.

I WAS ON deadline, so I almost didn't answer my desk phone. Voice mail picks up on the fifth ring and I could delete it at my leisure. But I caved at the fourth ring because asking a reporter to ignore a ringing phone is like asking a fox to ignore a rabbit, or a news director to ignore ratings, or a politician to ignore a parade.

"Riley!"

The voice on the other end of the line was Toby Elness, my pet-loving source who first introduced me to Shep. He was saying something about only being allowed one phone call. Ends up, he was in jail as a suspect in the kidnapping of Big Mouth Billy Bass.

"Why are you calling me?" I yelled.

"You know I'd never hurt any living animal."

"What I know doesn't matter, Toby. You should be calling a lawyer."

"I don't need an attorney. I'm innocent." Then I thought I heard him mumble, "This time."

He explained that the Animal Liberation Front was a leaderless resistance of like-minded souls whose members helped mice escape from laboratories or freed deer from game farms.

"But we're being set up here," Toby said. "We wouldn't harm other fish just to save one."

He made sense, sort of, but I was no expert on the group's ideology and truth be told, even though Toby had brought me a monster of a tip about pet-cremation scams last year, I still thought him slightly wacko when it came to animal rights. I enjoy a good steak and if turning rats into medical guinea pigs finds a cure for cancer, what's wrong with that?

"You know the police are probably taping this whole conversation," I warned him. Law enforcement isn't supposed to listen in when inmates speak with their attorneys, but cops have no such prohibition about eavesdropping on criminal suspects talking to reporters.

"Doesn't matter to me. I haven't told you anything I haven't already told the police."

"What else have you told them?"

"That amateurs sent you that note. When our members want to claim responsibility for success, they anonymously notify our press office which sends out news releases electronically with photos and video attached as proof. We don't use glue and scissors to get our message out."

"You have a press office?"

"We're very well organized."

"You know I'm going to have to report your arrest."

"Go ahead. We don't receive nearly the media attention our cause deserves."

Hmmmm . . . I had a feeling that was about to change and wondered whether the Animal Liberation Front might have something else to gain from the disappearance of a champion bass. Like having their name on the front page instead of buried in the back of the Metro section.

A computerized voice came on the line and told us we had only one minute left before our call would end.

"Well, Shep says hi," I told Toby. Since I wasn't sure when I'd get home, I'd brought Shep to work with me. Now he was sleeping by my feet. Snoring, even. Hard to imagine he was comfortable amid all the phone, computer, and audio and video cables snaked under my desk. But he and the dust bunnies had apparently made friends.

"Shep's there? Put him on." Toby sounded less businesslike and more joyful. "I want to talk to him."

I nudged Shep in the ribs and held the phone down. "How you doing, big guy?" I heard Toby make what sounded like kissy noises. "Do you miss me?"

Shep barked enthusiastically several times before the line, thankfully, went dead.

I took Shep to the alley behind the station for a quick bathroom break before going to Noreen's office to tell her the latest news about Toby.

We'd need to decide whether to actually name him in the story or to simply report that a member of the Animal Liberation Front was in custody in the Billy Bass Case. Legally we could use his name. He had been arrested. That was a fact. But Channel 3 and most of the other mainstream media in the Twin Cities had long held an ethical standard of only naming suspects actually charged in crimes. Because if he was arrested—then released—who could restore his reputation?

In high-profile cases, that standard was starting to slip away because of the advent of so many online news outlets crying out for immediate content. To compete, traditional media organizations were becoming more ruthless. So the newsroom policy had morphed into not naming suspects unless it was a really, *really* good story.

Noreen had company in her glass-walled office and as I got closer, I realized her visitor was the FBI guy. He either had a closetful of dark-gray suits or was wearing the same one from yesterday.

"You got a lot of nerve coming back here," I told him as I walked in.

Before he could answer, Noreen explained that Agent Jax (oh right, that was his name) was here at her request. "Agent Jax was just telling me how unhappy he is about the leak in the case."

Agent Jax nodded. "Loose lips can jeopardize Operation Piscis Absenti."

I wanted to let him have it right then and there, right smack in those loose lips of his. But I suspected Noreen would prefer a verbal punch, so I simply stated, "I think we all know where the leak came from."

"Excellent. That's what I'm here to find out," he said.

Noreen must have sensed that I wasn't done sparring because she jumped in. "Agent Jax was just asking me if anyone from our newsroom might have—"

"Might have what?" I cut her off. "Tipped the competition to our exclusive?"

Then she cut me off. "And I was just explaining to him how unlikely that particular scenario was."

She and I both glared at him. And he got the message.

"I didn't tell the newspaper," he said. "You have to trust me on this."

"Trust?" I said. "So whose fingerprints were on that letter besides mine?"

He paused like he was considering giving me the usual

can't-comment-on-an-active-investigation line that cops like to use to blow off reporters.

"So where are your loose lips when *I* need them?" I continued.

"Yours were the only prints we recovered."

"Where did he get your prints?" Noreen asked.

"He stole them."

"That's not true. I used a routine law enforcement technique."

"Where did he get them?" Noreen asked again, louder.

"He took them off a glass I was drinking from. Don't you need a search warrant for that?"

She reached for her phone and asked Miles to come downstairs.

I picked up her wastebasket and dumped the trash on the floor in front of Agent Jax's feet. "Want to go through our garbage while you're waiting?"

"Riley!" Noreen said.

The move was not as spontaneous as it appeared.

Going through Noreen's garbage was an actual fantasy of mine. As I looked down at the mess, my reporter instincts and ability to read upside down kicked in. Amid a coffee cup, a *Broadcast News* magazine, and some old expense forms, I saw what seemed to be a crumpled copy of an anchor contract for Tom McHale and wondered if there was any way to slip it under my jacket without my boss noticing. As a ruse, I apologized for my outburst and started cleaning up.

"Just leave it," she said.

"Maybe I should go." Agent Jax stood up.

But just then Miles arrived and Noreen brought him up to speed on the situation. Now there were three of us glaring at the FBI guy. It felt good to have him so clearly outnumbered even though he was armed with a gun and all we had were our wits. That elation died when Miles told us that Agent Jax actually had the law on his side when it came to swiping my prints.

"Unless, of course, you think the restaurant wants to make a claim concerning the missing glass."

Noreen reminded Agent Jax that she still expected to hear from him when they made an arrest.

"They already have," I said. "That's what I was coming back to tell you. He broke that end of the deal, too."

More glaring at that now tight-lipped FBI guy.

"Toby Elness just called me from jail. He said they're holding him as a suspect."

"Isn't he that animal guy who used to own Shep? The one in last fall's pet-cremation story?" Noreen asked. "He always seemed so gentle."

"Bingo. He says their group wouldn't risk harming the other fish just to free Billy."

"Actually, economic sabotage is a trademark of the Animal Liberation Front," Agent Jax said. "What's a few busted aquariums when they've already destroyed lab equipment and bombed buildings?"

"Want to say that on camera?" I asked.

That threat settled him down some. Feds hate going on camera. He explained that it was not unusual for some of the Animal Liberation Front's rescuees to actually perish in the rescues. Apparently a bunch of minks recently suffered that fate after being freed from a southern Minnesota fur farm.

"And what do you think the group's response was?" the FBI guy asked. "Better they die free than die skinned."

That actually sounded like something Toby might say.

"I'd be surprised if you have a strong enough case against

127

Mr. Elness to charge him before you have to kick him," I said. Prosecutors must charge a suspect within thirty-six hours or release him from custody unless a judge approves an extension.

"Maybe we have more than you know," he said.

"What about Toby, Noreen?" I asked. "Do we name him on air now or wait and see if charges come down?"

This was a hard one for Noreen. Show mercy or get the scoop? "If we report there's been an arrest but don't name him," she said, "one, maybe all, of our competitors will."

"And we'll look stupid," I conceded. As fond as I was of Toby, I got the feeling this could be one of those times when mercy might not be practical.

"If we don't report there's been an arrest, it'll leak out anyway." She threw a pointed glance in the direction of Agent Jax, who once again denied being the newspaper's anonymous source.

"And we'll look stupid." I could see where this decision was headed. After all, I wasn't stupid.

"Try smoothing things over with Toby if you can," Noreen said. "But we have to run his name."

I directed my next question to Agent Jax, making a point of remembering his name since he seemed like he was going to be a pain in my life for some time. "So what do you actually have on Toby Elness?"

"Actually our best evidence against him is you."

"What do you mean?"

"They chose you to receive the letter. So we went looking for ALF members with connections to you. And we found one."

"I think the animal rights group picked me just because I broke the story that Big Mouth Billy was missing."

One scoop often leads to another as interested parties

perceive which journalist owns a particular story. Everyone likes to back a winner.

"And who did provide you with that juicy nugget?" Agent Jax asked.

That was Miles's cue to act all lawyerly again. "I think we're through here. We're not going to be discussing news sources with the FBI."

Miles was right. Minnesota has perhaps the top reporter-shield law in the country, though I wasn't sure how much protection it offered in a federal investigation. Typically the way it works is that for journalists to be compelled to name sources, the government has to prove the information is vital and cannot be obtained by any other means.

In other words, they can't simply go on a fishing expedition.

CHAPTER 17

While searching through the back of a closet for a Frisbee for Shep, I found my own wedding gown. The dress was crammed against the wall in a cheap plastic garment bag. Calling it a gown was probably an exaggeration. It was bought off-the-rack, on the fly, at an open-all-night store in Vegas. My choices were that, rent a dress, or get married in my street clothes.

But there's something tactile and sensuous about wanting to have and to hold your own wedding gown. And there's something about the pageantry of wearing white that I didn't want to compromise—even if I was eloping.

Wedding gowns were not always white. Queen Victoria started the trend in 1840. White also had nothing to do with virtue—it was all about wealth. Back then, being married in white signified that a woman could afford to buy a dress that she would never be able to wear again because white was so very difficult to clean. In fact, many brides dyed their white dresses navy after the ceremony for everyday use.

Then, in the 1920s, Coco Chanel unveiled the first short wedding dress and that runway moment cemented white as the preferred bridal color.

My dress was also short and white, but not high fashion. What I spent to play virgin was nothing close to what Madeline Post's gown cost. That got me thinking about the emotional sway of her wedding dress as a prop. News directors love props, especially on the set. I'd never describe Noreen as a romantic, but even she might not be able to resist the NEVER WORN story if she saw Madeline's wedding gown up close and personal and felt its silky magic.

I held my own wedding dress, labeled polyester, tight against my body. Then moved over to the mirror and closed my eyes.

MADELINE SAT AT a small corner table when I walked into Ursula's Wine Bar, owned by a guy named Kurt who must have figured he couldn't create an exotic atmosphere if he called it Kurt's Wine Bar.

I pulled out the chair across from Madeline and settled in. She handed me a wine list and made a recommendation that I couldn't pronounce. Fine with me.

"You're early," I remarked. I tried not to sound disapproving, but I like being the early one for off-site meetings. I feel like it gives me an edge.

"I wanted to make sure we got a table," Madeline said.

Probably a good idea, I conceded. The place looked exclusive, yet cozy, with room to seat at most a couple of dozen people. A diner at another table apparently recognized me from the news. She casually pointed me out to her companion, but was too polite to interrupt my meal.

Madeline was meeting me because I had told her I had some new information regarding Mark's disappearance.

And that meant I needed to come up with some new information regarding Mark's disappearance. Because I could hardly say let's get together so I can grill you about the night you and your fiancé got engaged. Or how about I swing by and borrow your wedding dress because my boss is unenthusiastic about your misfortune? Those are the kind of topics best broached after developing a trust relationship over alcohol. So we were off to a promising start.

In our case we also shared an interesting cheese-and-fruit plate with crunchy bread while I shared the new information I had acquired. And yes, I actually did have new information.

After an evening of playing cyber detective, Xiong had retrieved three interesting items from Mark's laptop.

The first was a nude photo that his ex-girlfriend, Sigourney Nelson, had sent to him a few days before the wedding. She thrust her breasts toward the camera, perky nipples up close. Her hands were clasped against her stomach in an understandable attempt to hide an extra ten pounds. Her pose wasn't obscene, but it wasn't FCC-approved material either. We could air it, as long as we put black bars in strategic places.

Mark hadn't replied to her and had even tried deleting the photo, but Xiong found it anyway. I wasn't going to share that picture with Madeline. Not yet, at least. I'd tried contacting Sigourney at her e-mail address but had heard nothing back. Either she was ignoring me, or it was a dead address.

Xiong also discovered an e-mail from the best man, Gabe Murray, sounding a little more anxious about the two grand he loaned Mark than he admitted to me. Mark responded with a relax-I'll-have-the-money-soon e-mail. Gabe sent a few more, asking his buddy where he went and when he was returning. The notes started out curious and grew increasingly panicky.

Mark never replied.

"Was Mark in any trouble financially?" I asked Madeline, trying to appear casual.

She shook her head. "Mark didn't have the same means I did, but he also didn't have the same wants. So money wasn't an issue between us."

I was trying to decide whether to tell her she'd been courted on borrowed money when our entrées arrived, mine a sautéed chicken breast with lime sauce, roasted Roma tomatoes and grilled asparagus, Madeline's a penne pasta with shrimp, goat cheese, pine nuts, and red and yellow peppers.

While we picked at our plates, I also weighed the best approach to bring up the most intriguing thing Xiong pulled from Mark's computer. That was the real reason I'd invited Madeline to dinner, specifically so I could press her about a Web site her groom had accessed the week before he disappeared.

Escapeartist.com—a how-to guide on restarting your life abroad.

"Was this anything you ever discussed?" I asked Madeline.

She shook her head. But my reporter's gut told me she didn't seem as surprised as she should have been under the circumstances. I expected an outcry of "What?" or a denial of "Not my fiancé!" Instead she mumbled something about how everyone fantasizes about getting away from it all.

That's when I explained why it's important that journalists have the full picture during an investigation.

"You're not keeping anything back, are you, Madeline?" I asked.

"What do you mean?" she replied.

"Like who asked who to marry them?"

"Oh that." She apologized for her "little white lie," explaining she hadn't known me very well then and felt embarrassed talking about her engagement.

I explained why journalists talk to multiple sources for a story, especially one this complicated. And when we get conflicting versions we start asking ourselves whether our source is on the level. Or whether they have hidden motives.

"No more secrets?" I asked.

"None," she assured me.

Over the next few minutes, the two of us started acting like gal pals. Because my work hours are so crazy, I don't have a whole lot of girlfriends. So dinner with Madeline was a fun, airy kind of evening. And I think she felt the same way, even joking that if she ever got engaged again, she wanted me to be her maid of honor.

And she'd make me wear peach.

"Listen," I told her, "if you're fishing to be my maid of honor—it ain't going to happen."

She misunderstood me, and offered reassurances that someday I'd meet Mr. Right, and would feel about him the same way she felt about Mark.

So I told her how I was married once and couldn't ever risk that pain again. She touched her fingers to her lips and gasped at the potency of my misfortune. She'd heard about my husband's death. Most folks had. It had made the front pages coast-to-coast and had run continuously on cable news channels. After all, Hugh Boyer died a hero. Saving a politician who didn't deserve it, and schoolchildren who did. But Madeline hadn't realized that he had been *my* husband.

Then we laughed in a very subdued way about our personal losses and parallel pain.

And she asked me what it was like being married.

I could tell she wanted a straight answer and wasn't just seeking mealtime chatter.

So I told her it had been the best two years of my life. And I had never felt anything that intense before or since.

"Hugh was my soul mate," I said. "When I lost him, I lost my way." Saying it aloud sounded uncharacteristically sappy, but it was the truth. I didn't get into my struggle with survivor's guilt.

"Oh, Riley, that's how I feel about Mark. Lost without him."

So that's when I pushed the girlfriend button and asked her the question that had been on my mind from the start.

"So, Madeline, why weren't you more freaked out when he vanished? Why weren't you dialing 911 till your fingers bled? Or at least clutching your cell phone till the battery died?"

That's what the wife of Tom Burnett, a Minnesota native and hero of Flight 93 did when she could no longer reach her man on September 11. Her phone was dead, her fingers numb, before she accepted he wasn't calling home.

Madeline didn't answer. She looked away, at the contemporary paintings of wine casks on the wall; I could tell she was close to tears. But if Madeline Post was too tough to cry on camera, she was certainly too tough to cry in public, in an intimate, upscale restaurant, where word might get back to her society friends.

I signaled for the check, complimented the owner on the excellent meal, and when we got outside Ursula's, Madeline revealed that she still had one more secret. And it was a doozy.

"After the rehearsal dinner," she whispered, "I saw a woman kissing Mark out in the parking lot."

Her observation either raised a lot of questions or answered a lot of them. "Was he kissing her back?" That seemed an important distinction.

"I'm not sure. He said he wasn't."

"So you asked him about it?"

"I made some kind of choking sound and ran inside and he followed me and I said, 'Who was that woman?' And he told me she was a comedy club fan who'd been stalking him."

I thought of the hot chicks surrounding Chad, but Chad had looks and Mark did not. "Did you believe him?"

"I believed him then. He told me it was an occupational hazard for entertainers, but once he was wearing a ring, they'd know he was off-limits."

"And you believed him?" Sometimes journalists ask the same question twice, just to see if we get the same answer.

"Yes, I believed him." She buried her hands in her face. "I believed him because I had sort of stalked him, too." Subtle tears streaked her face. "But the next day when he didn't show up for our wedding I didn't know what to believe anymore. I thought maybe he ran off with her."

"What did the woman look like?"

"I don't know. It happened so fast."

"Did anyone else see her?"

"No, most of the wedding party was gone. My family was still there, but they must have been inside."

"Did you tell anyone about this kiss?"

"Not until now."

I motioned Madeline toward my car and opened the passenger-side door. "I have something to show you."

I slid into the driver's side, turned on the dome light, and grabbed an oversized purse from the backseat. Then I pulled out the photograph of Mark's old girlfriend that I got from his mother. In this one, she was clothed.

"Have you ever seen this woman before?" I asked.

"Who is she?"

"An old friend of his."

Madeline stared at the picture without replying. I gave her more time, but still she said nothing. All I wanted was a simple yes or no. "Do you think she might be the parking-lot kisser?"

Madeline remained uncomfortably silent, avoiding conversation and eye contact. At that point, I'd have settled for a hesitant maybe.

"Madeline, talk to me."

But she didn't.

"At least look at me."

But she didn't. Madeline seemed focused inward, not catatonic but eerie.

"Let's go back to the scene," I suggested, "maybe that will jog your memory." So I drove her a half mile to the parking lot outside the White Bear Country Inn.

"Show me where they were standing." We got out of the car and she pointed to a spot on the ground. "Okay, that's good," I told her, setting my bag down to mark the place. "Now show me where you were standing." We walked back toward the restaurant entrance until she stopped and turned around.

"About here," she said, trying to cooperate.

The distance was only ten yards. It was dark, but the lot was well lit. And identification seemed plausible.

"Work with me," I urged her. "Does this woman seem at all familiar?" I handed her the photo.

"I . . . don't . . . know."

This was not helpful. But if she couldn't tell, she couldn't tell. The last thing I wanted her to do was guess just to please me.

I was about to drive her back to her car and utter an exasperated good night, when her shoulders started trembling.

"I can't tell if it's the same woman because I *can't tell*."

"What are you talking about, Madeline? You can't or you won't? You're not making any sense."

That's when Madeline Post proved she was not too tough to cry in a dark parking lot where no one else could see her tears.

And in between stifled sobs, she told me what she swore was her final secret.

"I'm face blind."

It took a minute or two for me to understand what exactly she was saying. She could see my eyes, nose, and mouth. She just couldn't put them all together and identify me. Or anyone else apparently. Much less the woman kissing her fiancé.

"I can't even recognize my own mother on the street," she said.

Now I was the speechless one.

There was even a scientific name for face blindness, she explained, prosopagnosia.

Please, God, I remember thinking, don't make me ever have to pronounce that live on the air.

CHAPTER 18

Some people never forget a face. Not Madeline Post. As soon as she looks away, the image is gone.

Face blindness sounds bizarre, but a search of the Internet later that night assured me that Madeline was not nuts. And I didn't have to comb obscure medical journals to learn that what most of us take for granted—the ability to recognize our friends and family—is a foreign language to the face blind. Mainstream media such as *The New York Times*, *The Wall Street Journal*, and even *People* magazine were giving big play to fascinating research being done at Harvard University.

That's where Madeline was first diagnosed with the developmental disorder. She was attending a college near Boston where her roommate knew somebody who knew somebody in the Prosopagnosia Research Center looking for subjects for a facial recognition study.

"She thought I was stuck up because I couldn't be bothered to say hello to her outside our dorm room," Madeline said. "I kept telling her I just didn't see her."

All her life people had teased Madeline about being a rich snob because she ignored them on the street. But her eyesight always tested 20/20. She thought she was just bad with names. A ditzy blonde. Or an absentminded-professor type.

So for Madeline—when she couldn't even recognize pictures of Elvis or Abraham Lincoln in the experiment— the word prosopagnosia spelled relief. And during a follow-up interview—when she talked about how she and her mother became separated at an Easter egg hunt when she was a little girl, and how they both became hysterical, and had to be reunited by the event organizers because neither could recognize the other—the researcher saw himself moving one step closer to proving that face blindness is inherited.

But according to Madeline, Mrs. Post refused to participate in the study. She didn't dispute her daughter's diagnosis or that she herself suffered from the same affliction. She just didn't see any point in dwelling on what couldn't be changed. So unless Harvard found a cure, she saw no need to get involved.

No matter that researchers speculated that prosopagnosia could solve some of the remaining mysteries of the brain. It was enough for her that face blindness explained some family mysteries, like why Madeline never knew who to throw the basketball to during games. And why Roderick enjoyed watching movies while neither his mother nor sister did. After all, who could keep a plot straight when all the actors looked like Matt Damon?

Vivian had found ways to compensate for her condition and so did her daughter. Soon after that Easter egg hunt episode, Vivian had two sets of trademark birthstone brooches designed. Mother and daughter always wore matching ones in public to identify each other. She encouraged her daughter to wear her hair long and distinctive. For casual charity events, she insisted the attendees wear name tags.

Madeline explained to me that whenever she's meeting someone somewhere she suggests a small, intimate place and gets there first and grabs a table so they come to her. Like with me at Ursula's.

And when she's in front of a mirror in a crowded bathroom, she makes a face to see which reflection is hers.

She told me that once she'd even left her dinner date to go to the restroom and when she came back she sat down at the wrong table with the wrong man, picking up the conversation right where she'd left off. Until her real date objected. And walked out. And never called her again.

So finding love was hard for Madeline. Since everyone looked the same, it was hard to connect emotionally.

Then she saw Mark.

And experienced what she imagined must be that love-at-first-sight phenomenon she'd always heard so much about.

"I could *see* him," she said. "Riley, it was amazing."

I'd already heard how they met. She'd watched his comedy act, then recognized him later that night at a bar. Only now did I grasp the significance of the word "recognized."

"I'd never remembered anyone's face before," she said.

His hair, eyebrows, mustache, scar. To the rest of us, the combination came across as a bit much. But to Madeline, it set him apart from the pack. And made him irresistible.

More than being her soul mate, Mark was her face mate.

CHAPTER 19

The next morning I came to work early and tossed twelve yards of billowy white fabric at my boss in the middle of an empty newsroom. Flustered, she caught it. She opened her mouth to chastise me, but I spoke first.

"Yes, Noreen, this is *the* dress. The NEVER WORN gown from the newspaper ad. Just imagine how the hearts of key women demos ages 18 to 49 will beat a little faster when we flash it on the set during the preshow tease?"

She closed her mouth and eyes to live that fantasy and started fingering the satin.

"Why do you hate the wedding-dress story so much?" I whispered the question, not expecting an answer.

"Because it reminds me that I'm married to my job and at the end of the day only my dog is glad to see me and that's probably never going to change."

Those words were as introspective as I'd ever heard from my news director. And she seemed uncharacteristically sincere and somber. Then she posed a similar question back at me.

"Why do you hate the fish story so much, Riley?"

"Because I was married to a man who liked to fish and all I did was complain like a harpy. And fish remind me that he's gone."

My words were unexpected. A revelation, even. Society isn't sure how to treat young widows. People are uncomfortable discussing death. And frankly, I'm uncomfortable listening.

That moment made me question my own motivation for the wedding-dress story and why I was drawn to the want ad. My marriage ended too early. And here I was, fascinated by a marriage that never started. I had no satisfying answer for my own personal experience of love and loss. Maybe that's why it was so important that I find one for Madeline.

Noreen might have been undergoing the same self-examination because, without saying a word, she carried the gown to her office, laid it on her desk, and wrote NEVER WORN on the storyboard. Then she turned and hugged me.

Even though I know Noreen, I still didn't like her touching me.

"AREN'T WE SUPPOSED to be looking for that fish?" Malik asked on our way back to Mark's mother's house.

"Sure. Look out the window as we drive over the river."

I shouldn't have snapped at Malik. But I hadn't a clue how to catch any fish, much less Big Mouth Billy, and despite playing nice with Noreen, I was not eager to tackle the project. I tuned out my cameraman while I replayed the latest developments on the fish case.

Toby Elness had been released from jail because police confirmed his out-of-town alibi. But even if he wasn't directly involved in the Mall of America attack, the cops made it clear that they suspected he knew more about the missing fish than he was letting on. If he did, he wasn't sharing his insight with me and continued to claim the Animal Liberation Front had been set up.

"Somebody is trying to pin the blame on animal activists," he told the media as cameras surrounded him outside the jail. "But that note didn't come from any of my people."

However, I could see why investigators were sticking to their theory: without it, they lacked an obvious motive. And cases are easier to solve when the motive is obvious. A murder for insurance gain has a small, fixed number of suspects. A random sexual homicide can have a seemingly infinite number.

Garnett had telephoned me the previous night from Washington, D.C.

"What are you doing out there?" I had asked.

"Business." Since he volunteered nothing further, I didn't press. The Mall of America, having a braggy name and being a symbol of conspicuous consumption, was on a national terror watch list. But that wasn't the reason he'd called.

He'd heard that the Bloomington police had checked out former Underwater Adventures employees as suspects but hadn't found anyone disgruntled enough to take it out on the fish.

"Keep me posted if you hear anything else," I had told Garnett. "Noreen is pushing me hard to break the Big Mouth Billy Case, but I've got nothing."

"I'm not surprised," he'd said. "All you TV chicks generally fish for is compliments."

"Do you like my hair?" I'd replied, without missing a beat.

We had both laughed comfortably and Garnett had also

shared that Agent Jax was irritating the local cops who considered him pompous, but couldn't do much about it because he was a fed.

My only consolation was that, much to Agent Jax's ire, none of the media stories—print or broadcast—had used the term Operation Piscis Absenti.

Garnett and I had chuckled over the government moniker and chatted about getting together when he got back in town.

Then Malik interrupted my thoughts. "Riley, let's stop and get gas before we cross the river."

The van's tank was nearly empty and because Wisconsin has a dime per gallon higher gas tax than Minnesota, I got off at the next freeway exit and pulled into the first gas station.

Since I'd been doing all the driving, I made Malik get out to fill 'er up. He'd only pumped about five gallons, when he stopped and put the nozzle back.

"Hey," I banged on the window at him. But he ignored me, raced around to the passenger side of the van, and jumped in.

"Follow that car!" he shouted.

"Oh, please."

"Hurry, Riley, the gray SUV!" Malik squeezed between the seats and reached for his camera gear in the back.

Luckily, I'd used a credit card so the station wouldn't label me a drive-off. I resisted peeling out of the parking lot because to follow a target without being made, you have to be inconspicuous. It also helps to have additional vehicles on your team. Solo is no-go.

"Want to tell me why we care about this guy?" I asked. I couldn't see what he looked like because I was trying to keep a couple of cars between our vehicle and his.

By now Malik had his camera ready. "I recognize him. He came to my parents' house after my sister died."

"So? What did he want?"

"He wouldn't say. That's why they called me. He wanted to check her room. He claimed she had something belonging to him."

"That sounds creepy."

"I told the man to leave and never come back. I think he was one of the drug people my sister was involved with."

"Any particular reason?" I could see the traffic light ahead of our chase car was turning yellow. I sped up and passed another car to avoid being stuck at the intersection.

"We found cash under her mattress. Nearly five thousand dollars."

I gasped at that piece of news—a lot of money for a young woman without a steady job. But I held back on my questions for the moment.

We followed the gray SUV for another mile. Then it turned down a gravel industrial road lined with heavy equipment and trailer trucks. That's when we, inexplicably, lost him. Seconds later, we heard a horn honking, slowly and deliberately. Malik spotted the vehicle, parked between two semis. All four doors were open wide and our target leaned against the hood, arms crossed.

I hit the brakes, skidding dirt and sand, not wanting to get close enough for him to read my license plate. I couldn't see the expression on his face, but he opened his arms as if in welcome, momentarily freezing in that position.

"What's he up to?" Malik asked as he shot the scene from the backseat, through tinted glass, camera perched on his shoulder.

To me, our target's body language couldn't have been clearer. "He's saying, the door's open. Let's talk."

"Great. I'll put a wire on you."

He grabbed a wireless microphone from his equipment bag, anxious to clip it under my sweater and tuck the receiver in my pocket. From inside the van, he'd be able to listen to my conversation with the brute.

Instead, I put the vehicle in reverse, skidding more sand and dirt. Malik scowled, not just because he wasn't buckled in and smacked his head against the window to protect his camera lens, but because he wanted action. Even closure.

"That could have been a big break for us," he said.

"No," I answered. "That could have been a big trap."

"But you said he wanted to talk."

"Then why lead us here? Why not just pull into that strip mall we passed a mile back? Open space. Lots of witnesses. Too isolated here. The advantage all his. No thanks."

Malik considered what I said and nodded. We retraced our route back to the gas station and filled up the tank.

"Did you at least get his license plate?" I asked.

"Yeah, I zoomed in." He rewound the tape and watched it through his viewfinder, calling out a combination of letters and numbers.

I called Xiong back at the station and asked him to run the plate on the gray SUV, but it checked to a vehicle leasing company. A dead end as far as public records go.

"So what'd you do with it?" I asked.

"With what?" Malik answered.

"The money. From under your sister's mattress."

"My parents anonymously left it in various churches and mosques around the cities. A hundred dollars here and there, so as not to draw suspicion. They didn't want to call the police because Muslims with large amounts of unexplained cash sometimes go on terror lists."

He was probably right about that.

Soon we were back on the freeway heading east to Wisconsin. As we passed over the St. Croix bridge, Malik dutifully glanced out the car window at the river below for Big Mouth Billy. No bass leaping from the water, but we noticed a squad car behind us, gaining. I pulled over because, well, damn it, I *had* been speeding. While the Minnesota State Patrol cuts me slack for driving offenses in honor of my late State Patrol–officer husband, neighboring states do not.

But the lights and siren passed us like we were standing still. Which we were. A mile later, the same thing happened all over again.

When we finally turned onto the road to Mrs. Lefevre's house and saw all the police vehicles, I feared she'd suffered a heart attack or stroke. As we got closer and spotted crime-scene tape surrounding her home, I feared something much worse.

I stopped by the front door and Malik jumped out, threw his camera on his shoulder, shooting wildly, while I parked the van down the block. I ran up to a sheriff's deputy standing watch at the yellow-and-black line. He ignored me when I asked what was going on.

"We have an appointment with Mrs. Lefevre," I insisted. "She's the woman who lives here."

"Do you know what she looks like?"

"Yes." And I started to describe her.

"Wait here." And he went inside.

Another deputy came out and told me to head back to the station. No story here. "Do you see any other media?" He waved in all directions.

"I'll decide what's a story," I replied. "Now what happened? Did someone kill Mrs. Lefevre?"

"You need to listen closer to your scanner. This is a 10-56."

A 10-56. That didn't make any sense: 10-56 was . . . suicide.

"She would not have killed herself," I maintained. "I had a meeting set with her. I saw her earlier in the week."

"How did she seem then?"

"Her son is missing. She was worried. Otherwise she seemed fine."

"So you could make a positive ID of the victim?" I nodded. He motioned me to come behind the tape, but for Malik to stay behind. "Don't touch anything."

He led me through her kitchen to the living room. A body lay on the floor with blood congealed around the victim's head. An old revolver lay nearby. The weapon didn't have the firepower of its modern successors so there was still enough of her face for me to recognize Mrs. Lefevre.

"It's her," I told the officer.

My reaction should have been horror. After all, she and I had been chatting amiably in this very room days earlier. And now look at her. But seeing my fourth dead body in six months, all I could muster was a clinical vein of curiosity.

"Did she leave a note?" I asked.

He pointed to a scrap of blue paper in a plastic evidence bag on a coffee table, but wouldn't let me read it. Then he escorted me back outside. I explained that she had given me permission to look through her son's boxes in the garage and asked if there was any chance I might carry out her last wish.

He said they would have to locate next of kin before releasing anything from the scene. Lotsa luck, I thought. But when the officer opened the garage door so I could point out the pile, my question became moot because that corner of the garage was empty.

The boxes were gone.

*   *   *

MY EYES HURT. So I ducked in the station's green room to take out my contact lenses and put on my brainy-girl glasses. I walked into the newsroom just in time to see Noreen erase the NEVER WORN slug from the storyboard.

"News doesn't cover suicides," she said. "Drop the story now and never mention it again. The last thing we need is anyone suggesting that your interview contributed to her death."

Malik had told Noreen that I'd made Mrs. Lefevre cry, and she and Miles ordered me to destroy the interview tape.

"But the missing boxes proves it wasn't suicide," I said. "Whoever killed her, took the boxes."

Except that wasn't how the cops saw the situation. They concluded that Jean Lefevre became depressed over her son's disappearance and gave his belongings away because they were too painful to look at. Then took her own life.

"But, Noreen, she had things she was looking forward to," I said. "Like the blooming of the corpse flower. She wouldn't have killed herself before experiencing that."

Noreen gave me the same kind of look I probably gave Mrs. Lefevre when she first mentioned the corpse flower, so I explained what a botanical treasure we had in our viewing area. And Noreen waved her hand and told me to go tell the assignment desk the news.

Sitting in my office, I called Nick Garnett because I needed someone to talk to who wouldn't dismiss my homicide theory simply because the local authorities did.

He had just gotten back to Minnesota and was rushing to find his car in the sprawling airport parking garage. He didn't have time to get together just then, but I asked him to keep his ears open for any buzz.

"It'll be tough, being a Wisconsin case," he said.

Cops are territorial, not just about their turf or snitches

but about their information as well. Two departments, working the same case, fighting for jurisdiction, don't necessarily share data with each other, much less with outsiders.

"But I'll see if I can find someone who knows someone who knows something," he said. "Just for the record, Riley, suicide cases typically cause more problems for cops than homicide cases."

"So you think she probably did kill herself, huh, Nick?"

"I didn't say that. And also, just for the record, suicidal women don't generally shoot themselves in the head. That's a macho thing. The ladies, they go more for pills or hanging."

I tried shutting that image out of my mind.

Garnett and I also made plans to meet for a movie the next night to hash over the shooting, hash over the missing bass, and hash over our lives.

We'd often met in movie theaters over the years to hand off documents clandestinely. Now that he wasn't a homicide detective, we didn't have to sneak around, but we both fancied ourselves film aficionados.

"Don't worry, Riley," he said, "it's not like it's a date."

But it would be the first time we'd be alone together in a social setting since last fall when our friendship nearly took a dive. Perhaps that's why he was so quick to establish boundaries. I felt a tinge of regret at his choice of words, wondered where that sentiment came from and why.

"You don't worry me any," I answered before saying goodbye.

I had plenty of real worries. Even though Noreen had again nixed the missing-groom story, I needed to get some things straight in my own mind. I stuck my interview of Mrs. Lefevre in a tape deck, shut my office door, and hit Play. I wanted to watch it before erasing it.

151

I got to the part where I pressed her about why she hadn't called the police earlier when her son went missing. I watched her cry. And then I almost cried when Noreen knocked on my door and Miles held out his hand for the now controversial videotape.

"It's better if this video doesn't exist," he said.

I handed it over, but I made one last pitch to save it. I reminded him of our policy to keep everything from our news-gathering process for investigative stories, because the station stands a greater risk of being sued in those reports. Notes. Tapes. Documents. Miles had always maintained that these items would prove, to a jury if necessary, how thoroughly we check each story before airing it.

"There's an exception to every rule," he said.

"And besides that," Noreen added, "our save policy only applies to stories we air, and we're not airing this one."

Miles took the tape, about the size of a deck of cards, and he and Noreen turned and walked down the hall.

For about ten minutes I pouted at my desk with the door shut. Then I e-mailed Xiong to run a criminal background check on Jean Lefevre. Within minutes it came back—clean—except for a huge stack of parking violations, still unpaid. That proved how little effort the police put into her son's disappearance. If they'd even run her name, they'd have run her in and made her settle up. Instead, they assumed Mrs. Lefevre to be an overly protective little old mama.

And I learned during my college years, from an old journalism professor at the University of St. Thomas, what happens when we assume.

Ass-U-Me. We make an ass out of you and me.

I ducked my head in the newsroom to look for Noreen and tell her we shouldn't just assume Mrs. Lefevre's interview tape meant trouble. But I saw her standing near the news control booth, lecturing the anchors and technical staff on avoiding gaffes with wireless microphones.

A CNN anchorwoman had left her wireless mic turned on when she took a bathroom break during a presidential speech that morning. Her ladies-room gossip was broadcast live coast-to-coast before she was alerted that her mic was hot.

I could hear the techies arguing with the talent over whether the debacle was the anchor's fault for not turning off her mic or the audio guy's fault for not potting it down after her last read.

Then Noreen started stressing how That Better Never Happen Here. Her monologue sounded like it might go on for a while, so I backed away lest I get drawn into that distraction. I didn't want to be forced to take sides. Whoever's position I didn't pick—anchor or audio—would be mad and just might remember this tiff the next time I had to sit on the news set or go to the bathroom.

CHAPTER 20

hen we meet people, we size them up. Often by their face. Honest or shifty. Attractive or not.

Unlike the famed Helen of Troy, my face would not launch a thousand ships. Maybe not even a bass boat. But in my line of work, what I have going for me may be better: my face opens doors.

Physically, I look safe. Sympathetic. Ordinary. On some level, my face inspires trust. For a journalist, that's a gift.

Often my colleagues and I are knocking on strangers' doors on the best or worst days of their lives. Maybe they've just won the lottery, or recovered a missing child. Or maybe they've just learned their daughter was killed in a school shooting, or discovered their son was the shooter. We want their stories. They want to be left alone. Sometimes to celebrate. Sometimes to grieve.

Yet more often than not, when I knock, they open.

We have this saying in the news business: you can't get the interview if you can't get inside. The most obvious interpretation means inside their house. But often you have to get inside their mind as well. Sometimes they need empathy. Other times, information about what's happening with their case or how the media works and what options they have.

If I sense nervousness about appearing on live television, I offer to tape the interview, so they can start again if they stumble. If I sense nervousness about being edited or having their comments taken out of context, I suggest a live interview.

Being the first reporter on the scene can certainly help lock in an exclusive. But not always. Subjects might ignore the buzzer or slam the door in reporters' faces. They might regret that move, but can't change their mind without admitting a mistake. So if I come along later, after the media mob has given up, and make a new offer, pitched a different way, they can tell themselves they were smart to wait.

Because that's what I tell them.

But Madeline clearly wasn't taken in by my face. So something else must have drawn her to me.

"Never heard of this face-blind business," my buddy Nick Garnett said.

We were chatting over the phone while I was curled up in bed, Shep sprawled across my feet. But Garnett was insisting that some people are simply better at reading faces than others. "It's a talent."

He told me about a street cop in Detroit, a Legend at the law enforcement shoot/don't shoot training camps. The cop and his partner watched a man approaching their vehicle on foot. Legend rolled down the window and shot him dead, no questions asked, horrifying his partner, who was riding shotgun. But investigators found the dead man had a flamethrower and was just yards away from turning their squad car into an inferno.

In another episode, the same cop refrained from shooting at a teen waving a gun—a real gun. Later, after he'd disarmed the youth, all he could tell his backup was, "I knew he wasn't going to fire."

Both times, Legend explained, he could judge his adversary's intent by his face.

"How about you, Nick?" I asked. "Can you read truth in a perp's face?"

"No way. Not something you learn at the academy. That's why cops like lie detectors. Takes the pressure off. Me, I can't even tell truth in a woman's face, much less a perp's."

I wished we weren't on the telephone for that particular exchange. I would have liked to watch his face as he said that last line, because his emphasis suggested he was suggesting something.

I WAS WALKING through downtown Minneapolis, just past the statue of Mary Tyler Moore throwing her hat in the air, when my cell rang. I'd been rethinking my face theory and by the area code could tell that Professor Emmett Vasilis, the prosopagnosia researcher from Harvard, was calling me back.

As journalists, we use our occupation as an excuse to call up just about anybody and ask just about anything and we usually get answers. Especially from scientists who don't get a lot of public recognition for their work. To them, questions are the ultimate compliments.

"Face blindness is very real, Ms. Spartz." Professor Vasilis was flattered by my interest and urged me to try an experiment sometime. "Pick up a handful of stones."

"Wait," I said, stopping. "I can do that now." I bent over and grabbed some grayish landscape pebbles from a foliage display on the outdoor pedestrian mall.

"Name each stone," the professor told me.

"Name them what?"

"Whatever you want."

Seemed like a crazy experiment, but I leaned against a storefront, followed his instructions, and named the stones after the seven dwarfs.

"Put them in your pocket," he said. I complied, still not sure where this would lead. "Now take them out. Call them by name."

I couldn't tell Dopey from Doc or Sneezy from Sleepy.

"That's what it's like to be face blind," Professor Vasilis said. "Not everybody suffers to that degree, but a surprising number do. Some studies suggest perhaps 2 percent of the population might be impaired to some degree."

While he was talking about the part of the brain that controls facial recognition I staged an obvious experiment of my own and removed my brainy-girl glasses and walked down the street, gazing at the blurred images approaching. But when I shared my findings with the professor, he disputed my methodology and conclusion.

"That's not prosopagnosia," he said. "For them, the faces would be blurry, but the rest of the scene would be in focus." As another example he explained that the face blind can tell cars apart, just not faces. And they can also discern expressions, like whether a particular face is happy or angry.

"A face is integral to being human," he said, "that's why it's easier to recruit doctors to fix cleft lips in Third World countries than to treat AIDS victims."

"And that's why there was so much controversy over the first face transplant," I said.

"Exactly."

Then the professor and I talked about how "face" has become a part of our vernacular. Face the facts. Face the truth. Face the music. Face the consequences. Face the voters. Face the jury.

"In some parts of the world, face is even synonymous with honor," I said. "In Japan, status is all about saving face."

"Very true," he replied, "yet it would be a mistake to limit the concept of face to Far East geography. The Cuban Missile Crisis hinged on neither side losing face while the world watched. Understandable. Humiliation requires witnesses."

Quite understandable, I thought. If Mark had simply called off the wedding, Madeline could have moved on more easily. As it was, three hundred guests witnessed her shame. I decided to weave her case into our discussion.

"Are some faces simply more recognizable than others because of certain characteristics?" I asked. "Like if a person had a facial scar?" I was thinking of Mark and what made his face so special.

"A scar could make someone more memorable," he said. "As could facial hair, like a beard or mustache." Mark's Groucho Marx look seemed obvious. "While long hair isn't actually part of the face, it might be useful to distinguish individuals. A person of a different race in a homogeneous population could be recognizable to someone suffering from prosopagnosia."

"Let's say a woman is severely face blind." I was careful not to use Madeline's name. The last thing I needed was patient confidentiality to bring our conversation to a halt if he realized we were discussing one of his research subjects. "But one day she meets a man whose face is recognizable to her. How big a deal might that be?"

"It could be a life-altering event."

He explained that face-blind people are often socially

isolated and have difficulty bonding. "They're searching for a connection they might never find."

"Sounds a little like sociopathy."

"Not exactly." Professor Vasilis laughed. "Sociopaths are focused on themselves, not on relationships. They don't really care about human interaction. People afflicted with prosopagnosia seek a personal connection, sometimes desperately, and don't understand why it isn't happening for them."

"And if it suddenly does?"

"Conceivably, it could feel like winning the lottery," he said.

I stopped walking and sat on a cement bench in Peavey Plaza across the street from the station. A couple of Canada geese were swimming in a concrete pond with fountains outside Orchestra Hall. City officials would have preferred swans, but this is goose country.

The professor continued analyzing my hypothetical example. "It might not matter to the individuals if their love interest isn't suitable on other more traditional levels, like age or education."

"You mean if a wealthy, face-blind person is suddenly drawn to a person of low economic status, they could still find happiness?" I asked.

"Exactly, but let's say we're dealing with the opposite concept, a person of low status is drawn to someone of high status, if the love interest does not reciprocate, the attraction could turn into an obsession. Such a rejection could be brutal because they might go their entire life without finding anyone recognizable again. Worst case, it could develop into a stalking scenario."

His insight gave me so much to think about that I didn't realize he was waiting for me to speak.

"Do you know of such a case?" Professor Vasilis repeated the question. "I'd be interested in interviewing the person for my research."

"Let me talk to her first."

Then I thanked him for his time and left open the possibility of calling him back with follow-up questions.

While I sat, absorbing all this new information, I tried skipping one of the seven dwarfs over the pond in front of me. Not flat enough to catch air, it sank abruptly. Just like my chances of airing this story. I tossed the rest of the stones in the water in a single throw and they made a scattered series of splashes.

CHAPTER 21

A crowd gathered around the dock by Tally's, a small bait shop and marina on the east shore of White Bear Lake. Black ducks tried swimming but weren't making much headway against a brisk spring wind. Shep barked at them and they scattered like a school of minnows while we walked along the path that hugged the shore.

My mind was processing the new piece of information I'd just obtained over lunch at Rudy's Redeye Grill, where Madeline and Mark's rehearsal dinner had been held. I schmoozed the owner, a guy named Bill, not Rudy, who must have figured Bill's Redeye Grill lacked a certain panache. But Bill also owned the hotel that housed the restaurant. And by dessert, I'd confirmed that Sigourney Nelson had been a registered guest at the White Bear Country Inn the night before the wedding.

What was she doing there? Besides kissing her old boyfriend in the parking lot? And that didn't require a room.

Shep barked again and brought me back to the present.

White Bear Lake was staging a premier Minnesota bass

competition to kick off the season. For some time, the town had lobbied to host the Governor's Fishing Opener, a tradition dating back sixty years in honor of walleye season. The outing is a cooperative venture between the resort industry, the media, and public officials. But politics seemed to decree that the annual event to pay homage to Minnesota's state fish be held outside the metro area to build name recognition for more obscure lakes.

The White Bear Lake Chamber of Commerce became convinced their time would never come, even though they'd sent smooth-talking emissaries, dressed like fish, to make their case before the governor. So they'd spent the last year making plans to buy an insurance policy should a lucky angler catch a state-record-breaking bass in their water.

The winner of such a trophy fish would net half a million bucks, plus prestige throughout the bass world. If no record fish was landed, the top bass of the day would net a new pickup truck and ten grand for its captor.

A record bass would also benefit the town: its namesake lake would become a tourist magnet for bass lovers. And that image meant full hotels, bars, and restaurants for fishing seasons to come. The *White Bear Press* had been absolutely giddy in its editorial endorsing the idea.

Even without a record-breaking fish, town leaders could use the contest to demonstrate their organizational skills in pulling out all the stops in the name of fish. That might land them a step closer to luring the actual Governor's Fishing Opener to their shores the following spring.

Because the area is a Republican stronghold, the current governor was forced to accept the mayor's gracious invitation to join him and the bass on the water even though it carried some political risk. A governor who gets skunked fishing in public loses the confidence of his people.

Governor Wendell Anderson set a high bar in 1973 when he was featured on the cover of *Time* magazine holding an impressive walleye to illustrate "The Good Life in Minnesota." Minnesota governors ever since know that their political virility is measured each spring by the size of their catch.

Our current governor, Tim Pawlenty, had slipped up during a recent live radio interview, revealing that his wife preferred fishing to sleeping with him.

I walked up to a guy wearing a sweatshirt that read WOMEN WANT ME, FISH FEAR ME and hoped he wasn't in charge. Thankfully, he pointed to a man at the end of the pier, surveying the lake.

"So you're the mastermind behind all this," I gushed. He beamed.

He seemed mildly interested when I introduced myself as a Channel 3 reporter, but when he realized I was the one covering the Billy Bass story, I had his full attention.

"What a beauty! A fish of a lifetime." He introduced himself as Russell Nesbett, the president of the local chamber of commerce. "But call me Russ. I've been following your story closely."

Suddenly a new motive for taking Big Mouth Billy came to mind.

"That prize money you're offering, seems like very attractive bait," I said. "What if the thieves aren't animal rights activists but just stole Big Mouth Billy to rig the contest?"

Russ pooh-poohed that theory fast. "Some of the top bass anglers in the world will be here competing. What do you think it would do to our credibility if we had lax security?"

"You have security?" I asked.

"Absolutely. No contraband fish are getting into this competition."

He explained that every boat and cooler would be inspected at manned entry points to ensure no bootleg fish were smuggled in. Fish police would also patrol the shorelines to make sure no one parked a lunker under a dock.

"It's part of our insurance contract," Russ said. "Lloyd's of London is making us."

He seemed proud of all the precautions they were taking, some of which I promised to keep secret, and he even showed me an X-ray machine to ensure that the winning fish hadn't been loaded with lead weights.

"More ways to cheat than I could ever imagine," I said.

"You'd be surprised. What's a little fish fraud when a half a million bucks is at stake?"

We both shared a nice laugh while Shep panted like he was in on the joke.

"Maybe I'll get myself some fishing gear before the competition and join you," I said.

He shook his head and explained that organizers capped the roster at one hundred anglers, and it was full. White Bear Lake, about 2,400 acres in size, was the second largest lake in the Minneapolis–St. Paul metro area.

"If we let too many boats in, the lake gets crowded. This way it's also more exclusive and we can justify the one-thousand-dollar entry fee."

That seemed like a lot of money to sit in a boat all day. But I didn't want to debate those merits with him.

"I'd love to do a preview story," I said. "Can I get a list of the entrants?"

"Oh I can tell you off the top of my head who the big names are," he answered. "One of them is your news anchor, Tom McHale. He's such a big bass fan, he entered to show his support for the competition."

"That's great, but I can't really interview Tom because

he and I work together. Also, I'd like to talk to some ordinary folks, those whose entire lives could be changed by just one fish. A half a million bucks would mean more to them than to Tom."

"That's true," Russ said. "He's entering it more for the honor and legacy that comes with landing a record fish. We all dream that dream. Landing a champion brings immortality."

He weighed the pros and cons of releasing contestants' names, such as privacy, but I dangled the idea that a preview story would pay off with a little extra publicity for my new hometown, White Bear Lake. Wink. Wink. A few minutes later, Shep and I left with a computer printout of potential suspects in Bassgate.

On our way back to the station, I answered my cell phone reluctantly because the caller showed as RESTRICTED on the screen. RESTRICTED or UNKNOWN usually meant the newsroom assignment desk. TV stations like blocking their phone numbers so folks on the other end don't know it's the media calling. I feared being hijacked by the desk to cover breaking news or a reporter out sick. But this call was actually welcome.

"Hey, that flower you've been asking about," Ozzie, the assignment editor said, "it's blooming and word is it smells blooming awful."

"The corpse flower?" I asked. "Great. It emits the odor of rotting flesh. But it only lasts about eight hours." I felt like I owed it to Jean Lefevre to pay the famed flower a visit. "It's really quite rare."

"So we hear. Since you know so much about it, how 'bout you do a live shot while you're there?"

Hard to back out now. But going live meant finding a

bathroom and putting my contacts back in. Noreen didn't like viewers seeing me in my brainy-girl glasses.

"I have to bring my dog along," I said.

"Keep him out of the shot this time."

The line to view the horticultural celebrity stretched outside the conservatory. A Como Park security guard kept the flower crowd under control. My media pass got me to the front, but my dog almost kept me out. Once I explained that Shep was a K-9, we were inside. From there, locating the plant was as easy as following my nose.

The closer we got, the worse the stench. I tried taking short, shallow breaths. But I still felt like barfing. Shep appeared immune—infatuated, even, by the smell of death. He strained on the leash to try to get a closer inspection, but another guard kept the crowd behind a ribbon barrier.

The plant stood a little over two feet high in a pot much too large. Purplish interior leaves unfolded slightly from a straight green trunk with narrow white streaks. No mistaking the source of the odor.

"This assignment stinks." Malik met me with his camera gear, claiming he drew the photographer short straw. Then he complained about the nauseating working conditions he was exposed to. "Give me a sweatshop any day."

My nose adjusted to the smell, but my throat felt sore, like the plant pollen was burning it. During the next few minutes Malik shot cover of a kid plugging his nose and a red-hat lady racing to the door with her hand over her mouth. Then we grabbed a few quick man-on-the-street sound bites from conservatory guests lamenting the pungency.

An academic type came over to make sure I knew that *Amorphophallus titanum*, the official name for the corpse flower, was Greek for misshapen giant penis. I didn't know. But once he said it, that's all I could think about.

"Thank you," I said, "I'll make sure the newscast producer gets that information. But we're on deadline now and need to go outside and put together our story."

Besides, the corpse flower was starting to attract flies.

XIONG WAS PACKING up to leave when Shep and I finally got back to Channel 3. He made a sharp remark in his native Hmong language that sounded unkind when I showed him the list of bass fishing contestants and explained what I wanted.

Besides doing computer work for the station, Xiong also produced newscasts, so he was growing irritated with all the extra cyber tasks I was throwing his way this sweeps month.

"I know, Xiong, I'm sorry. Of all the stories I'm chasing, this fish caper is the one I care least about, but Noreen cares most."

"This list contains one hundred names," he said. "And none of them have dates of birth, middle initials, or addresses. I do not have time for this. You want it done, you do it."

Normally, Xiong is territorial with his computer databases. He'd married birth records with death records with crime records with vehicle records with hunting records with voting records with property records and any other electronic public files he could convince the station to buy. And he doesn't like anyone messing with his creation. So I was surprised at his reaction.

He showed me where to type in each of my fishing entrants to see what background information popped. When he felt certain I could be trusted not to wreck his genius, he left me on my own. With Shep curled at my feet, asleep.

Xiong was dressed edgier than normal. Instead of a Mister Rogers sweater he wore a denim jacket. And when he said good night, he had a nervous smile on his face. I suspected he had a date and I felt a flash of envy.

I looked at the calendar hanging over his desk and recalculated again how many days I'd gone without sex.

TYPING ONE HUNDRED names was the easy part.

A couple of hours later, after sorting through dozens of nicknames and middle names to match people to addresses and ages, my eyes were blurry. Folks from out of state made up about a quarter of the list. So the computer run was useless for them. Of the rest, I printed a lot of data, but didn't know what it meant. A few had criminal records, but nothing screamed fish thief.

CHAPTER 22

Since I remained in computer-think mode the next morning, I worked at home a few hours, trying to ignore Shep chasing red squirrels from window to window.

I made a list of all the hard data I had about both the fish case and Jean Lefevre's suicide. Sometimes that technique helped me better organize information or see it in a different way.

Even though Noreen opposed probing the woman's death, and might even blame me for it, I couldn't just forget about Mrs. Lefevre. When you meet someone one day and see them dead soon after, you need to make sense of the violence. Unfortunately, most of the time it's senseless.

My eyes still hurt from looking at the fish-contestant names, so I put that file aside and reached for the suicide. I looked through the notes of my impressions about Madeline, her family, and all the other players I'd met. I also scanned the e-mails Xiong found in Mark's laptop. The correspondence from the best man and old girlfriend still seemed the most promising leads.

Then I noticed the background check revealing Mrs. Lefevre's erstwhile parking habit. The wave of tickets dated back a couple of years and seemed to cluster in St. Paul, across the river from her home and business in Wisconsin, making them more difficult to enforce.

Curious for a such a seemingly God-fearing, law-abiding mom. What had she been up to?

XIONG CAVED TO my pleading, and because it involved a new task that interested him, he agreed to plot out the tickets geographically. An hour later he showed me the results. Three locations on the map, near and around downtown St. Paul, seemed most popular.

"I guess I better drive over and see what's there," I said. Sometimes there's no substitute for hitting the streets to follow a lead.

"Wait a minute," he replied. "Let us try this first."

"What is it?"

"Just watch."

After a few minutes of downloading, then clicking and dragging across his computer screen, Xiong positioned a satellite map of the city over the clusters of parking-ticket images. The aerial view of downtown was amazing. The state capitol, the Cathedral of St. Paul, the First National Bank building, and the Mississippi River gave me perspective.

And I knew immediately where to head next.

I thanked him and made a big show of hugging him tight. The assignment editor even glanced over from his perch in the newsroom to see what was happening. Xiong beamed at our success.

Two of the ticket clusters were near hospitals. I ignored

those, figuring them to be business stops for flower drops. The other location was familiar to me.

"SHE WAS ONE of the last souls I would have expected to commit suicide."

"Why is that?" I was talking to Father Mountain about the death of one of his parishioners: Jean Lefevre.

"It's unusual when someone so devout takes her own life." He spoke freely because he didn't consider me a reporter, rather one of his flock. By happenstance, Mark's mother and I had my childhood priest in common.

"Does that mean she can't be buried in a Catholic cemetery?"

"No, Riley, that's still a common misconception, especially among the elderly . . . and those who only attend Mass on *Christmas and Easter.*" He gave me a judgmental look. "But canon law was changed about twenty-five years ago. While the Church doesn't condone suicide, we believe victims may not understand their actions and that their families deserve compassion."

"She didn't seem suicidal when I interviewed her," I said. "And she specifically mentioned believing that suicide was against her faith when I asked whether her son might have taken that route."

I told Father Mountain about my investigation into Mark's disappearance and how his mother's trail of parking tickets brought me to the door of his church.

Then Father Mountain dropped a bit of a bombshell.

He was at Madeline's botched ceremony, waiting along with everyone else for the musicians to play the wedding march and the bride to walk down the aisle.

"The prairie grass there reminded me of my rural parish

days, back when I baptized you, Riley, and started you on a path to knowing God."

Madeline was Lutheran and wanted to exchange vows outdoors. Mrs. Lefevre insisted on a priest being present to give a Catholic blessing. I already knew how that story ended. No groom. No ceremony. No blessing.

But at least I now had a neutral eyewitness I trusted.

"What did Mrs. Lefevre say when Mark was a no-show?" I asked. "Was she angry? Worried? Embarrassed?"

Father Mountain wasn't nearly so chatty now. I pressed him, why not?

"Things were said in confidence."

"Confidence?" I echoed. "She's dead now. What difference would telling me make? Except maybe to clarify things."

"She shared a personal secret with me."

Everybody in this investigation had secrets. Madeline. Mark. Now even the mother of the groom. Luckily, I'm in the business of outing secrets. Other people's secrets, that is. My own, I like keeping cloistered.

"Do you think it's a secret she wanted to take to her grave? Maybe she told me her secret already, but I didn't grasp the significance."

"I don't think so." Father Mountain made the sign of the cross. Probably to keep away the media demon.

I decided to use church law to make my case. "Was her secret shared during the sacrament of reconciliation?"

I could tell Father Mountain was giving serious thought to my question.

"Unless there was a confessional out in the woods," I continued, "I don't think you're obligated to keep her secret. I think you should ask yourself what she would have wanted now. After all, she was cooperating with my story."

I didn't tell him her cooperation was a little fluid—obviously she'd made a decision the other day to keep something back from me. But Father Mountain apparently decided disclosure would not mean betrayal.

"She and Mark had a fight the previous night, just before the rehearsal," Father Mountain said. "He was remarking that it was too bad that his dad and Madeline's couldn't see them get married. He told her that they were including a special prayer honoring their deceased fathers."

"Okay, what's to fight about?" I asked.

"Mrs. Lefevre isn't a widow. Her husband didn't die. He ran off and left them when Mark was little. Deserted his family. She told him his father didn't deserve a prayer."

"So she lied to him all these years about his father being dead?"

"Yes, she concocted a story about him being killed in a car accident out west and them scattering his ashes in the mountains. That was to explain why they never left flowers on his grave."

Mrs. Lefevre was beginning to sound more like a professional liar than a sweet little old lady. I wondered if she had laid any whoppers on me. "Seems like a bad plan destined to get worse."

Father Mountain nodded. "She felt like she was protecting her son emotionally and physically when he was young. Apparently her husband was abusive and gave Mark that scar across his face. So she never tried finding him and moved around enough so he couldn't find them."

"Why didn't she get a divorce?"

"Divorce was out of the question for her because of her faith."

"Then I guess she's lucky he left."

I could understand Mark being upset about being misled.

Madeline had money. He didn't. Madeline had looks. He didn't. Madeline had youth. He didn't. Growing up fatherless was something they had in common. Although Mark might have read more into that connection than Madeline did. I didn't want a long drawn-out discussion with Father Mountain about her obsession with her fiancé's face.

If she had been infatuated with her own face, that would be the sin of vanity. And I'm sure he'd have plenty to say about that. As to face blindness, I figured Father Mountain wouldn't have much insight there. So instead, I pressed further on the history of Mark's missing father.

"Why would any of that make Mark leave his bride at the altar?" I asked.

"After the rehearsal dinner, Mark told his mother that if his father couldn't be at the wedding, he didn't want her there, either."

"Seems an overreaction."

"That's what she thought. So she showed up thinking they'd work things out. But they never got the chance."

"What do you think happened?"

"Only God knows his fate," Father Mountain said. "At first Mrs. Lefevre blamed herself: he didn't show up because she did. Then she started thinking maybe he went to look for his father. Later she worried *like father like son*, did he leave Madeline the way his father left her?"

Neither of us had much to say after that. Jean Lefevre had plenty of reasons to be a troubled soul.

"Okay, Father, you've convinced me. She killed herself. I just hope I didn't push her closer to the edge."

He shrugged his shoulders. "Men of God have no special powers to anticipate tragedy, why should you?"

To lighten the mood he told me a joke about Pope Benedict getting bird flu from the cardinals. Father

Mountain collected church jokes and liked to weave them in his homilies. He started to tell me how much Mark appreciated his humor.

Just then I got a text message from the Channel 3 assignment desk: CAUS OF DTH N WIS CASE CHNGD 2 MRDR.

I flashed the screen at Father Mountain, explaining that I needed to leave to meet my photographer at the news conference.

"Just as well," he replied. "I have a funeral to plan."

THE SHERIFF STOOD at a podium with the seal of the state of Wisconsin on the front. Sheriffs are elected officials so anytime they get a chance to appear on TV on their terms, they generally take it. He indicated that he would read a statement, but allow no questions.

"New evidence has caused us to reclassify Jean Lefevre's death from suicide to homicide."

"What new evidence?" another reporter eagerly asked, forgetting, or ignoring, the prohibition on questions.

"No comment," the sheriff responded. "We are continuing our investigation and believe her murder to be a domestic."

A domestic, I thought, means a family member. I didn't know she had other family.

The public takes comfort when a victim ends up knowing her killer. Then we can tell ourselves we're safe. Our spouses and friends and children would never harm us. But random homicides give us the chills and make us all feel vulnerable.

I'd done enough Fear Grips live shots to understand those dynamics. That's where a reporter stands in a cul-de-sac strung with crime-scene tape and says something like "Fear grips this once quiet neighborhood while a killer roams free."

Yep, random homicides make residents panic. And put pressure on police—which is why cops prefer domestics, too.

The sheriff continued. "We do not believe her assailant poses a direct threat to other residents of our community, but he could be dangerous if cornered so we ask anyone with information on his whereabouts to contact us and not approach him directly."

Could the sheriff be referring to her estranged husband? Could her ex have tracked her down after all these years?

"We are making public a photograph of the suspect, her son, thirty-four-year-old Mark Lefevre. Anyone with information on his whereabouts is asked to call the St. Croix County Sheriff's Department."

Then the sheriff turned and walked away. I was so stunned I couldn't speak, which explains why I was the only journalist in the room not shouting questions at his shadow.

Noreen was ecstatic when I returned. She'd already slated me to lead tonight's late news. And NEVER WORN was back on the May board.

My competition didn't realize the prime suspect was also a missing person, so that gave me a big scoop. And changed the focus of my initial story as Mark shifted from victim to villain.

((RILEY/ON SET))
A MAN MISSING SINCE LAST
 FALL IS NOW SUSPECTED IN
THE MURDER OF HIS
MOTHER.

The other media also had to settle for the driver's license photo authorities released of Mark Lefevre, while I used a shot of him sitting on a couch with his now dead mom and the home video of him making a toast at the rehearsal dinner.

((RILEY/SOT))
MARK LEFEVRE VANISHED
ON THE EVE OF HIS
WEDDING. HIS BRIDE HAD
NO IDEA OF HIS
WHEREABOUTS . . . AND
WORRIED FOR HIS SAFETY.
((BRIDE/SOT))
WE LOVED EACH OTHER. HE
 WOULDN'T JUST LEAVE
WITHOUT SAYING
ANYTHING.

None of my competition had video of the crime-scene tape, either. And none of them had helped authorities identify the victim. I struggled to work that in without sounding too boastful, trying to make it seem more like a public service than a news exclusive.

((RILEY/NAT))
CHANNEL 3 ARRIVED ON
THE MURDER SCENE AFTER
LAW ENFORCEMENT
RESPONDED TO A CALL
THAT A DELIVERY MAN HAD
FOUND THE FRONT DOOR
AJAR.

I blamed Noreen for the one missing element that might have made the story a national award winner: an on-camera interview with the deceased. My boss regretted that business about destroying the tape, but tried to throw the blame on me by saying I should have fought harder to save it. I had to settle for a few cover shots of Mrs. Lefevre in her house because they were on the same tape as the old photo albums Malik had shot.

((RILEY/NAT))
AUTHORITIES INITIALLY
CALLED THE DEATH A
SUICIDE.

After leaving the sheriff's department, I had phoned Madeline because I didn't want her to turn on the radio or click on the Internet and learn the news unexpectedly. I also didn't want her to take any other media calls. It was not an easy conversation to have over the phone. I resisted using the obvious good news/bad news approach. *The good news is police have a lead on your missing fiancé; the bad news is he's a killer.*

Instead I gave it to her straight.

Madeline didn't believe me. Oh, she knew Mark's mother was dead. And she, too, was troubled by the notion of suicide and felt some guilt that she hadn't stayed in closer touch with her almost mother-in-law.

But she didn't believe for a minute that her betrothed had anything to do with murder.

((RILEY/NAT))
AUTHORITIES SAY NEW
EVIDENCE CAUSED THEM

TO CHANGE THE CAUSE-OF-
DEATH RULING . . . BUT
THEY DECLINED TO GIVE
ANY DETAILS.
((SHERIFF/SOT))
NO COMMENT.
((RILEY/ON SET))
BUT CHANNEL 3 HAS
LEARNED THAT SEVERAL
BOXES CONTAINING ITEMS
BELONGING TO THE
SUSPECT ARE MISSING
FROM HIS MOTHER'S
GARAGE.

"I'd like to know what this new evidence is," Madeline said. "Those lazy cops probably just made it up to frame Mark."

"Madeline, you need to watch more *Law and Order* on television. Police gain nothing by calling a suicide a homicide. It creates more work for them, not less."

"But none of this makes any sense. She was the only family he had. Why would he harm her?"

Mark clearly hadn't confided to her that his mother had deceived him about his father. But to me, that deception didn't merit murder.

"You don't know him, Riley, but I do. He is not a man of violence."

"But, Madeline, you only knew him for three months and much of that time you were registering for linens and picking out colors."

"Three minutes was all I needed to know what kind of man he is." Then she hung up before I could ask her about his pre-wedding confrontation with his mom and what Madeline knew about her fiancé's father.

The mother of the bride apparently didn't share her daughter's confidence in her almost son-in-law's character. When Vivian Post heard that Mark was wanted for murder, she hired a private security firm to protect her family. And to keep the media away.

She said that included me.

CHAPTER 23

After the late news I headed to the Mall of America for my movie meeting with Nick Garnett. We had seats in the back of a nearly empty theater for a late-night show. I insisted I wasn't hungry but he made a trip to the concession stand and brought back hot dogs, a giant pretzel, pizza, and a couple of drinks. Popcorn, too. Greasy.

Garnett insisted I eat *something*. "You've had a long day and it's a long movie."

Earlier, I'd told him he could pick the flick, so I was stuck with a Jackie Chan martial-arts film that I had little interest in watching. But the popcorn smell drifted my way and I realized I was hungry after all and reached for the pretzel.

He told me repairs had been made at Underwater Adventures and the aquarium would reopen tomorrow. I told him about my suspicions that the fish thieves would try to smuggle Big Mouth Billy into the bass contest to collect half a million bucks.

"And my boss expects me to find him before sweeps end," I said. "That gives me just over two weeks to fail."

Garnett laughed and replied, "Tell her there are some fish that can't be caught. It's not like they are bigger or faster than the other fish. They are just touched by something extra." He said the line with twinkling eyes and I recognized the challenge in his voice.

"Very funny," I replied. "Ewan McGregor. *Big Fish*, 2003. I win." I associate movies with news events near their release date. And I distinctly remembered seeing a *Big Fish* film ad run next to a promo about U.S. forces capturing Saddam Hussein, and thinking, Two big fish in one commercial break.

"Good catch." Garnett raised his drink in a playful toast.

"As amusing as this game is, Nick," I continued, "and as certain as I am that you're setting me up for that quote from *A River Runs Through It*—"

"You mean the 1992 one," he interrupted me, "where the narrator says, 'If our father had had his say, nobody who did not know how to fish would be allowed to disgrace a fish by catching him.' "

Garnett looked pleased with himself, like he'd reeled in a winner.

"Yes, that's the one," I conceded. "But I need to shift the talk back to business. Hear the homicide news from Wisconsin?"

"Oh yeah," he answered.

"So what do you think?" I asked.

"I think I'm glad it's not my case."

"I'm starting to wish it wasn't my story." Just when I was willing to give up NEVER WORN, my news director was giving it top priority. "This isn't what I signed up for. The last thing I want to do is chase another killer. I just wanted to help find a missing person."

"Your problem, Riley, is you think you can tell Norman Rockwell from Norman Bates."

I opened my mouth to contradict him, but Garnett put a finger on my lips and shook his head. "Distinguishing good from evil isn't that simple, even though you media types would like it to be."

The lights in the theater were starting to dim, so I quickly turned our discussion from abstract villainy to the real reason for our meeting.

"Find out anything about this new evidence Wisconsin's referring to?" Finding that could be the key to finding Mark.

"I was waiting for you to ask," Garnett said.

"Really, Nick? You know something?"

A preview for a Will Smith superhero film started rolling, so he whispered. "They had to outsource the autopsy to the Ramsey County medical examiner here in Minnesota because that county doesn't have their own ME. Plenty of rural counties don't. Lots of buzz going on."

"Like what?"

"They're pissed because the investigators in the field forgot to bag her hands."

The image startled me.

"Is that cop talk?" I asked. "I love it when you talk cop talk." Unsub. Blood splatter. Chain of custody. Cops have their own exotic language.

Garnett explained that the field team neglected to put paper bags over Mrs. Lefevre's hands to preserve evidence. That meant forensics couldn't draw a firm conclusion whether she fired the gun or not, even though her finger-prints were the only ones found on the weapon. "That meant the sheriff's office had to establish suicide with the other evidence. And it pointed in the opposite direction."

"Do you know what the new evidence is?"

"It's the suicide note," he said. "Handwriting doesn't match the mother's. It matches the son's."

I recalled the blue piece of paper near Jean Lefevre's body. "Where did they get copies of his handwriting?"

"Probably the missing person file. Often cops ask for handwriting samples just in case bank accounts are opened or closed suspiciously. Helps them rule out identity fraud."

I had more questions, but the movie was starting and Garnett shushed me so he could pay attention. The last scene I recall was a kung fu confrontation that seemed to go much too long.

Then Garnett was shaking me awake and the closing credits were ending. The theater was empty and still dark. I was groggy and our evening seemed like a dream and our faces were close together. *I* probably should have just kissed *him* and avoided an awkward conversation; but I sometimes overthink and overtalk. This was one of those times.

"Nick, do you ever think about that time last fall when you kissed me?"

I think I asked because I wanted *him* to kiss *me* again.

But Garnett kept his lips to himself, and not just because the lights had come up and the ushers had arrived to collect the garbage.

"Riley, if you're looking for something personal, you should know I'm a once-burned, twice-shy kind of guy."

He obviously remembered our previous kiss had ended badly.

"You know how I feel about you." As he whispered, I felt beard stubble brush against my cheek.

He reached over to tilt my chin up with his hand and gaze into my eyes, perhaps as if trying to read truth in the face of a woman. Something he admitted that he had no talent for.

I stopped breathing because I was certain a kiss was seconds away. Then he threw our botched buss back at me.

184

He delivered his next words like he'd practiced for this moment.

"I think I need to hear the L word first."

L? Love? Now he seemed to be the one overthinking and overtalking. In my experience, men typically kissed first and questioned later. And those queries were more likely to spell the L word l-u-s-t than l-o-v-e.

I wasn't looking to lock into a complicated romantic relationship; I was just craving a kiss. After all, a mere kiss between old friends wouldn't jeopardize my new virgin status. Would it?

I was afraid of where this conversation might lead, so I kept my mouth shut on love and friendship and suddenly remembered I needed to get home and let the dog out.

CHAPTER 24

Well after midnight, I pulled into my garage just as headlights from another vehicle turned into my neighbor's driveway. Shep was unhappy I'd been away so long. As I opened the door to get in, he ducked out for his doggy business. A couple of minutes later, I heard the slam of a screen door and saw a man leaving my neighbor's house. Shep and I watched as he climbed into his vehicle, backed out, and drove away.

Another quickie visit, I thought to myself. The family living on the other side of George had told me a few days earlier they found the odd comings and goings irritating in the middle of the night. This latest visitor didn't bother me because it wasn't like I was trying to sleep, and when I did sleep, I slept deep, oblivious to headlights in the window and car tires on asphalt.

I GLANCED AT the overnight numbers posted on the bulletin board by the coffee machine in the newsroom. A 28 share. Mediocre by last year's measure. But exceptional now, considering the network gave us a rotten lead-in show and some viewers were still mad about the writer's strike. Mrs. Lefevre's murder was as close to gold as I expected to strike during this ratings book.

I pulled the sheet down and headed for Noreen's glass-walled office because I needed a shot of praise. But she was already in a meeting with two guests I would never have expected: Toby Elness and Blackie, his black Labrador. The Lab's rather obvious name made perfect sense to Noreen—after all, she'd named her own dalmatian Freckles.

"What's going on, Toby?" I asked. "Were you waiting for me?"

Noreen looked miffed for some unknown reason; Toby looked confused, probably from being cooped up too long with my news director. She sometimes had that effect on me, too.

Toby's face drooped like a basset hound's—large nose, sad eyes, and longish ear lobes, but I knew him to be as loyal as a collie.

"We were discussing options in the missing bass case," Noreen said. "You've been so busy, Riley, I thought Toby might have some insight."

She glanced his way with a smile that seemed like a fake attempt to flirt by someone who was out of practice. I wanted to tell her to save it—Toby didn't respond to feminine manipulation. But I ignored her sham and put the question to him plain.

"Do you?" I asked Toby. "Have any insight?" If he did, I couldn't imagine why he wouldn't have already told me.

"Not really," he answered. "I was just telling your boss—"

"Please, call me Noreen."

"I was just telling her I don't know anything about the kidnapped fish. I don't know how many times I have to say that the Animal Liberation Front would never harm other fish just to save one."

"And I was just telling Toby how I genuinely share his concern for animals," Noreen said. "And how, should he find himself in a position to witness the release of Billy into the wild, Channel 3 would love to broadcast some home video so our viewers could see the important work being done for our earth's creatures."

Noreen's face had that special glow she gets when she's in love with a story. And then she delivered *my* closing line— the one I'd told her I often used with reluctant sources who didn't want controversial documents or information traced back to them.

"Toby, this television station gets baskets of mail each day, should a package arrive with a videotape and no return address and no signature, we'd have no idea where it came from, and that's what we'd have to tell anyone who asked."

Then she insisted on walking him and Blackie out the front door to pay for their parking. While they were seated in her office, Toby seemed taller than Noreen. But that was an illusion, I now noticed as Blackie led them down the block. Side by side, they were the same size, but Noreen's height was in her legs and she moved like a greyhound, slim and sleek. Toby's legs were shorter, and closer to the ground, and he took more steps to keep up with her.

Toby later told me Noreen suggested they meet at a local dog park with their pets sometime soon.

Noreen later told me she suspected authorities were right and Toby did know more about that missing fish than he was letting on.

Back in my office, I was going through my e-mail spam filter, counting all the different ways to misspell Viagra, when my cell phone rang. Madeline needed to see me. Urgently.

"I'm in downtown Minneapolis," I told her. "How about if I stop by after work?"

"The police were here, asking questions about Mark."

"That's to be expected. Just tell them what you know."

"I didn't know anything. What I need to talk to you about is what *they* told *me*."

MADELINE CLAIMED SHE needed to get outdoors and breathe fresh air, so she gave me directions to Tamarack Nature Center in White Bear Lake. I figured I could dash home afterward and let Shep out. I pulled into the parking lot next to her Mercedes.

"Hello, Madeline, it's Riley." I called out my name, understanding that she wouldn't recognize me otherwise.

A man wearing dark glasses watched us from another vehicle. She explained he was her bodyguard, retained by her mother. "But he's agreed to follow at a distance."

How exotic, I thought, a bodyguard. I wonder if he's carrying a gun? I wonder if he would protect me if trouble came? More likely I'd be sacrificed to save the heiress. You get what you pay for in life.

Madeline motioned for me to follow her down a wood-chipped trail into the woods. Easy for her, she wore walking shoes. I moved clumsily on the uneven ground because of my heels.

"This is one of my family's favorite places." She waved her arms wide and spun around. "My grandfather donated the land."

We entered a clearing and she explained that this prairie was where she and Mark were supposed to get married, surrounded by rows of rustic benches for the guests.

Normally weddings aren't allowed, but in her case an exception was made. Her bodyguard stood about thirty yards away, on the line where woods and meadow met.

"Mother and I planned and planned for the wedding. There was so much to get done in such a short time. I thought the only thing out of my control was the weather," she said, "but it was a perfect Indian summer day."

She breathed deeply, reminiscing. "The way things turned out, the groom was out of my control and has been ever since."

"What happened in your meeting with the police?" On the phone she'd hinted at a break in the case.

"They wanted to know if I'd given Mark any money. But I hadn't." She paused briefly. "They found $98,000 in cash in a safe-deposit box under his name."

My feet stopped, but my mind kept moving. Nearly a hundred grand. In cash. My first thought was drug money. And I was sure that's where the cops were headed with this. After all, nobody ever mentioned Mark winning the lottery. And most folks would want to be earning interest on all that dough. Secret wads of cash suggest other secrets.

"Seems like a lot of money for him to have stashed away," I said, trying to keep my voice neutral.

"I know," Madeline answered.

Without saying anything we walked down another trail toward a pond. I surveyed the view over the water. Birch trees with peeling white bark and oaks with fresh, pointy leaves. The colorful autumn forest must have made for a magnificent wedding backdrop. I could see why Madeline had wanted to get married here and I told her I admired the fact that she didn't let memories of that day keep her away from such splendor.

But I also asked, gal pal to gal pal, if maybe it was time

for her to drop that Stand by My Man routine, now that her man stood accused of matricide.

"I mean, Madeline, how good could the sex have been?"

"That wasn't the part of his body that did it for me, Riley." She looked more anguished than angry. "It was his face. There's no way for you to understand the *intoxication*. When I made love with other men, I closed my eyes. But when I was with Mark I could not take my eyes off him. I kept them open until they hurt."

She was right; I couldn't understand an affliction like face blindness.

"I'm sorry, Madeline." We followed a loop around a wildflower garden and headed back. I watched a park worker shovel wood chips from a wheelbarrow on another path.

"Maybe it's just as well Mark and I didn't get married." She shrugged, more in resignation than conviction. "There seems to be a lot about him I didn't know. What's hard, Riley, is I can't forget his face. When you close your eyes, you can conjure up any face you want. All I see is him. It's like he haunts my soul."

Out of the corner of my eye, I spied a shadow, but it was Madeline's bodyguard and not her AWOL fiancé or the ghost of his murdered mother.

Mark's father was easy to find but hard to reach, though he lived only half an hour away. A couple of mouse clicks and Xiong located him serving life in the Minnesota Correctional Facility at Stillwater. Murder topped off a list of more modest crimes.

I'd contacted him by letter after Father Mountain shared Jean Lefevre's secret. Now Felix Lefevre had my office phone number, with a note to call me collect and put me on his visitor list.

Felix's conviction ten years ago wasn't for a particularly interesting murder. Just one thug shooting another. Never made the news.

When prison inmates hear from reporters, they always hope we want to prove their innocence and free them. So Felix was disappointed to learn I only wanted to discuss his son. And all I really cared about was whether Mark had been in touch with him. That answer was no.

I'd gotten that much over the phone and could have simply thanked him and said goodbye. But on the chance that he might still hear from Mark—or know something else newsworthy going on in the slammer, or like many snitches was doling out information one piece at a time—I went to meet Felix. I was his first visitor in quite a while, and it had taken some back-and-forth with prison officials to make that happen.

Stillwater was one of the oldest prisons in Minnesota. Unlike some of the state's newer correctional facilities, Stillwater looked like a prison. Stone walls and steel bars. The inside door crashed shut behind visitors just like in the movies.

I held a photo of Mark up to the visitor glass for Felix to see.

"So that's what he looks like?" Felix said. They shared the same frizzy black hair. "Kind of forgot I had a kid."

He didn't follow the news, so didn't know his estranged wife was dead and his son a murder suspect. If he cared, he didn't show it beyond mumbling something about his kid taking after his old man.

So much for the theory that Mark left to find his father.

CHAPTER 25

My neighbor's yard sale had expanded when I got home. I noticed some lawn gnomes that hadn't been there earlier along with a white wicker picnic basket and a wheelbarrow. After walking to the post office to buy stamps, Shep and I went next door to check out the new stock and try making nice with George.

A bearded man I'd seen there a couple times before was carrying an ugly multicolored vase to his pickup truck parked by the curb. He set his purchase on the ground to open the door.

"Hope you didn't pay more than a buck for that," I teased.

Shep pushed past me to stick his nose in the vase and paw against it. "Stop that," I told the big dog.

I apologized for my nosy canine companion. But when the bearded man grinned, his teeth looked brownish. His smile, disgusting.

After he drove away I realized I might have just witnessed Shep's classic drug-alert signal. And I recalled Shep pawing in the garage the other day, too.

Wouldn't it be something if my neighbor's yard sale was a front for dealing drugs? That would explain the odd traffic patterns next door. And why so many of George's customers seemed to be regulars. And why my neighbor didn't need a real job.

MALIK'S CAMERA WAS set up inside my dining room facing out the window at my neighbor's driveway early the next morning. Shep and I sat on the porch with a newspaper and some breakfast treats, waiting for the YARD SALE sign to go up.

The first customer, a middle-aged man with a receding hairline, seemed to leave empty-handed. That didn't mean he didn't have some contraband tucked in his jacket. But Malik and I figured we could only test two patrons before George became suspicious and pulled a gun or whatever drug dealers do when their neighbors piss them off. We decided not to make a move until we could visually confirm someone had made a purchase. But we did shoot his license plate.

So even though Shep wanted to leave for a walk, we waited some more. After another hour, a young woman with a toddler walked into the garage and left minutes later with a used Twister board game.

Shep and I went into action on the guise of putting a letter in the mailbox. I greeted the woman while she was trying to buckle her squirming son in his car seat.

"Would he like to pet my doggy?" I asked her. Then, turning to the tot, "If you're a good boy and sit still for your mom, I'll let you pet my dog."

The board game lay on the floor of her minivan. The mother seemed to be sizing Shep up. His tongue hung out of his mouth so he looked fairly harmless.

"Doggy, doggy," her little boy chanted. So while he was happily patting Shep's back, and his mother was snapping him in, Shep was sniffing and pawing at the Twister box in the same distinctive manner he had earlier. Malik had a clear shot because the van door was wide open. He got her license plate as well.

The outcome was the same when I flirted with a large man with colorful tattoos on one arm just as he was getting on his motorcycle to drive away. He'd left the garage carrying a hooded sweatshirt with a large front pocket that Shep found irresistible.

George walked to the curb, craned his neck as if to check on us, but by then Mr. Biker had left and we were back on my porch. I gave him a small wave. He turned without saying anything.

Opportunity allowed us to add a control element to our experiment. I helped an elderly woman across the street unload her groceries, but Shep showed no curiosity toward any of her packages, not even a plastic bag containing pork chops.

"SO WHAT DOES it prove?" Noreen was excited over the prospect of a drug story now that it involved video of a dog. What it lacked was concrete proof my neighbor's garage actually contained illegal drugs. So I wasn't surprised when Miles prohibited broadcasting anything without additional verification.

I was still sore about his legal advice to destroy the mother-of-the-groom interview, but Noreen didn't appear to hold that episode against him. What he called advice, she took as gospel.

So the following morning, I'd gone next door to George's yard sale, wired with a hidden camera. I surveyed the merchandise, pulled a worn copy of *All the President's Men* off a shelf, winked at my neighbor, and asked how much.

When he replied a buck, I winked again. And said, "Are you sure?" hoping he'd slip a little dope or speed between the pages and jack the price up.

"All right, fifty cents." George pretended not to get my drift and seemed in a hurry to get rid of me.

Xiong had cross-checked the license plate with criminal records. Only the minivan mom had a drug offense, but it was three years ago and, as Miles reminded us, people change. I had the county e-mail me her mug shot and she could have been a poster child for one of those "before and after" anti-meth billboards along the freeway showing pleasant wives and mothers reduced to street people. Trouble was, I couldn't be sure which image—minivan mom or jail-house junkie—was her real persona.

Bottom line, our attorney refused to take Shep's word on the matter. Even though the big dog lay at my feet on the floor of Noreen's office looking sober and responsible.

"So whose word would you take?" I asked.

"If your neighbor had a history of drug sales or even other illegal activity, that would help," Miles said.

No luck. I'd pulled George's last name from his license plate and he came up clean.

"All we have is your hunch that this is how the dog behaves around illicit drugs," Miles continued. "And you're not a trained K-9 officer."

Oh, but I knew a trained K-9 officer. And in this business, sources are everything.

I checked with the hospital and found out Emily Flying Cloud had been discharged two days earlier. She wouldn't be ready to go back in the field for some time yet, so I called her at home. When she answered, she sounded like I woke her up.

"Emily, just checking to see how you're feeling." I started off reminding her who I was, but she remembered me easily. "I'm going to be in your neighborhood this afternoon, are you up for any company? I'll bring the doughnuts."

I wanted to keep things casual and not let on I needed a favor. Especially since it was the kind of favor she'd probably insist on clearing with her boss first. But she said fine, so I put the video of Shep pawing on a DVD and grabbed a portable DVD player, not knowing the sophistication of her home electronics equipment.

I left Malik back at the station because I didn't want her calling her department public information officer because a television camera was on her stoop. And I'd left Shep with Noreen in the newsroom because I wasn't sure if Emily was ready to face the big dog in person. More than likely he'd jump all over her stitches in his glee at seeing her again.

Emily was slow answering the door. She wore a baggy sweat suit, easier to slip on and off. Definitely a step up from a hospital gown. But physically, she looked ragged out.

We visited a few minutes before she asked about Shep.

"I brought some video of him," I said. "Would you like to watch?" That prospect cheered her.

Normally journalists can't go around showing people, especially law enforcement officers, unaired video because then the cops start thinking they are always entitled to our work product. And that would make news organizations an arm of the government. Which would contradict the First Amendment. And diminish our status as the Fourth Estate, something the press is touchy about. But in this case, I was seeking Emily's reaction to the videotape. That's part of my job, to seek reaction to events. That context makes all the difference.

So I got out the DVD player and set up the scenes by telling her, "Shep's greeting some shoppers leaving my neighbor's yard sale." Then I hit Play.

Emily watched Shep pawing the board game. Then pawing the pocket of the sweatshirt. "Let me see that again," she said. Rewind. Play. "Riley, explain what I just saw."

"Actually, Emily, I'm hoping you can explain it."

I told her my suspicions about my neighbor's never-ending yard sale. She confirmed the pawing motion was Shep's drug-sniffing alert.

"I'd bet anything your neighbor is running meth. It's big business in the suburbs. And dealers need false fronts to stay under the radar. That's what his yard sale is all about."

Just the confirmation I needed. To celebrate, I opened the doughnut box. Emily picked a real looker with chocolate frosting and vanilla pudding in the center. I settled for an apple fritter over your basic raised glazed because fruit is healthier. We discussed the damage meth has done to our state and to people we knew. But my elation came and went with her next words. "You're not thinking about putting this on the news, are you?"

I mumbled something resembling "Well . . . yeah . . . sort of." And then made like my mouth was too full to talk.

"You can't do that, Riley. Your neighbor will destroy all the evidence before police can move in and stop him."

Another legal/ethical dilemma. One more encounter with Miles and Noreen might be one more than I could handle.

Luckily, Emily had an idea. "Just hold off for a day or so. I can file a search warrant affidavit based on your tape. You can run your story after the police go in."

That *would* give Channel 3 the ultimate confirmation of

any drug activity. Police have to make public what they confiscate during such raids. So Emily and I agreed to talk to our bosses. A more complicated task for her because that conversation would involve multiple law enforcement agencies, but first she needed a nap.

"In the meantime, Riley, stay indoors. Don't spook your neighbor."

CHAPTER 26

((RILEY/LIVE/CAM PAN))
I'M LIVE IN WHITE BEAR
LAKE . . . WHERE EARLIER
TODAY POLICE RAIDED THIS
HOUSE AND DISCOVERED
WHAT THEY ARE
DESCRIBING AS A MAJOR
METH-SALES OPERATION.

The cops had debated waiting to further develop the case, but had concerns that I might, knowingly or unknowingly, raise suspicions in the neighborhood. So they busted George the next day. Naturally, Malik hid at my house to record the action.

((RILEY/NAT))
HERE YOU SEE THE
OWNER . . . GEORGE
MAURICE . . . TAKEN INTO

CUSTODY IN
HANDCUFFS . . .
AUTHORITIES SAY HE RAN A
LARGE-SCALE DRUG
OPERATION FROM HIS
GARAGE WHERE HE HELD
YARD SALES AS A COVER-UP.
THE REAL HERO IS THIS
DRUG-SNIFFING GERMAN
SHEPHERD WHOSE NOSE
PICKED UP ON THE RUSE . . .
WATCH AS HE PAWS ITEMS
THESE CUSTOMERS
PURCHASED . . .

Miles made us blur their faces because the mom and the biker guy, nonpublic figures, hadn't been officially accused of anything. I suspected authorities were negotiating a plea bargain to get them to testify against George.

((RILEY/NAT))
THAT'S THE DOG'S WAY OF
INDICATING DRUGS ARE
HIDDEN INSIDE.
((RILEY/LIVE/SHEP))
AND HERE HE IS, WITH ME
NOW . . . THE DOG OF THE
HOUR.

Just like Lassie, Shep barked on cue.

And of course, the overnight numbers went through the ratings roof at Channel 3. Helped along, no doubt, by a promo that ran all through the network's prime-time lineup.

201

((PROMO/SOT))
EXCLUSIVE! SEE RILEY
SPARTZ'S BIG BUST
TONIGHT AT TEN.

I only found out because my mom called me, all embarrassed, checking to see whether she dared tune in at ten.

She and Dad live outside the Channel 3 viewing area, but bought a satellite dish for Christmas just so they could watch my stories and tell me how good they are. At first, she thought she misheard the promo, but when it ran again half an hour later, she tried to alert me but I let her call roll over to voice mail and didn't find out until too late.

Noreen apologized that no one at the station caught the double entendre. Then she abruptly changed the subject by asking me how I was coming along on the fish story.

I DIDN'T KNOW it at the time, but Emily's hunch about Shep being in danger was more than pooch paranoia. Among the 30 share audience watching my reports on the yard-sale bust must have been the meth cartel seeking to eliminate Shep.

To protect him from revenge seekers, I'd been careful not to mention Shep's name on the air. Or that I lived next door to the drug raid. Or that the hero dog temporarily lived under my roof. But this kind of information apparently gets around in criminal circles. And George Maurice probably viewed my actions as less than neighborly and likely ratted me out to any drug kingpin or peon behind bars who'd listen.

So while I definitely started getting the feeling someone was watching me, I guessed it was Mark. Figuring he'd seen my news coverage about his mother's murder, he might have been interested in eyeballing me without a television screen separating us.

As a wanted man, he'd be easy to recognize. So many fugitives blend into the crowd, usually resulting in false sightings and tying up law enforcement teams in far-flung geographic areas on squat. That hadn't happened in this case. Police received absolutely no tips reporting the missing groom/suspected murderer. They attributed this to his skill in lying low. After all, he'd vanished months ago without leaving a trail.

Madeline insisted he'd not been in touch with her. Best man Gabe Murray claimed the same.

But during the last twenty-four hours I felt certain he was out there, watching me, and since I didn't have a bodyguard, I was glad for the row of news trucks parked conspicuously on my street and the company of a big dog with sharp teeth. But tomorrow, Shep would be reunited with Emily, so tonight we went for a last run together.

It had a parade quality.

A couple of times people recognized us and cheered.

When we passed Ursula's Wine Bar, the owner chased us down and insisted we take a break on his patio. He poured me a glass of what he called his finest red and served Shep a slab of raw sirloin under the table. He asked if I'd mind if he put our visit in his monthly newsletter under "celebrity sighting."

The sun was nearly gone, but I didn't want the day to end. Also without Shep's protection, starting tomorrow, I'd want to be home by nightfall. So we ran west into the end of the sun and the start of the moon.

A white full-size van pulled up alongside us as we raced and I waved to the driver, who I assumed was another fan.

Then I saw a man in the passenger seat raise a gun. The illumination of a streetlight just then revealed that neither man was Mark.

"Shep!" I called and turned off the street, cut through a dark industrial park, over some railroad tracks. Soon I found myself in the Tamarack Nature Center parking lot. The vehicle followed us from the street and sped straight toward us, flying over speed bumps. I sprinted for the trees with Shep on my heels. A car door slammed. Then the sound of running feet.

I changed directions several times and heard a voice shout something like "Make sure you get the dog this time."

That's when I realized that instead of Shep protecting me, I needed to protect Shep.

And I wished my dog was named Nitro.

ON THE PRO side: I had a head start, was familiar with the park after my walk and talk with Madeline, and was highly motivated to stay alive.

On the con side: I was tired, had a dog to keep quiet, and my pursuers were armed, dangerous, and highly motivated to kill.

The prairie where the wedding didn't happen was straight ahead. Hiding seemed my best option. I ducked under some bushes, pulling Shep with me, and we rolled and pulled until we were wedged deep in a briar patch. This seemed as good a place as any to make our last stand.

"Hush," I whispered to my dog, wrapping my arms tight around him and closing my eyes. Then I listened, heard nothing except my beating heart. Or was it Shep's? My cell phone was gone. I spread one hand across the ground, reaching and searching for something metallic, but felt nothing except damp leaves and soggy moss.

Shep struggled against my grip, so I loosened it, whispering for him to sit still. But he wanted to stretch. Then he wanted to sniff. Then he wanted to move.

I tried to coax him back in the direction we came, thinking by backtracking we might find my phone. He ignored me, heading the opposite way. I trailed behind, praying our opponents didn't detect our movement. I recalled Madeline saying that Tamarack was more than three hundred acres, which seemed like plenty of space for all of us to get along. I couldn't let our paths cross with the gunmen or Shep would attack and lose badly.

He stopped and started smelling the ground. Then pawing it in a now familiar manner. "Not now," I whispered. "Lie down, boy. Please."

But he continued, sniffing and pawing, like on a mission from a drug czar. Then he started digging.

Great, I thought, he'll probably unearth ten kilos of heroin. And then those thugs will get rich wasting us. Why can't you just chase cats like other dogs?

I pulled at what seemed to be a cloth bag wedged under the dirt, thinking the sooner we finished this, the sooner Shep would settle down. As the fabric tore, the hole deepened, and while I couldn't see the contents, the smell told me we had not uncovered a secret stash of illegal drugs. The smell actually reminded me of the corpse flower, which couldn't be all that rare if they also grew wild in the woods of Tamarack Nature Center.

Shep kept digging and I kept pulling and suddenly, we were not alone.

In the moonlight, a human face stared back from the hole in the ground.

CHAPTER 27

My Jamie Lee Curtis scream started Shep barking. Movement seemed to come from different directions and I guessed the bad guys had split up looking for us. I wasn't sure which way to go, then I heard repeated gunfire and turned the opposite way.

I tripped, landing in the dirt. I blamed my clumsiness on a tree root until I realized it had a handle and a blade. Piling dead, damp leaves over Shep and myself, I kept one hand on the shovel in case I needed a weapon. Then I flattened my body and tried not to breathe.

I prayed some nosy neighbor might have heard the gunshots and called the police to report poachers in the nature center.

Minutes later, sirens.

"OVER HERE," I called out when I could see uniforms behind flashlights.

The two officers were skeptical of my story until Shep led them through the brush and showed them the corpse at our feet—the fifth dead body I'd seen in just under six months.

By their reaction, I suspected it might have been their first.

One of them took my statement while the other called for the homicide team. The parking lot had been empty when the squad cars arrived to investigate the sound of "shots fired." The cops decided to walk up to the park lodge to make sure the building was secure when they heard me hailing them down the path. The only detail I could provide was a vague description of a white full-size van.

"Sure they weren't after you instead of the dog?" one of the cops asked.

"I'm very sure."

"Usually thugs don't go after women with dogs," the other insisted.

"That's the whole point," I explained again, "they weren't after me, they were after him."

I explained that Shep wasn't just any dog. Leaning against my legs, he seemed to nod.

Over the next hour, more questions. "Tell me again why the dog started digging." That query came from Detective Leo Bradshaw, a homicide investigator with the White Bear Lake Police Department.

Even though there seemed little connection between the men chasing me and the corpse in the ground, he pressed for minutia. "Are you sure you didn't get a look at either of them?"

Like most Minnesotans, they were Caucasian. But that's all I could offer. Then I remembered how K-9 dogs in Europe are used in scent lineups, and suggested Shep might be able to identify the men if they were captured. Detective Bradshaw shook his head.

By morning, state crime lab technicians would finish unearthing the body and begin forensics. In the meantime, additional investigators arrived to string crime-scene tape and sweep the nature center for evidence. That's when they found a freshly dead drug dealer shot in the heart, apparently by his careless accomplice in the darkness.

That made six dead bodies I'd seen in just under six months.

WHEN WE GOT home, Shep slept in my bed with me. A squad car stayed parked in front of my house all night and escorted me to Emily Flying Cloud's place the next morning where I returned her four-legged partner.

They delighted in seeing each other again. She looked much stronger than the last time I visited. We agreed, at the moment, that Shep was safer with her than with me. I shook the big dog's face, traced the scar on his ear with my fingers, and told him goodbye. He barked, but didn't try to follow me out the door.

I left lonely.

Sitting in my car outside her house, I switched through radio stations until a sad song from the seventies stopped me. I listened to Sylvia's mother advising a caller that her daughter was too busy to come to the phone. Now I really felt lonely.

So I called Nick Garnett for an early lunch. We met at a Mexican restaurant in south Minneapolis where few of the help or customers seem to speak English—a good place to meet a source since no one can understand your conversation. That same reason also makes it a good place for a rendezvous, except it lacks romance.

I hadn't decided where I wanted this encounter to lead. My latest brush with death made me want to cling to someone without fur and a wet nose. I wanted to touch and be touched. Intimately. Just to reassure myself I was still alive and could still be thrilled by passion.

But Nick didn't seem to want me unless I wanted him. I could sort of understand his position. I had rejected him once—pretty convincingly. So I almost made the first move and reached across the table to squeeze his hand; instead I chickened out and reached for salsa and chips.

"If I hadn't lost my cell phone," I told Garnett, "I would have called you last night and said, 'I see dead people.' "

"You would have been better off dialing 911 because I'd simply have answered, 'Haley Joel Osment, *The Sixth Sense*, 1999,' and hung up on you."

We talked about how neither the police, the public, nor the media get too excited over drug dealers killing each other. Newsrooms shrug off drive-by shootings unless they result in the death of an innocent, like a kid doing homework who's hit by a stray bullet through a window. That kind of murder will spark a neighborhood to protest the violence and energize activists to call for change.

But as innocents keep dying and nothing seems to change, so does the community fervor to try to do something about it.

LEST YOU THINK I buried the lead, it wasn't until later in the day that authorities announced the buried body was the missing groom. The news didn't exactly stun me—remember, I'd gotten a glimpse of the face.

He wasn't badly decomposed, because the ground had frozen so early. Some insect larva had invaded his flesh, but crawly things don't freak me out. I grew up studying entomology as a hobby and taking my insect collection to the county fair each year to compete for a blue ribbon. An unusual hobby, but I was a poor farm kid and bugs were free. So my level of squeamishness differs from that of most women; better that I found Mark's body, than a young child exploring the nature center for buried treasure.

So in retrospect, Mark Lefevre had an acceptable reason for missing his wedding: he was dead.

He hadn't run off with an old girlfriend.

He hadn't killed his mother, either.

And the discovery of his body in a shallow grave was a development that the police, the public, and the media cared intensely about. Especially since he hadn't died from the bullet in his chest. Certainly loss of blood was a contributing factor, but the medical examiner found traces of dirt down his trachea and in his lungs, concluding that Mark had technically suffocated—been buried alive.

The next night, after the crime lab had cleared the scene and the police tape came down, I went back with Malik to shoot a moonlight stand-up bridge for my story.

((RILEY/STAND-UP))
THIS IS WHERE I STUMBLED
UPON THE SHALLOW GRAVE
CONCEALING MARK
LEFEVRE'S BODY.

Noreen had assigned coverage of the police investigation to another reporter because I was in pretty deep. Finding the body of the missing groom took me well beyond my role as journalist and made me a witness. But my boss still wanted me to track a how-it-happened sidebar story as I walked viewers through the woods.

While I waited to lay my voice track in the truck and

feed it back to the station, I practiced variations of my sign-off line: "This is Riley Spartz, Channel 3 News."

I like my name. Some journalists, such as CNN's Anderson Cooper, have two last names stuck together. Others, like NBC's David Gregory, have two first names. Both work well for them. To me, Riley Spartz sounds strong and confident, and that counts for something in the news business.

"This is Channel 3's Riley Spartz . . ." "From White Bear Lake, this is Riley Spartz reporting . . ." "Reporting from White Bear Lake, Riley Spartz, Channel 3 News . . ." I kept it up until my photographer called me annoying and asked me to please turn off my wireless mic.

A couple of crews from the other stations were already laying cable in the parking lot for their own live shots. Their biggest challenge was telling the story without mentioning my name or television station, otherwise viewers would switch channels mid-sentence from them to us. No reporter enjoys following a competitor's big scoop. We try glossing over that detail with vague references to "News reports say . . ."

On an earlier evening I might have walked through these woods thinking, Isn't the park beautiful at night? But now I all I could think was, Isn't it creepy?

The killer must have been familiar with Tamarack to pick that place to bury Mark. Or have known Mark well because I considered it a real in-your-face move to bury him near the site of his own wedding. That seemed to rule out a random serial killer, carjacker, or robber.

Garnett, using his old police sources, had unearthed another reason, not yet made public, why robbery could be ruled out. He'd just called to tell me Mark died with a big wad of cash in his wallet: five one-hundred-dollar bills.

But money wasn't the biggest clue in this case. Not even close. Forensics showed the same gun killed both Mark and his mother.

Investigators were having a hard time making sense of those test results, particularly because a different jurisdiction was handling each murder. But to me, it seemed fairly reasonable to conclude that if the same gun was behind each homicide, the same finger pulled the trigger both times.

The Wisconsin cops still believed the big stack of cash in the safe-deposit box suggested Mark was connected to something dark and dangerous—like drugs. The cash in his pocket also supported that theory. Whatever the Minnesota police made of the evidence, they were keeping it to themselves. And I hadn't heard anything to suggest either team of investigators had made any headway recovering the boxes taken from Jean Lefevre's garage.

I had seen the murder weapon. Briefly. Though I was distracted by Mrs. Lefevre's body sprawled on a blood-soaked carpet. The gun used wasn't a drug thug's firearm of choice. Instead of a semiautomatic pistol, it was some kind of old revolver, likely retrieved from the top shelf of a dusty closet, where it had been hidden years ago.

To me, Mark's slaying screamed crime of passion. And since he clearly hadn't run off with his old girlfriend, I wondered again about Sigourney Nelson's whereabouts—both now and in the hours leading up to the doomed wedding.

To be fair, I also vowed to press the Post family—mother, daughter, son—a little harder on their individual timelines following the rehearsal dinner. Problem was, they tended to corroborate one another's stories. And they'd had months to get them straight.

If investigators hadn't reclassified Mark's mother's death

as homicide, Jean Lefevre would have been a tempting target for authorities to wrap up loose ends. The cops could have concocted a theory—she killed her son out of rage; killed herself out of guilt—blaming her for not wanting her only child to marry and start a new life. But they'd already played their cause-of-death flip-flop card and now had to stick by their homicide ruling or else look like idiots.

Minneapolis police closed their missing person file on Mark Lefevre. Didn't matter that he'd been found dead. All that mattered was he'd been found. Their work was finished. They could mark another case solved.

I would have liked to read that file, but those records remained sealed because they'd been folded into White Bear Lake's homicide case and that department had a whole lot of work ahead before they could mark anything solved.

THE DARKNESS REMAINED macabre that night without Shep as I stared out the window of my home office. I no longer feared a missing groom lurking outside. But murderers and drug dealers remained fairly high on my worry radar.

I'd owned a gun, briefly—or rather, I inherited my late husband's service Glock. Police confiscated it last fall as evidence in a suicide committed by a serial killer at close range to me. Once I, and the cop on the scene, were officially cleared in the shooting, authorities offered the gun back to me. I declined, perceiving the weapon as tainted. But tonight I wished I was armed and dangerous.

A friend once worked at a TV station in Laredo, Texas—market size 198, small by television standards. A firearm store couldn't come up with the cash to cover its advertising bill, so the station was paid in guns. Every employee got a .22 Magnum as a Christmas bonus that year. But this is the Twin Cities—market size 14. And all we get at Christmas is a gift voucher for a sport watch, toaster oven, or some other civilized home-electronics gizmo.

I glanced around the room for a suitable weapon to keep close by. A shelf of journalism awards drew my interest and I reflected on past stories that had gone much better than my current batch.

I stroked a national Emmy, but the shiny gold figurine was too beautiful and delicate to swing at an intruder. I quickly dismissed the bronze Sigma Delta Chi medallion as better suited for a coaster than a weapon. The pointed corners of the Edward R. Murrow trophy might inflict some damage but lacked heft. The silver duPont-Columbia baton fit nicely in my hand but was too short to cause serious harm. I settled on an American Women in Radio and Television Gracie Award. Nothing feminine about this stat-uette, except its name and curved shape. The four pounds of solid pewter could crack a skull as decisively as a metal baseball bat.

I laid Gracie on the pillow next to me as I turned off the lights, soothed by her company.

CHAPTER 28

Without Shep to feed and walk and brush, I got into work early the next morning. I bought a hot chocolate, topped off by whipped cream, at the coffee shop down the block from the station and settled in at my desk, content with my treat.

The St. Paul and Minneapolis newspapers gave major play to Mark Lefevre's murder. I skimmed both versions but didn't see anything new. Just as journalists hate following a competitor's exclusive, we also hate getting scooped on our own story.

Checking the normal comings and goings at Tamarack, the cops had narrowed Mark's time of death to a twelve-hour window after he left the White Bear Country Inn. Otherwise they figured he'd have shown up for the ceremony. They speculated the killer had buried him before park workers arrived the next morning. Certainly the deed had been completed before the big snowstorm hit less than forty-eight hours later.

I continued charting clues in my office and focused on

people who might want Mark dead. The bullet markings tied his death to his mother's. I had no solid idea why she ended up dead, but I had a hunch—find the killer's motive to harm Mark and I might solve both murders.

I put Mark's name in a circle in the center of a board hanging on my wall. I drew lines outward for suspects like spokes on a wheel. Each getting equal weight. Now came the time for brainstorming. No idea too outlandish at this stage. Get them down. Flesh them out. Eliminate later.

Mark's old girlfriend came to mind. I wrote down SIGOURNEY NELSON on one of the spokes, but was no closer to locating her than when I'd hypothesized that she and her old beau might have reconciled and run off together. Clearly that hadn't happened. But maybe that kiss in the parking lot had been the kiss of death.

The comedian who replaced Mark seemed to get a career boost after his rival's disappearance, so I added CHAD GRISWOLD to another spoke. He hadn't returned any of my phone calls. I pondered how much to read into that and how best to handle the situation.

I wrote DRUGS on another spoke. And it felt solid. Could Mark be involved in dealing? That much cash in a safe-deposit box was suspicious since Mark didn't appear to be living high and loose. He even owed his best man money.

Or could the murder motive be as simple as that? Revenge on an unpaid debt. Seemed unlikely, especially since Mark would be in a good spot to pay back the loan after his honeymoon. But I wrote GABE MURRAY on the board just to keep all options open—after all, people have killed for bus money.

My ad hoc theory about Mark's mother returned. Since Mark hadn't murdered her, could the cops have been right about her committing suicide? Might she have been driven

216

to it over the guilt of murdering him? That, more than parking tickets, might explain why she waited to contact police. The suicide note, in his handwriting, gained in importance. I wrote down JEAN LEFEVRE.

Though it seemed a long shot with the prenup, I wrote down VIVIAN POST, mother of the bride. Although she'd assured me she was happy for Madeline, if I had a daughter and a bunch of money, I'd have done more to help when her lover went missing. I recalled how quickly Mrs. Post hired a bodyguard. How come she never hired a private eye? Maybe she had hired a professional—a professional killer. But in the case of such a methodical murder, Mark's body probably would have been hidden better, encased in cement, and never been found.

I had one spoke left and I wrote down MADELINE POST.

I recalled my conversation with Professor Vasilis, the Harvard prosopagnosia researcher, and what he said about obsession and stalking should affection go unreturned. His research indicated facial recognition of a specific individual could be an astonishingly powerful lure to a face-blind subject.

What if the anonymous parking-lot kiss had been a prelude to Mark telling his bride the wedding was off? How might Madeline have reacted to such a rejection?

The timing required to shoot and bury a man seemed too tight for her to have left her mother's mansion without her absence being noticed. But I'd never pressed Madeline, minute to minute, where she was following the rehearsal dinner. That shallow grave in Tamarack was not far from Peninsula Road, so while I considered her involvement improbable, I no longer considered it impossible.

CHAPTER 29

Onstage, the man sweated. Whether from nerves or the overhead lights, I couldn't be sure. I was even sweating a little myself.

I sat near the front of the comedy club, but kept my head down and my collar up so Chad would not notice me in the crowd. I wanted to observe him up close to get a better feel for his speech pattern and body language. The bright lights and rambunctious audience might skew the results, but since he wouldn't meet with me or call me back, this approach would have to suffice.

Chad's name was listed last in the program. The closer for open-mic night. That meant he got seven minutes to wow the crowd instead of four. So I tried to relax and enjoy the preceding laughs. That's one thing about laughter—it's distracting. Amid the giggles and guffaws, I'd forgotten about my nerves until Chad walked onstage holding both hands against one shoulder, pretending to cast a fishing line into the audience. He opened his act with a joke about the best way for men to get their wives to let them spend more time fishing.

"Give them a choice," he said. "Wake them up real early in the morning and offer to leave and go fishing or stay and have sex."

The crowd laughed and several men stomped their feet in an atta-boy fashion.

"Either way, we win." Chad pretended he had a bite on his imaginary line and mimicked trying to reel in a fighting fish.

"Don't be surprised when she rolls over and mumbles those sweet words: 'Honey, don't forget to close the garage door.' "

A predictable punch line, but the audience clapped amiably. I'd purposely grabbed an aisle seat so I could follow Chad out once his seven minutes of glory ended.

He pretended that his next joke was also fishing related but it was actually a fairly juvenile double entendre about "hooking up."

"And how about that big fish that went missing?" he asked the crowd.

My ears perked up. What about Big Mouth Billy?

"Did you hear about that case?" Audience members nodded and murmured that yes, they were knowledgeable about local current events.

"That fish was the pride of the state. Any guy who'd do that has to be a real basshole."

I clapped spontaneously, along with the rest of the crowd. That "basshole" line was probably the cleverest of the night. I made a mental note to tell Tom McHale so he could work it into his anchor chitchat between weather and sports. Nothing the Federal Communications Commission could do about that. But then I wondered if appropriating "basshole" might be considered stealing material, and didn't want to get Tom in trouble.

"Good thing Lent's over or the FBI would be raiding every church fish fry," Chad continued. Several women in the crowd tittered in amusement at that image.

"I don't want to *cast* aspersions on law enforcement." Chad did that funny casting motion again. He seemed fond of physical comedy. Also of using puns. He followed with a couple of humorous observations about the lack of progress in the investigation with a special emphasis on *fishy*, *smells*, and *scales* of justice.

"When a fish goes missing, it's serious business. Seems we should have a special Amber Alert for those cases. Oh wait, we do. It's called a bobber." A few men groaned and seemed to be tiring of the bit. I sure was.

"And what about the media?" he asked.

Yeah? I wondered suspiciously. What about us?

"They don't seem to be closing in on the fish thief anytime soon."

Noreen must be putting him up to this.

"And there's that TV chick who claims she got a note from the fishnappers." That would be me. I glanced around but Chad seemed oblivious to my presence. No one in the audience appeared to recognize me, either. "Next time I tune in to the news I expect she'll be looking for suspects by doing one of those man-on-the-street interviews." He took the microphone off the stand and held it out like he was a reporter. "Where were you when the fish went missing?"

A handful of folks laughed at his impersonation, but not me. I hadn't realized I was standing until I started speaking. "Actually, Chad, I'm more interested in where you were when Mark Lefevre went missing."

No chuckles, only confusion.

I had always figured comedians would be naturals at

ad-libbing, but many aren't. Interrupt their easy, practiced delivery with a heckle and many spook like a deer about to be whammed by a pickup truck. Same thing with some TV anchors. Lose the teleprompter and they lose their cool.

Chad was one of those. First he froze. Then he seemed to forget the crowd and took an angry step toward me.

"What are you talking about?" None of his friendly banter, he sounded pissed.

Some of the crowd might have started out thinking I was part of the act, but by now the scene was verging on uncomfortable.

"You heard me," I said. "Do you have an alibi for the night Mark Lefevre disappeared?"

A few people gasped at the implication. After all, many in the crowd were familiar with Mark's name. First, because he regularly did stand-up at the club for the last several years. Second, because his name had been banner headlines and lead TV news-story material for the last forty-eight hours. A whisper on my left suggested someone realized I was the journalist who found his buried body.

Chad remained silent.

"You wouldn't *kill* for a laugh, would you?" I tried remembering some of the jokes Jason Hill, the club manager, and I had improvised the other night concerning the fine line between comedy and violence.

Then I heard a noise behind me, but before I could turn around, Jason and a bouncer-looking guy each grabbed me by an arm. No courtesy tap on the shoulder, they simply picked me up and moved toward the nearest exit.

"You're not funny," Jason said.

The crowd picked up on that and began chanting "not funny, not funny." That hurt.

Chad suddenly got creative and shouted, "And let's have a big round of applause for Channel 3's Riley Spartz!"

He acted like our confrontation was all part of his act. The crowd bought into it and the last thing I heard and saw before being carried out the door was their standing ovation for my apparent cameo.

My feet didn't hit the ground until the pair dropped me on the sidewalk outside. Off balance, I fell on my knees on top of cigarette butts and other unpleasant street litter. Jason leaned down and put his face next to mine.

"Don't come back to the club," he said. "Ever."

Then his gorilla companion pushed me over and added his own one-liner: "Or the club will take a club to you."

The sign of a mediocre joke is if the only one laughing is the guy who told it. Neither Jason or I laughed at the chuckling goon. But I got the message.

NOREEN HAD A scowl on her face. Miles sat in a corner of her fishbowl office with a dark lawyer glare on his. As usual, I was the cause of their unhappiness.

"You practically accused a man, in public, surrounded by witnesses, of being a murderer," Noreen said.

"And that's no laughing matter," Miles said.

How they could know that, one day later, puzzled me. But then Noreen pulled up an e-mail on her computer screen and clicked on an attachment. Video loaded and played. Closed-circuit security-camera video inside the comedy club.

The shot was wide so we could see Chad onstage, doing his fishing motions. We couldn't hear his monologue because the tape had no audio. But that also meant that while Noreen and Miles could see me stand up and confront Chad, they couldn't hear what either of us said.

In my mind, that made the whole incident a draw.

"That's not how we see it," Noreen said.

"And that's not how Chad Griswold's attorney sees it," Miles interjected.

"If he's not guilty of anything," I asked, "how come he's so quick to get a lawyer?"

I was especially curious after Miles explained that Chad's attorney was Benny Walsh, one of the best criminal attorneys in Minneapolis.

Garnett had used him last fall when he was unfairly charged with the murder of a city councilwoman. Glib and confident, Walsh made it clear to me then that he didn't much care whether his clients were killers or not—just whether they could afford him and whether the media spelled his name right. I couldn't imagine that Chad could afford him.

"Benny Walsh has other legal specialties, too," Miles said. "One of them is slander."

"Slander?" I said. Slander meant Benny might take the case on a contingency, instead of making Chad pay up front. Suddenly Chad could afford top legal counsel.

"That's right," Miles continued. "Slander. The verbal defamation of one's character. Accusing someone of murder certainly falls into that category."

When Miles described my actions like that, he made me sound real bad.

Noreen banged her fist on her desk and a pen with a station logo rolled off the edge. "If this gets ugly, you're out on your own. We'll make it clear you were not representing nor on assignment from Channel 3 at the comedy club."

I felt as isolated as her pen, now lying on the floor, waiting to be stepped on by powerful feet.

I braced myself in case Noreen's next sentence included

the F word. Fired. With media organizations in a financial free fall, I wouldn't put it past Channel 3 to be looking for reasons to terminate employees for cause.

But then I realized if the station *was* sued, they'd have to circle the legal wagons around me. Benny Walsh wouldn't settle for a judgment against little old Riley Spartz; he'd be drawn to the deep pockets of my employer.

"He offered to settle for fifty grand," Miles continued, "and he said he wouldn't file any paperwork in court, plus his client would sign a confidentiality agreement."

"That's extortion," I said.

"No," he said. "That's a common legal maneuver."

"I think we should tell him she went off her meds," Noreen said. "And promise it won't happen again."

"What meds?" I asked. "I'll sue you for slander if you say that about me."

Noreen continued to brainstorm solutions that made me want to brain her. "What if we put Riley in rehab?"

I reached across Noreen's desk but Miles waved his hands like a sports referee to separate us. "We might still get out of this. I declined Benny's settlement offer. Then I thanked him for the videotape and told him it would be excellent evidence when we press charges against the comedy club for manhandling our reporter."

That Miles is good.

Then he told me to keep quiet about what happened and cross my fingers that it might all blow over. "And stay away from that comedian. I don't want you within a mile of him."

"The club owner told me not to come back," I said. "Actually he phrased it more like a threat."

"Then it's trespassing if you go back after you've been told not to. So don't."

I promised.

After he left, Noreen let me know where I stood with her. I believe the technical term is shaky ground.

"Riley, I don't care how good the numbers are on this story. I'm suspending you a day without pay."

"What?" The money meant nothing, the principle did. My face must have reflected my shock.

"Don't give me that betrayed look," she said. "I'm the one who should feel betrayed. Until this happened, I thought we were finally developing a good working relationship."

I wished I could take back that confrontation with Chad at the comedy club, but I couldn't. But I also wished that Noreen could grasp that sometimes in the course of a chase, stuff happens. She was a desk head, with no field experience. She didn't complain when I used unconventional approaches and things worked out. But hit a snag, and finger-pointing became second nature. It was that old We're Behind You One Hundred Percent Until You Get in Trouble policy.

"You should have talked to me before you went to that comedy club," she continued. "I might have gone with you. I could have pulled you back in your seat and prevented all this craziness."

Was Noreen suggesting that she actually wanted to get out in the field? Or just hang with me? For a girl night? I was starting to wonder if her anger might stem from her own circle of loneliness. Then, just as I was feeling sorry for my boss, she reverted back to beast mode. The empathy passed immediately.

"And maybe if you'd spent more time looking for that missing fish, we wouldn't be in this legal jam."

I kept my mouth shut, not reminding her that I'd already

found a meth dealer and a dead body this sweeps month. It seemed greedy to expect me to find Big Mouth Billy, too.

I CALLED NICK Garnett from my office to tell him what happened at the comedy club, and because I needed to hear someone tell me not to worry, that things could only get better.

"I don't know about that, Riley. In my experience, things are never so bad that they can't be made worse."

He made me so angry that I hung up without saying Humphrey Bogart, *The African Queen*, 1951.

AS I LEFT the station to walk to my car, a man came up to me and asked if I was Riley Spartz. Just what I needed, an autograph hound.

"Yes." I sighed, reaching for a pen.

He handed me some papers. "You're served."

When I read the word "defamation," I turned and went back inside the station where Noreen greeted me with "What are you doing here? I thought I told you to leave."

I handed the libel lawsuit to Miles, who quickly paged through it, then suggested Noreen forget the whole suspension thing. Under the circumstances, he didn't think it wise for the station to take a formal position that I'd done anything wrong at the comedy club.

But Noreen insisted, saying we'd make it a "private" suspension. By then I didn't care anymore. A day away from the station was actually starting to sound like an overdue vacation.

GARNETT'S PREDICTION OF things getting worse continued to play out the next morning when I opened the Minneapolis *Star-Tribune* and saw a picture of me being physically ousted from the comedy club in the local gossip column. The story noted that the entire video could be seen on their Web site and also reported a rumor that I'd been suspended.

Noreen was quoted as saying Channel 3 doesn't comment on personnel matters.

CHAPTER 30

"Let eternal rest be given to the departed."

Father Mountain was presiding over a double funeral for Mark and his mother, arranged by the Post family. Low-budget compared to the almost-wedding. A trio of tasteful floral wreaths reading MOTHER, SON, FIANCÉ decorated the closed caskets.

Short obits. No lunch. Small turnout.

I went to pay my respects even though I wasn't being paid to attend in my role as suspended journalist. But I'd slept late and that was almost worth the grief over Noreen.

For the funeral, Madeline wore a short black dress with a small black veil as if unconsciously spoofing the wedding she never had. She appeared in genuine mourning, yet also held her head high, relieved to have a reasonable explanation for why her groom pulled a no-show on the most important day of her life.

That clarification seemed especially important to Madeline, maybe even more important than exactly how Mark ended up dead. Since I'd met her, Madeline had seemed tormented that her groom's disappearance was a rejection of her. Spurned. Jilted. Ditched. Somehow my finding his body in a shallow grave validated that she remained undamaged goods. So while she was unlucky in love, she was not unworthy.

"While on earth we cannot understand the evil amidst us," Father Mountain was delivering the eulogy since no one else offered.

Madeline's mother and brother sat beside her, each holding one hand. I saw no sign of the bodyguard and figured his gig ended when Mark proved no menace.

"Jean Lefevre saw beauty in the world around her and cherished flowers as a gift from the Almighty," her priest continued.

The best man, Gabe Murray, got there late and scooted in next to me even though the church was practically empty. He whispered did I think there was any chance the police would pay him back the money Mark owed him out of the safe-deposit cash? That nugget hadn't been reported in the news, so I figured the local gossip grapevine to be at work. I ignored Gabe's question and wished I'd stayed home, but I also know sometimes the killer shows up at his victim's funeral.

The police know this, too, and a plainclothes detective casually waited in the back of the church. We caught each other's eye, but gave no overt sign of recognition. I first noticed him lingering near the guest book, watching who did or didn't sign in. Upstairs in the choir loft, another cop discreetly videotaped all the observers.

Except for Libby, the maid of honor, I didn't recognize the other female mourners. Mostly older women, probably friends of Mrs. Lefevre.

My comic nemeses, Jason Hill and Chad Griswold, sat in a pew in the middle of the church along with a few other performers from the comedy club. They looked uneasy, like they'd rather be joking than praying. They were probably trying to prove that brotherhood-of-comedians thing and downplay any talk of jealous rivalry.

I was also uncomfortable, since I'd promised Miles I'd stay away from those guys. But I felt I had more of a right to be at the funeral than Chad, who claimed to barely know Mark. And if I left now, in the middle of the ceremony, people might talk.

"Mark Lefevre saw humor in the world around him and cherished laughter as a gift from the Almighty," Father Mountain told his flock.

The row from the comedy club nodded in agreement and gave one another friendly punches on the shoulders in a display of comic camaraderie.

But Father Mountain's remark about the gift of humor also elicited a sound best resembling a snort of indignation. I glanced behind me and that's when I saw her sitting near a stained-glass window depicting Madonna and child.

Mark's old girlfriend.

When Sigourney Nelson stood for the Our Father, she looked like an extremely pregnant scarlet woman in a snug, screaming-red T-shirt with black leggings. Her belly was obvious, but at least covered, probably because we were in church.

Father Mountain sprinkled the caskets with holy water and incense and said a prayer about an escort of angels. The funeral workers wheeled the Lefevre bodies out of the church to the sound of an uplifting tune on the organ. The best man reacted to Sigourney's lack of waistline with widened eyes.

But Madeline walked by Sigourney like she'd never seen her, or even a picture of her, ever before. Face blindness in action.

I missed the graveside ceremony because I wanted to steer clear of Jason and Chad. They seemed to feel the same way and avoided eye contact with me on their way out.

I also had another reason for skipping the interment. I wanted to chat up Sigourney. I unobtrusively clicked a full-body photo of her with my cell phone to document her pregnancy. Then a head shot. She'd stopped dying her hair black, trading her goth look for a mousy but natural brown. I walked up and introduced myself.

"Yeah, I know you," she said. "I've seen you on TV."

"Did you know I've been looking for you?"

"Yeah, but I don't want to be on TV." Sigourney used both hands to frame her stomach. "This baby's already added forty pounds to my girlish figure and I hear the camera adds another ten."

She turned and walked away, a defiant look on her face.

"I'm trying to piece together Mark's final hours," I said, catching up with her outside the church. "When was the last time you two spoke?" She continued to ignore me. "Come on, Sigourney. You must still feel *something* for him. You came to his funeral."

That got her attention. "Let's get one thing straight," she said. "I came to say a prayer for his mother. Not him. Far as I'm concerned, no amount of prayer will keep that man out of hell."

I was right. She still did have feelings for him. Contempt.

To keep her talking, I apologized for causing her to miss the burial service, but she just laughed. "Don't you worry about that, I got plans to come back later, with my baby. Together we're going to spit on his grave."

That remark didn't leave much doubt as to who the father of her child was.

And I was starting to have a strong suspicion who Mark's

killer was. Sigourney suddenly owned the leading motive. But if she was guilty of murder, she certainly had style.

I stopped short of thinking he asked for it, but admired her irony in burying him near the place where he was supposed to be married to another woman. A murderess with chutzpah. Take that, you philanderer!

I pressed her for a phone number in case I came across some new information, or in case I was actually able to build a criminal case around her, but she refused.

"Sorry, no interest in being on TV."

I suspected her goal was not so much avoiding a television appearance as avoiding a prison sentence.

As she awkwardly fit her stomach under the steering wheel of a compact car, I told her I knew about the kiss in the parking lot.

She denied knowing what I was talking about.

"A witness saw you kiss Mark the night he died," I said.

"You're confusing me with someone else."

But when I confronted Sigourney about being a registered guest at the hotel during the rehearsal dinner, she admitted that she'd hoped to see her old beau that night, but had fallen asleep.

"Wait till you're in your first trimester," she groused, patting her belly.

I made a note of her license plate as she drove away. I didn't try to follow her, because if she had already killed two people, I didn't want to be Father Mountain's next funeral.

CHAPTER 31

The next morning, my "suspension" over, I returned to the newsroom, waved at the assignment desk, but said nothing to Noreen. Half an hour later she brought me a high-end coffee drink from down the block and tried to engage me in a discussion about the fish story, but I wasn't biting.

A couple of hours later, I decided feuding with her wasn't worth the effort.

THE AIR WAS brisk so I was glad for the life jacket over my sweatshirt out on the boat that afternoon. Malik seemed comfortable in the outdoors gear he often wore when doing live shots in inclement weather.

"The deepest point of the lake is over there." Russ Nesbett pointed somewhere in the direction of open water. "Eighty-four feet straight down."

The developments in the missing-groom case, as well as the drug bust next door, had distracted me from the upcoming largemouth bass contest. Russ had insisted on

233

taking me out for a spin in his new bass boat, sleek, shallow, and speedy. He hoped to net some publicity for the town.

"But not all publicity is good publicity," he explained, confiding that he wished I hadn't done the meth-neighbor story because now viewers might think White Bear Lake has a drug problem and that could affect property values.

"I'll keep that in mind next time."

As the boat banked, a spray of water hit my face. I wiped it off, smiling politely, while telling Russ that I was feeling cold. Instead of heading back to shore, he handed me a wool blanket. Malik looked amused at my discomfort.

"So how long could you live if you fell in this water?" I asked. I wasn't trying to be negative. I just like knowing my odds.

"That depends," Russ said. "The water temperature's probably around sixty-five degrees. If you lived long enough to die of hypothermia, that might take a few hours. But you could die in a matter of minutes if you drowned or suffered cardiac arrest or your larynx went spastic."

All unpleasant-sounding ways to go.

"Holding on to something that floats, like a capsized boat," he continued, "would help prevent the loss of body heat. You lose more heat when you swim or tread water."

I was glad I wore a life jacket. And I made it a point to sit low in the boat, especially on the turns.

"Let me show you some of the basics of bass fishing." Russ steered the boat near the shallows and pulled out a rod and reel. "Bass like hiding under sunken logs."

"I thought the season hadn't opened yet."

I was looking for a plausible excuse for why we shouldn't do this. Calling the sport boring wouldn't faze him. He probably heard that from dames all the time.

"We're just going to practice your cast." Russ showed me

that his blue-speckled fly had no hook. "We'll use this, though bass really like to bite on live crawfish."

He demonstrated how to hop the bait across the shallows into the shade, then handed the fishing rod to me.

I recalled my husband had been especially fond of, even superstitious about, a particular red-speckled fly. He'd once landed a lunker with it. Not just a fish story, either, I'd seen photographic evidence. I smiled at how he'd employed that angler trick of holding the fish out toward the camera to make his catch look bigger. I now regretted giving away his tackle box and wished I'd kept that special lure.

"Just a minute," Malik called out.

He got repositioned low on the bottom of the boat to take no chance that I'd knock his camera overboard while I was casting. To save money, Channel 3 recently dropped insurance on most of its equipment. Malik knew if he lost the camera, he wouldn't be fired until the station worked the replacement cost out of him.

He hoisted the camera to his shoulder. "I'm ready."

Then Russ reached his arms around my shoulders to demonstrate how to pull back and flick my wrist. "Gentle. Gentle."

I didn't answer, but concentrated on achieving a perfect cast so I could thank him and we could head back to shore.

"We'd make a great team," he said. "With your media connections and my business know-how, I know we could land the Governor's Fishing Opener next year and really put this town on the tourist map."

To distract him from thinking of me as his public-relations maven, I asked if we could look at some of the historic lake houses from the water *on our way back*. I knew many of the estates started as summer homes for St. Paul's elite in the late nineteenth century. But Russ filled me in on vivid lake lore like how famous gangsters such as Ma Barker, Pretty Boy Floyd, and Al Capone hid out in the fashionable resort town during Prohibition. And how the lake got its name from an Indian legend that a Sioux warrior saved his beloved by killing a white bear and the animal's spirit still lives in the area.

I must have looked skeptical about a polar bear being this far off course, but it occurred to me that the lake's namesake was most likely an albino black bear. By then Russ was insisting that Mark Twain even referenced the tale in *Life on the Mississippi*.

"And that's an American classic," he added.

That would also be easy to check, I thought, confident the volume sat on my bookshelves at home.

We were approaching the Post family's landmark Peninsula House. I hadn't seen the view from the water before. Situated on a cliff, the mansion looked formidable. Russ steered the boat around the point, emphasizing the coveted shoreline location. I encouraged Malik to shoot exteriors, just in case we ever needed them.

Next Russ pointed out the White Bear Yacht Club, and I paid close attention because Madeline and Mark's wedding reception was supposed to have been held there. I tuned out Mr. Civic Booster's running commentary of all the celebrities who had played golf on that course, to admire the vast wall windows in the clubhouse. As part of the lake history Russ mentioned that F. Scott Fitzgerald and his wife, Zelda, rented rooms at the yacht club one summer in the twenties before being kicked out for disruptive parties.

Russ's historic gossip was starting to make me feel special, sharing the geographic shadow of noted authors. Especially when he told me that Fitzgerald's short story "Winter

Dreams" (generally considered the precursor to *The Great Gatsby*) was set in White Bear Lake.

"Except he called it Black Bear Lake in his story," Russ explained.

I tried discussing what he thought Fitzgerald was saying about women and greed in *Gatsby*, but it became clear that Russ wasn't much of a reader, just a collector of local trivia.

That became further apparent when he echoed a hooker's cheer, "Go, Bears!," from the 1996 movie *Fargo*, and proudly explained, "That came from White Bear Lake High School."

I'd forgotten that scene and made a mental note to try to stump Garnett with it.

Yet I walked on literary air when I returned home. With so many bedroom communities popping up overnight around suburban shopping centers and convenient freeway access, it felt nice to be living in a community rooted in real history. After all, Mark Twain and F. Scott Fitzgerald were among America's most influential novelists. And if White Bear Lake was good enough for them, it was good enough for me. I was even considering talking to a real estate agent once sweeps month ended.

I flopped onto my couch and flipped through my copy of *Life on the Mississippi* and sure enough, Mark Twain did visit the area. I read his discourse with great interest until I got to the part where he wrote "connected with White Bear Lake is a most idiotic Indian legend."

Idiotic? My newly adopted hometown? I slammed the pages of his American classic, thinking, How judgmental of the old coot.

CHAPTER 32

Madeline ran her hand across a shelf of books and complimented my fiction collection. She pulled out a copy of Gaston Leroux's *Phantom of the Opera* and flipped through the pages. Her choice, a novel featuring an emotionally tortured adversary with a disfigured face, fascinated me, given her diagnosis of prosopagnosia.

"Yeah, if this TV thing goes south," I said, "I'm hoping to be a librarian."

She lifted her eyebrows in surprise at my answer. "Come on, Riley, not a writer?"

"Too solitary." I shook my head. "At least librarians get to mingle at the check-out desk and explore the stacks."

"I'd like to write a novel, but right now I'm working on short stories." Madeline explained that she held degrees in both English and business. "English for me. Biz for my mother. She says we all have a duty to understand the workings of money so we can put it to good use. But I'm more drawn to words than numbers. Statistics lack soul."

"Madeline, that last line of yours is quite profound. I

think you might have a natural flair for writing." Better to encourage that career path than a job dealing with customers and having to remember faces.

"Oh, what do you know about my writing?" She said it dismissively, but blushed in a pleased way.

"You wrote a six-word novel. Remember your want ad that brought us together? 'For Sale: Wedding Dress. Never Worn.' Your work rivaled Hemingway's. Even if yours was self-published."

She looked puzzled at the compliment and I explained that literary legend had it, Ernest Hemingway, arguably the finest American novelist of the twentieth century, wrote six words—"For sale. Baby shoes. Never worn."—to win a bar bet among other writers for the shortest story.

Silently, Madeline considered my words and the very direct comparison to the wedding-dress want ad that started our odyssey.

"Some say he considered it his best work, Madeline."

Then I dropped the subject because I'd made a mental vow not to discuss her deceased fiancé tonight and we were veering close to that forbidden topic. Mark might be buried, but Madeline's emotions were still very close to the surface.

She and I were riding together to a charity benefit in downtown St. Paul honoring the 125th anniversary of the Schubert Club, formed to salute classical music. Tonight's event included a chamber concert featuring a world-class cellist, followed by a four-course dinner.

I wore a little black dress with pearls because that seemed safest in uncertain social situations. Madeline wore a little black dress with an emerald brooch.

Madeline had invited me to join her family at the Post table. I'd initially declined because I didn't want to accept anything of value from them. That policy generally keeps

239

things cleaner in reporter-source relationships. But she'd convinced me that my presence was an added bonus to the event. That guests enjoy mingling with news celebrities. And couldn't I spare just one night out of my busy schedule in the name of charity?

So I reconsidered, but insisted on driving and paying for parking so as not to be a total mooch. Madeline agreeably left her cobalt-blue Mercedes parked outside my house and climbed into my middle-class Toyota Camry.

After the concert we walked next door to a ballroom and checked our coats. I regretted wearing my stiletto heels. While balance was my biggest obstacle, the evening would be even more challenging for Madeline and her mother on the face front. Nearly all the women in attendance wore little black dresses and nearly all the men wore black suits and ties.

The guest list represented a who's who of St. Paul's most influential and wealthy. Name tags were out of the question because it was *such* a swanky affair. Suddenly I suspected the real reason Madeline invited me.

"You need me to help you work the room," I whispered, "and make sure you don't confuse the mayor with the waiter?"

She had the grace to look embarrassed. "All right, Riley, it did occur to me you'd probably recognize many of the people here. So if you can just greet them or elicit an introduction, I can follow your lead."

"You make me feel like a guide dog."

She smiled, explaining that Roderick usually escorted their mother while she'd be left to fend as best she could because it looked odd for the three of them to cluster together too much.

As if on cue, I spotted her family on the other side of

the room. We headed in their direction, mixing along the way with the chief of police, the CEO of a large insurance company, and the general manager of the Saint Paul Hotel.

Madeline made seamless small talk. But when the head of a nonprofit group, who we'd just conversed with minutes earlier, approached her again, she was clueless until I put him in context with a couple of precise remarks. Men looked at Madeline with interest; she looked at them like they were invisible. Unlike Mark, she couldn't see any of them. Well, maybe she could see them, but she couldn't tell them apart.

"Here's Vivian and Roderick," I said, as we closed in on her family. Roderick didn't look as much like Malik tonight, but I'd never seen my cameraman don black tie and slick his hair back.

"Yes, I see Mother," Madeline said.

"How?" I asked. "You told me you couldn't even recognize your own mother on the street."

"We wear our brooches at large events like this." Madeline patted the jewelry pinned on her dress. I then realized Vivian wore an identical emerald brooch. My sister was born in May, and I recalled emerald as the birthstone for that month.

Vivian politely thanked me for attending the event and hoped I was enjoying myself. Then while mother and daughter chatted, Roderick and I stepped away for refreshments. He took a glass of champagne off a server's tray; I took a chocolate-covered strawberry.

"Do you think it's safe to leave them alone?" I asked.

"I have my eye on them." He answered protectively, in a big brother/elder son sort of way.

"If they embarrass themselves too badly," I said, "they can always pretend they've had too much to drink."

He laughed, but then quickly lowered his voice and explained that Vivian was actually quite upset with

Madeline for confiding the prosopagnosia business to me. "Just so you're aware of that. If I were you, I wouldn't bring it up."

"Your mother did seem a bit cool tonight," I said. "That explains it."

"She has a very rigid philosophy about family and privacy."

"I told Madeline that I'm willing to keep face blindness off the record unless it somehow becomes central to the investigation, which seems unlikely."

"How goes your investigation?" he asked.

Roderick seemed more amused than interested. His tawny complexion and black tuxedo gave him a debonair look that I found sort of alluring. Like an exotic, young version of James Bond, though I doubted the Post son had done anything more adventurous in his life than move money electronically around the globe.

I glanced over, making sure Madeline wasn't close enough to hear us. I wanted her to enjoy a night out if she could. "I'm hoping the cops are making better progress than I am. Of course, they should be. They have access to the evidence. All I can do is ask questions."

"What if you question the wrong people?"

"Believe me, if I knew who the right people were, I'd question them instead. Any ideas?"

"I'm afraid not. Now I think I better get back to my family."

"They seem to be coping well," I said.

Actually Madeline and Vivian were huddled together, admiring a painting of a generous local cigar-chomping benefactor. I'd hoped to chat Roderick up more and gain some additional insight to the Post family. But he was already heading in their direction.

"Yes, however as the man of the house, I'm responsible for escorting my mother."

"I can tell she appreciates that."

"I certainly don't mind, and it's what my father would have wanted."

"How about your sister?" I wasn't sure what I meant by that remark and I could tell he wasn't sure, either.

"My sister prefers independence."

I'd have liked to follow up about his father, but Roderick was already greeting Vivian and Madeline.

The Post matriarch gave me a warmer welcome than she had earlier, which made me wonder what she had discussed with Madeline in my absence.

We ate a splendid but uneventful dinner. The table seating was assigned, which eliminated much of the face stress for Madeline and her mother. A lovely toast to the Posts for all their good works capped off the evening. And Vivian, normally unemotional, seemed gratified by the gesture from her peers.

I'D JUST THROWN my jacket on the couch back home, narrowly missing my Gracie trophy, which stood tall and proud on an end table.

"Good night, Gracie," I said, with affection.

I was beginning to feel a little like George Burns when I heard a noise on the porch and figured Madeline must have forgotten something. I opened the door, but instead of my slender dinner date, a heavy shadow lunged.

Chad Griswold shoved me back inside, shut the door behind him, and flashed his gap-toothed grin. It didn't seem as endearing up close as it did onstage during open-mic night at the comedy club. "Well, Miss North Dakota, we meet again."

His breath smelled of alcohol. He gave me another push and I fell backward over an ottoman, banging my head on the floor.

"Who's funny now?" he said, bending over me. I tried kicking him, but he caught my foot. "Chad, this isn't funny. Let go." I thought it best to try talking him down by keeping things casual.

"I know it's not funny. I'm the comedian, remember? I'm a pro at what's funny."

"Knock it off so we can talk."

Instead he twisted my leg. "Ow!"

"That must not have been funny, either," he said. "How about this?" And he threw his body against mine, knocking the wind out of me. "I don't hear you laughing."

But I could hear him laughing.

As for me, I could barely breathe, so laughter was out of the question. I struggled to escape his grasp, but he had me pinned against the floor and my dress was creeping up around my waist. I clawed at him, but my nails were useless as weapons. I keep them short and practical because I spend so much time at a keyboard. Now I wished I'd cultivated more of a femme fatale look.

I tried spitting in his face, but lying flat on my back made it hard to work up enough saliva without choking. Suddenly Chad pulled me to my feet, seeming to settle down. Then he whacked me across the face. As I fell, I knew I was in serious trouble.

"Chad. Please." I stumbled to find the right words to make him stop. My voice had a pleading quality that embarrassed me and my cheek stung.

"Remember the other night," he said, "when you asked if I'd *kill* for a laugh? Maybe tonight we'll find out." He yanked my necklace off and pearls scattered everywhere.

Then he slapped me again and my nose started bleeding.

"Laugh, bitch." Chad laughed so hard, he bent over double.

I knew no one would hear me scream. And I knew he'd never let me reach a phone. But lacking a better plan, I tried both tactics simultaneously. Easily, he caught me by one arm and we crashed to the floor, slipping on loose pearls.

I scrambled up first and saw Gracie.

Her heft felt good in my hand. And the cracking noise when I swung her against Chad's head pleased me.

Some blood, but no movement.

I kissed Gracie.

CHAPTER 33

C had wasn't dead. Chad wasn't actually named Chad, either.

"He tried to kill me." One of the officers took my statement while the other handcuffed Chad, who was starting to wake up and become verbally abusive. They'd called an ambulance, but I'd decided my attacker needed it more than I did. And I didn't feel like sharing a ride to the emergency room with him.

I explained Chad Griswold's connection to Mark Lefevre, confident his violence against me made him a shoo-in for Mark's murder. I felt sheepish about jumping all over Madeline as a suspect.

The officer wrote down everything I said while his partner patted Chad. No surprise he found no weapons, otherwise Chad would have shot instead of punched. The surprise came when he checked Chad's wallet and found several pieces of photo ID—all under different names.

"So who are you, buddy?" the officer asked.

Chad didn't answer. Perhaps he had a concussion or

maybe he just wanted to talk to his lawyer first. Seems hiring a top criminal attorney might have been a prudent call for him after all.

By then the medics had arrived and loaded "Chad" inside the ambulance. I followed in a squad car because the cops wanted me checked out to have a medical record of my injuries. As I suspected, I was fine except for a bruised cheek and swollen lip. But my assailant suffered a minor skull fracture.

Atta girl, Gracie.

Chad was really Rodney Sherborn. A fugitive from Iowa wanted for robbery. He'd served time for assault several years earlier, as well as piled up an impressive string of arrests for drunk driving and disorderly conduct. He'd stolen the identity of a dead cousin in Canada for his stage name; that's why Xiong couldn't find any criminal record.

Attacking me wasn't the brightest move on his part, since it got the cops all over him again. I don't know what his endgame was for me. Maybe he figured no problem—I'd be in no shape to identify my assailant.

Noreen was in an exuberant mood the next morning, torn between keeping me off the air until I looked better or promoting my bruises.

"Benny Walsh called me," Miles said. "His client offered to drop the slander suit if you drop the assault charges."

"Did you tell him we'd see him in court?" I asked.

"That I did."

"Legally, we should be in the clear now. Right?" Noreen asked.

"That would be my professional opinion," Miles said. "I can't imagine Benny would continue to take the slander case on a contingency after all this. And frankly I don't think your attacker can afford him for representation on the criminal charges. So unless Benny wants to do it for the publicity, our boy's looking at a public defender. And all he'll want to focus on is the crime at hand, not some nebulous civil long shot."

Apparently, after the funeral, Jason started feeling a little spooked by the whole murdered-Mark situation and did a little digging on his own. The reason Chad flipped out and came after me was because Jason Hill canned him after learning he wasn't who he said he was.

Chad blamed me.

The entire Channel 3 newsroom eagerly waited for the cops to add homicide to his list of arrests so we could break the story that the murder of the missing groom had been solved. But that never happened. Under yet another name, Chad was in jail for DUI in Milwaukee, six hours away, the night Mark disappeared.

CHAPTER 34

The license plate of the car Sigourney drove away from Mark's funeral checked to a Sven and Inga Nelson in Fridley. Since I'd erased Chad from the suspect chart on my office wall, Sigourney looked better and better. The dirt where her old boyfriend had been buried was soft and boggy. Easy enough for a dog to unearth in minutes. Digging the grave wouldn't have been difficult, not even for a woman.

An older man answered the Nelsons' door, but when I asked for Sigourney, he said she wouldn't be home from the hospital until tomorrow.

I had the feeling I might be talking to a new grandpa, but he seemed so Scandinavian stoic that I thought it best to play dumb because I wasn't sure just how happy everybody was about the pregnancy.

"I'm sorry, Mr. Nelson. I must have got my days crossed. I thought she was coming home today."

"No, she and the baby are still at Unity. My wife is leaving there just now."

He was talking about Unity Hospital, a few miles away. "Shall I tell her you stopped by?" he asked.

"No, I'll swing by the hospital. I want to surprise her." Boy, was she going to be surprised. "Has she picked out a name yet?"

For the first time, he beamed. "Ja, Sven."

"Oh, congratulations, Grandpa." I gave him a playful punch in the arm and said goodbye, reminding myself that Minnesota's Scandinavian stereotype exists for a reason.

I swung by Target to pick up a baby gift to help smooth my way into Sigourney's hospital room. I enjoy shopping for babies and knew better than to buy a newborn outfit that might already be too small. A maroon-and-gold University of Minnesota onesie beckoned from the racks of blue and pink. I selected a twelve-month size with a gift bag and some tissue paper. I inserted my Channel 3 business card in a "baby boy welcome" card as well as scribbling my congratulations for the arrival of little Sven into the world.

I'd put some heavy-coverage makeup on my face that morning, so my bruises just barely showed. Anyway, a hint of black-and-blue wasn't unusual in a hospital corridor. The receptionist at the patient information desk gave me Sigourney's room number and I headed up, carrying a pot of bluish tulips as well as the baby present, because bearers of flowers are generally welcome anywhere.

I counted three babies in the nursery window, all wrapped in pink, so I figured Sven was with his mother down the hall. From my perspective, Unity Hospital was the perfect place for us to talk about the murders of her former boyfriend and his mother. Holding a baby would make it more difficult for her to attack me. And if she succeeded, medical care was on-site.

Sigourney was nursing Sven and needed only seconds to recognize me as That TV Reporter. No face blindness for her.

"What are you doing here?" she asked.

"Just wanted to see the baby." I set the gift bag on the bed next to her and the tulips on the nightstand. With his frizzy black hair, Sven looked like Mark's baby picture. I thought it best not to mention the resemblance.

"Well, you've seen him," she said. "You can go now." She held Sven to her shoulder for a burp. He complied.

Both times I'd been with Sigourney were emotional events. Life and death. Birth and burial.

"Can I hold him?" I asked.

Please say yes, I thought to myself.

I really wanted to hold him. Not to use him as a human shield should his mother turn homicidal but because I like holding babies. I'd practiced on nieces and nephews, and on visiting infants in the newsroom. Recently I had to acknowledge that I might never hold my own. That reality didn't consume my waking thoughts, but it came up when friends became pregnant or babies stared at me from grocery-store carts.

Sigourney seemed to sense my sincerity, so she handed Sven over, opened his present, and politely remarked about the new outfit.

I snuggled him. He yawned, but didn't cry. "See, he likes me."

Please, Sigourney, I thought to myself, bring up Mark on your own. Don't make me have to go there. But it was as if she had taken a vow of silence and awaited my next move.

"So how are the two of you doing?" I coochie-cooed Sven as he kicked one foot loose from his blanket. His toes were so tiny, his toenails barely visible. "Going home soon?"

"We're fine. But you still haven't explained why you crashed my hospital room uninvited." She glanced at the red call button at her bedside, but didn't reach for it.

"I just wanted to check on you, Sigourney. Make sure you were okay after the funeral. You seemed agitated that day and I was worried."

"Well, nothing like motherhood to calm you down." She reclaimed Sven from my arms.

"I was hoping to learn a little more about how your relationship with Mark ended," I said.

"What's to know? He dumped me for the rich bitch."

"For a while, when I couldn't find you or him, I thought maybe you'd run off together and that's why he skipped out of the wedding."

"Well, you thought wrong."

"Did he know you were pregnant?" Her answer would say something about the kind of man Mark was and might also give Sigourney a chance to vent.

"I found out a few weeks after we broke up. It wasn't the kind of news I wanted to leave on an answering machine. I wanted to tell him in person, but he wouldn't see me. Then he started screening my calls and wouldn't even pick up."

That's when she decided to look for him after the rehearsal dinner. "And if his fiancée happened to overhear my news, fine."

"She did see you kiss him."

"Why do you keep saying that?"

If Sigourney would lie about the kiss, I wondered what else she was lying about. Sven suddenly fussed like she was holding him too tight.

"You don't think I killed him?" she asked.

Now it was my turn to stay silent.

"Look, the guy got what was coming to him," she said. "But I didn't do the honors."

Just then the door to her hospital room opened and Sigourney's reinforcements arrived. Grandpa Sven and an older woman, most likely his wife, walked in. He pointed at me like he was identifying a suspect in a lineup, and said, "Ja, she's the one who came to the house."

Baby Sven started crying full blast. And three generations of Nelsons made it clear that visiting hours were over.

CHAPTER 35

"See, this has possibilities." Noreen was reacting to a script she'd made me draft on Sigourney Nelson after she'd reviewed my expense sheet and spotted the baby gift.

>((RILEY/SOT))
>CHANNEL 3 HAS LEARNED
>THAT A FORMER
>GIRLFRIEND OF MARK
>LEFEVRE WAS A
>REGISTERED GUEST AT THE
>HOTEL WHERE HE WAS
>LAST SEEN ON THE NIGHT
>HE WAS KILLED.

I didn't expect this version to hit the air; it seemed a bit tabloidy: high on innuendo, low on context.

THE WOMAN, WHO
RECENTLY GAVE BIRTH,
CLAIMS LEFEVRE IS HER
CHILD'S FATHER.

But I also didn't object to writing it as an exercise to see where the pieces fit. Sometimes that simple task makes it clear whether you are close to nailing the story—or not. Even though Sigourney was my top suspect for Mark's murder, Noreen favored airing the report more than I did. But I didn't mind being ready if something new broke loose.

"I'm not naming her." I thought it important to point that out. "And obviously I'd seek reaction from her before we broadcast anything."

"Absolutely." Noreen nodded.

"Doesn't matter," said Miles. For once, our attorney came down against my boss. "She's not a public figure. She has privacy. So unless the police call her a suspect, it's dicey for us to hint that she should be."

"But everything in the story is true," Noreen insisted.

"Doesn't matter," Miles said again. "We'd be implying she was a murderer. We don't have enough for that kind of accusation."

"What about motive and proximity?" Noreen hated to let the story die, and I wondered if she sensed the ratings book slipping away.

But it was a good question, so we both looked at Miles.

"What about proof?" Miles responded.

Another good question, this time they both looked at me.

"I'm working on it," I replied.

"If we reported this and the cops never charged her, or even worse," Miles continued, "if someone else was convicted, she could end up owning this TV station."

So Noreen shook her head in regret, crumpled the pages into a paper ball, and threw it in her wastebasket.

I STOPPED AT the White Bear Lake cop shop on my way home, using the excuse that I was checking to see if they'd found my lost cell phone in the wilds of Tamarack Nature Center. But what I really hoped to learn was where their homicide investigation into Mark's death stood.

As far as I could tell, the city has had only two other murders in the past forty years and neither was routine. The most recent involved a high-profile bail jumper who allegedly killed his wife and set fire to their house. The other involved a woman who beat her adopted son to death, but wasn't prosecuted until his birth mother went looking for him some twenty years later.

Mark Lefevre's murder also promised to be anything but routine.

Detective Bradshaw checked some records and verified the cops had recovered my phone during a sweep of the woods, but said he'd have to check with the chief before releasing it to me.

"That's fine." I didn't want to make a big deal about the phone. I'd already bought a spiffy new cell with a full texting keyboard, Internet, and GPS. The wireless company had deactivated my old one so I didn't have to worry about a thief running up my bill. But I sweated the cops scrolling through my contact list with source names and numbers. Luckily my faves were under first names or nicknames. So I kept casual and admired a white bear figurine on Detective Bradshaw's desk.

"So how's the investigation going?" I asked.

"We'll call a news conference when we're ready to announce an arrest." That's cop talk for none of your beeswax.

"Any luck tracking where all that cash came from?"

"What cash?" he bluffed.

"The ninety-eight grand in Mark's safe-deposit box." I called.

His eyes narrowed. "How'd you know about that?" His inquiry was the verbal equivalent of throwing in his hand.

I ignored the question. Reporters don't like going there on how we know stuff, especially not with cops.

"I've held off reporting that particular detail," I said, "because I wasn't sure how relevant it was to the case. Specifically when I thought our comedian was the killer."

"We would have liked it to wrap it up with him, too."

"Do you have an alternate theory?"

"Are we on the record or off the record?" The detective was wise to clarify that point. Many a source mistakenly thinks that detail can be worked out after the fact.

"We can go off the record." If he said something earth-shattering, I'd try negotiating that nugget back on the record later. In most cases, this reporter source business is pretty one-sided. Our purpose is clear: we seek news. True, journalists need to take care they're not used for ulterior motives, like politics, revenge, or profit. But usually, our motives mesh with those of our sources. And in this case, we both wanted to find a killer.

"So what have you got, Detective Bradshaw?" I asked.

"Not much, I'm afraid."

Not worth going off the record for this. "Any idea where the money came from?"

"It's cash. Almost impossible to trace," he said. "We're thinking drug money. And the Wisconsin cops agree. That's pretty much the focus of our investigation. We've sub-poenaed his phone records, both cell and home, as well as financial records."

Those avenues certainly needed to be explored. But I pressed him about the gun linking Mark's murder with his mother's. "It looked like an old handgun to me. Not something a drug gang would use."

"They tried to stage an old lady's suicide," he said. "They probably figured she wouldn't have a semiautomatic lying around the house."

I did have one advantage over the cops; I'd been able to size up Mrs. Lefevre before her death. She didn't act like a woman worried about danger. "Why would druggies kill his mom?"

"He might have stashed some inventory and the killer went looking for it. Plus any cash and records he might have kept. They might have been chasing the loot and thought she knew something. As you know, boxes of his belongings are missing from his mother's garage."

I knew that. "How about old girlfriends? Have you checked them out?" After what happened with Chad, I didn't want to push Sigourney as a suspect any harder myself.

Detective Bradshaw shrugged.

News folks continually struggle with the edict that journalists shouldn't be the source of unpublished information for law enforcement. Or else the cops start wanting our notes and raw tape. Then sources dry up and subpoenas complicate life. So if I have stuff I'd like to share, I get around that quirk by phrasing it in the form of a question. Because my job is to ask questions.

So I decided to get specific. "Have you checked out his former girlfriend, Sigourney Nelson? The one who recently had a baby who sort of looks like him?"

He raised his eyebrows and asked me to spell her name, and double-checked whether Nelson was s-o-n or s-e-n. I was being especially careful to seek only his reaction and not to bring up any of my suspicions because the last thing I needed was Sigourney crying slander.

CHAPTER 36

Our station meteorologist claims he merely predicts the weather. Calls it as he sees it. Even though he was forecasting sunshine, his movements in front of a green chroma-key map earlier today looked enough like a rain dance that when a severe thunderstorm suddenly whipped through the area, viewers called to complain.

On my drive to Madeline's home, I watched as lake waves rippled over the water. Her building parking lot was flooded in many places and I was reluctant to leave the car. But I found an umbrella under the seat and made a run through ankle-deep puddles for her lobby. By then the rain was blowing sideways.

"It's Riley," I called out as I buzzed Madeline's condo. I could see why she lived in a security building. For her, a peephole was useless. I tried imagining life looking through one and never recognizing your visitor or anyone else.

She buzzed me in and was waiting with her door open when I got upstairs. "You look like a wet rat," she observed.

I'd been called a rat plenty of times so I took no offense.

She went to get me a towel while I shed my coat and shoes. I felt the warmth from her gas fireplace across the room and moved over there to dry off.

"Hey, Madeline, did you know F. Scott Fitzgerald lived in the place where you almost had your wedding reception?"

"Anybody who's lived in this town longer than a year knows that," she answered.

"Well, I guess I'm ahead of the curve."

She picked a framed photo of Mark off the mantel and held it against her chest and closed her eyes.

"I wish—" I never officially learned what she wished, because she started to choke on her words just then; but what she wished was obvious and impossible.

We talked about how closure would eventually help her move on, but how until Mark's killer was found, it would be difficult.

"I'm the only one he has," she said. "If I move on, who will push for answers?"

"You might not like the answers you find," I warned her, thinking again of the possibility he might have been involved in drug dealing.

"Better to know than not know."

I wasn't as sure about that philosophy as I once was. Mark had secrets. No doubt about that. What those secrets revealed about her lover might change Madeline's mind.

I hadn't told her about baby Sven because I was still waiting to see what the police found out about Sigourney.

"Do you ever hear from the cops?" I asked.

She explained that her brother and their family attorney stayed in touch with the police chief. "We were stunned when Mark's comedian colleague was cleared as a suspect. He seemed so guilty. Especially after he attacked you."

"I was just as surprised."

The boundaries between source and journalist were starting to blur between us. That's usually a bad idea. But when she asked me to come over because she needed someone to talk to, it seemed exploitive to only listen when the camera was rolling. So I'd said yes and ventured out into the rain. A loud clap of thunder lent sound effects to the storm inside my head.

To change the subject, I took the Mark picture from her grasp and put it back on the mantel. As I turned I knocked a small basket of light-blue note cards off. I apologized and as Madeline helped me pick them up off the floor, I noticed they each had a line or two of writing, but no signature. Some of the notes were romantic, others clever.

Those were Mark's trademark cards, she explained, he used them to write jokes for his stand-up routine and rearranged them until he had the pacing right. He picked blue because that's what his idol David Letterman uses to keep his jokes straight. She showed me a political one that probably was funny last year but didn't do much for me now. Mark also used the cards to pen one-line love notes to Madeline. She cherished them.

I didn't mention to Madeline that I recalled a blue note card by Jean Lefevre's body. Police initially called it a suicide note, until they learned the handwriting matched son, not mother.

If Mark gave such notes to his fiancée, it's possible his mother received some as well. Could she have been looking at one, reminiscing, when she was killed? That seemed too coincidental. Especially since the content was ambiguous enough to suggest suicide to the cops. Perhaps the note said something like "I can't go on like this." That's open to plenty of interpretation.

262

Could the killer have selected such a note from a personal collection and planted an appropriate one at the murder scene to confuse investigators?

Madeline had a stash and she knew I was going to Mark's mother's house to search through his belongings. I remembered sharing that information with the Post family at the Peninsula House. It's not unusual for reporters to reassure all players in a story that everybody is cooperating. That's how we keep everybody cooperating. Because they all want their role to be dominant. But could my own loose lips have put Mrs. Lefevre in jeopardy? She wouldn't have hesitated to open the door to her almost daughter-in-law.

"Riley?" Madeline nudged my shoulder and held out the basket for the last note card, still in my hand. It read "I am less without you and more by your side."

As I looked at her, I wondered if Mark might have a good reason to be haunting Madeline with his face. A crack of lightning mixed with thunder reinforced that thought.

"Riley?"

"Oh, sorry, Madeline, I zoned out just then."

"I can tell you're thinking about work," she said. "You need to step back now and then, and live life in the moment."

If she only knew my mind was considering whether she might have been so flipped out over the parking-lot kiss as to kill her groom. She'd have no choice then but to play jilted bride to cover up the crime.

Maybe being alone with Madeline wasn't such a good idea. I was starting to miss her bodyguard. If Mr. Muscle hadn't been chaperoning that day in Tamarack, she might have buried my body next to her dead fiancé. Maybe Madeline was a sociopath who got a sexual thrill walking so close to his covert grave, me unaware.

I glanced at my Swiss Army watch, pretending to be

surprised at the time, like I suddenly needed to be somewhere real important. As I dropped the final blue note card
in the basket I realized I'd concocted a highly implausible
scenario involving Madeline based on a piece of vague correspondence. Mark probably gave similar notes to lots of
people. Including his old girlfriend. Sigourney probably had
her own personal stash.

And she had a much more plausible motive.

CHAPTER 37

I t seemed like everybody in White Bear Lake, a place I'd only lived a few months, knew my name and my business. I grew up a fourth-generation farm girl used to small-town nosiness. And for the past 130 years, my family has coped with worrying about what the neighbors might think. But now I craved urban anonymity. So during my lunch hour I lost myself in the skyways of downtown Minneapolis.

Minneapolis has the largest skyway system in the world. Eight miles of glass tunnels, one floor above the street, linking attractions, buildings, and restaurants. Outside, rain still drizzled down, but I walked in climate-controlled comfort except for the final forty-yard stretch when I rushed from the Hilton lobby across the street to the back door of Channel 3.

Inside, I felt cooped up. My mind kept drifting back to the open grave, thwarted wedding, and suspect wheel hanging on my office wall.

I paged through my source Rolodex as a distraction. It needed updating—some had moved, one was serving time behind bars, and another no longer returned my calls because he'd recently been appointed to a post in the governor's office. I paused at Toby Elness's phone number. The animal rights activist was home and welcomed a visit. So I drove out to his place in the northwestern suburbs.

He owns a small, rundown farmhouse on an acre of land, enough for his menagerie to roam. His Lab, Blackie, and a husky named Husky greeted me as I drove up. What Toby lacks in imagination, he makes up for in heart. If I could be reincarnated as an animal, I would choose to be one of Toby's dogs. I can't imagine a more pampered pet life. Dogs sleep on his bed. Cats curl up on the dresser. Birds fly in and out of cages to perch on lampshades or shoulders. Even the fish in his tanks seem to be smiling.

Though the air was cool, I insisted on chatting at a picnic table outside because past visits had taught me that the house sometimes reeked of an unpleasant combination of fur balls and pet urine.

"Anything new on the Big Mouth Billy investigation?" I asked.

Toby shook his head. "I told your boss again the other day that the Animal Liberation Front is not involved with the missing fish, but I'm not sure she believes me."

"Again? This was after that day in the newsroom?"

"Yes, she insisted we meet at the dog park. She brought Freckles and I brought Blackie. The two got along well."

Noreen meeting with a source? So unlike a desk head to leave the office. She could only be trying to scoop me so she could rub my face in the fish story. She was probably in touch with that annoying FBI guy, too.

"You didn't tell her anything, did you?"

"I don't know anything."

"But if you did know something . . . now listen, Toby,

because this is important. If you were to learn something about the Billy Bass Case, I need you to tell me, not Noreen. I'm your first call. Got it?"

"Got it, Riley."

"Good," I told him. "And good doggy," I told Husky who was resting her head on my lap and gazing at me with happy good-doggy eyes. Then Toby and I spent a few minutes talking about Shep and all his K-9 adventures.

"You know I miss him," I said. "For companionship, but also for protection. I always sleep better with him around."

"Shep's meant for more important things than your sleep. And he's happiest as a working dog," Toby said. "But I could let you borrow Husky for a while."

Husky would be about as much protection as a pillow, so I declined.

BETWEEN THE DEAD groom, the missing fish, and my meth neighbor, Channel 3 should have been leading the May ratings book like a ring on the nose of a pig. But the overnight numbers told a different story. There'd been setbacks. Our network's prime-time shows were still dragging. Television viewers continued to migrate to the Internet for news and information. And our chief rival had gotten just plain lucky.

A record lottery jackpot was won by the great-aunt of one of Channel 10's news anchors. She happened to be a nun, took her vow of poverty seriously, and promptly donated her $203 million winnings to the Catholic Church. She was little-old-lady adorable from the hem of her habit to the tip of her veil. She spoke exclusively to Channel 10 and God. There was even talk of making her a saint. Or at least a co-anchor.

So despite me being shot at and roughed up, Channel 3 remained stuck in second place. A distant second place.

Still, we were better off than Channel 7, our competitors across town. Their big scoop—two poodles eating the partially decomposed body of their master after he suffered a heart attack at home—backfired as viewers switched channels in revulsion and stayed away.

I LISTENED TO a message from Detective Bradshaw, telling me I could pick up my cell phone anytime. When I got to the White Bear Lake cop shop, he handed it over like it was nothing special, which reassured me he didn't realize what a gold mine of data lay inside—sources who wouldn't want to be outed on my speed dial. He did make me sign a release form verifying I'd received the phone.

Then it became clear that the detective wasn't a complete chump and was using the cell as an excuse to chat me up, face-to-face. Just like I did with him the other day.

"So how long you plan on staying in our town?" he asked.

"What do you mean?" I replied. "I live here."

"I realize that. I wonder if you realize trouble seems to have followed you here."

"Trouble? Followed me?"

"Well, White Bear Lake was much quieter before you came along. Suddenly we're investigating meth dealers and dead bodies."

"Let's keep in mind, Detective, I haven't caused any trouble. I may have uncovered trouble, but it was here long before I came along."

I tried to make it sound like I was joking because I wanted to get the latest on the murder investigation. But suddenly I was glad I was renting, month to month, not paying his salary through property taxes and not tied to this town with a long-term lease.

Then Detective Bradshaw made sure we were off the

record. But it didn't matter because what he told me, I had no intention of broadcasting.

"The girlfriend lead isn't panning out." He said it like a simple, indisputable fact.

"What?" That hardly seemed possible. First Chad. Then Sigourney. Soon I wouldn't have any spokes left on my suspect wheel.

"Yeah," he continued, "and she's pretty sure you sicced us on her and she's plenty mad."

Oh great, I thought.

He must have been able to read my mind, or my face, because he assured me he had kept our conversation confidential.

"What do you think about the fact that she spent the night at the same hotel where Mark was last seen?" I asked, once again phrasing the information in the form of a question.

"Yeah, we liked her for that, too. But she's got an alibi for the mother murder. And we're convinced the same perp did both."

This was disappointing news. I'd already polished a new script about her arrest so I'd be ready to track my voice on short notice.

"What's her alibi for Mrs. Lefevre's shooting?"

"She had a prenatal appointment, followed by childbirth classes, then an evening shift at a fast-food joint. All corroborated by medical records, witnesses, and a time card."

Chad had an alibi for Mark's murder and Sigourney had an alibi for Mrs. Lefevre's. Unless the pair was working together (and I immediately dismissed that conjecture from my mind), they were both in the clear as far as the cops figured. How fortunate for them that they had alibis. Most people can't reconstruct where they were days, let alone months ago.

I certainly couldn't.

269

I don't remember Detective Bradshaw's next words exactly, but they were something along the line of me seeing suspects around every corner, wasting valuable investigative time and resources, and long ago ceasing to be amusing.

"I'm a little uncomfortable how connected you seem to be to this case and all the players," he said. "First you're a journalist. Then you're a witness. Maybe we should be looking at you as a suspect."

Nick Garnett and Humphrey Bogart were right. Things are never so bad that they can't be made worse.

"I'm wondering"—Detective Bradshaw leaned back in his chair, resting his thumb and forefinger on his chin, as if giving the matter deep thought—"if I ought to be asking *you* for an alibi?"

I wasn't sure how to answer him. He couldn't be serious because he hadn't read me my rights. Then I recalled that unless a suspect is actually in custody, Mirandizing is unnecessary. In fact, sometimes police chat suspects up while continually assuring them they're free to leave.

"Free to leave" sounds comforting but has a specific legal connotation. In reality, the term is cop code for "we think you're guilty, but have no evidence to actually hold you and want to avoid freaking you into calling an attorney who will shut you down before you say something implicating yourself." Police routinely assure suspects they're free to leave to ensure they don't.

So as long as the words "free to leave" didn't leave Detective Bradshaw's lips, I could relax.

"So where were you when these homicides took place?" he asked.

Not expecting him to be quite so direct so soon, I stammered something about not having a clue where I was. "Do I need to check my calendar?"

I pretended to be quipping; I could tell he was more interested in my reaction to his question than my actual answer. Some cops believe that if a right-handed suspect looks up and to the right during questioning, he's telling the truth. If he looks up and to the left, he's lying. Or is it the other way around?

Since I wasn't sure, I thought it safest to stare straight ahead. And keep my mouth shut.

Detective Bradshaw also remained quiet, employing the old interrogation tactic of silence to elicit an answer.

A long thirty seconds of dead air followed. I was fairly certain of the time because in TV news, thirty seconds is a magic number. The length of a standard television commercial. It's also an uncomfortable length of time for two people to simply stare each other down.

I looked away, deciding to go first. "Just to play along with you, Detective, what possible motive would I have to kill this man? I never met him."

"Maybe you did it for ratings." His voice sounded humorless, his eyes held no twinkle, but I remained convinced he was joking. TV stations do a lot of crazy things in the name of ratings, believe me, I know, but murder isn't one of them.

Suddenly Detective Bradshaw smiled, like everything was fine and he had been just kidding all along. "You're free to leave, Ms. Spartz, but first I'm wondering if this belongs to you?"

Free to leave.

I didn't hear what he said afterward. Suddenly he was opening a small, manila envelope and shaking something into his hand. "We found it in the victim's grave."

He held up a piece of jewelry, wrapped in clear plastic, like potential evidence.

An opal brooch.

"Is this yours?" Detective Bradshaw repeated the question. His eyes narrowed as he noted my hesitation.

I reached for the brooch and fingered the smooth October birthstone. White mixed with flecks of pastel blues and pinks. The contemporary setting showed no sign of tarnish, so I guessed it must be white gold, not sterling silver. Finest quality, to be sure.

"It's lovely." I shook my head, handing the opal back. "But no, it's not mine."

I realized he only showed it to me so he might eliminate it as evidence. If I claimed the brooch, that lent a reasonable explanation to its presence in Mark's grave and he could discount its value. If it wasn't mine, it remained one more mystery.

Detective Bradshaw never asked me if I had any idea who the shiny bauble might belong to, so I didn't have to lie.

I'd already sent the police on one wild-goose chase after Sigourney. And I'd gone on my own with Chad. Neither had accomplished much except to make me look stupid or suspicious in the eyes of the cops. I could argue that the elimination of suspects is an important part of any homicide investigation. But Detective Bradshaw would probably argue that these people were my suspects, not his.

We could go back and forth that the murder victim's old girlfriend and workplace rival certainly should have been on the police's short list. But that wouldn't change how Detective Bradshaw was staring at me. Like he might be waiting for me to confess, or at least let something damning slip.

So that's why I didn't tell him whose brooch I suspected fell off while she was burying her fiancé in a shallow grave.

And since I was free to leave, I did.

CHAPTER 38

The cop shop was just a mile from my house, but instead of heading home, I drove through rush-hour traffic back to the station. I knew I wasn't the killer, so I didn't bother checking my calendar for an alibi. My time seemed better spent gathering evidence of the real killer. So I reached into the NEVER WORN raw-tape box, pulled out the dub of the rehearsal-dinner home video, stuck it into a viewing deck, and hit Play.

The tape was second-generation home video and not shot particularly well. For all the money the Posts threw into the wedding, the rehearsal dinner came without bells and whistles. I wondered if Mark's mother didn't want the in-laws paying for everything and insisted on footing that bill herself.

A young Post cousin trying out a brand-new camcorder shot the tape. A lot of zooming, panning, and focus issues. Fast-forwarding, I stopped the video whenever I saw the bride-to-be. I scanned Madeline in four different places on the tape—greeting a guest, walking through the dinner buffet, kissing Mark, and twirling to some music—before a shot was clear enough to see the brooch pinned to her dress. The video wasn't perfect, but the stone certainly looked like an opal, surrounded by white gold. I wished I had Detective Bradshaw's piece of evidence to compare. Vivian Post appeared to be wearing its twin, but the shots of her were too brief or too far away for a definitive answer.

The next morning Xiong froze the cleanest clip, enlarged it, and printed a copy. He handed it to me without even asking why. I took it to Noreen's office and handed it to her. She immediately asked why.

To call the picture a smoking gun would be an exaggeration as well as a cliché. Noreen was enthralled by my premise, but had a practical concern: What if I was right?

"You tell me," I replied. "Her family's rich enough to cause trouble for us and the cops."

Miles was out of town, meeting with the network team in New York, but Noreen got him on speakerphone. I explained the situation, including my conversation with Detective Bradshaw.

"Wait a minute," Noreen said. "This part is news to me. Now the cops think you're the killer?"

"I don't think he really believes that," I said. "I think he's just messing with me to try to scare me off the investigation."

"I hardly think that tactic's likely to be successful," Miles said.

"We don't need any more messes," Noreen said. "This whole sweeps month has been one big mess."

She put her head down on her desk. Then she straightened back up, trying to look alert, but her eyes seemed dull—like she'd forgotten she was boss.

Television news is a business of people who live and work on the edge. They can snap at any time. You might think at the point journalists hit large-market or network newsrooms, the snappers would be weeded out. Not true. As audience size increases, so does the pressure. I wondered if Noreen was on the verge of snapping.

This May would be the last traditional sweeps month for the Minneapolis–St. Paul television market. The overnight numbers measure household ratings year-round—how many folks are watching the news. But advertisers are more interested in demographics—which station has the most women viewers or which newscast has the most young men. That helps companies decide where to run beer ads or dishwasher-detergent commercials. Getting that demographic data is difficult. Nielsen Media Research had always tracked individual viewing habits with paper diaries during special ratings months. The downside was viewers often wrote down what they thought they should watch, not what they actually watched, and they often forgot what they actually watched. Now Nielsen was pledging to monitor viewer demos year-round electronically.

Newsroom optimists say this will take the pressure off February, May, and November; newsroom pessimists figure it will just increase the pressure to produce big stories constantly. And increase the likelihood of snappers.

From Noreen's voice, Miles must have sensed something was off, so he picked up the bulk of the conversation. "Don't talk to this investigator anymore, Riley. If he wants to talk alibis, tell him to call me."

"Absolutely." I had no desire to play déjà detective with the White Bear Lake police. Free to leave or not.

"And meanwhile," Miles continued, "for the heck of it, even though you think that cop is just playing games . . .

check your calendar and assure me that someone can vouch for your whereabouts when these people died."

"You're kidding me, right?" Nick Garnett asked.

I shook my head. We were walking around the lower level of the Mall of America for some exercise, while at the same time I brought him up to speed on my encounter with Detective Bradshaw.

Garnett chuckled at my situation. "The two people who could verify your alibi for the night the groom vanished are dead? Both of them?"

"You know they are. You were there for part of it."

The first victim was ripped apart by a pit bull down the block from my house. The same dog had taken a bite out of Garnett as well.

About a week later, the second victim blew his brains out twenty yards away from me rather than face charges of being a serial killer.

Last November, both developments were good luck for me because both people wanted me dead. Their deaths were bad luck for me now when I needed their corroboration.

All I had were notes I'd made the previous October and a hidden-camera videotape Malik and I shot on the pet cremation story the same day our groom went missing. Yes, the notes and tape were dated, but I wasn't sure Detective Bradshaw would buy that as evidence any more than Malik would actually remember us working together that day.

Garnett smiled and took my hand in his as we walked. "Why don't you just tell them we spent the night together? I'm prepared to testify you never left my bed." He raised his other hand as if he was taking an actual oath.

I was halfway considering his offer until he suggested we

go back to his place and practice my alibi in case the prosecutor questioned him about what I looked like naked.

I snatched my hand away. "What about the L word? I thought you were so big on needing love. Suddenly it sounds like lust is all you need."

"I'm sorry, Riley," Garnett said. "For a moment, L stood for Lie. Which was what I thought you were asking me to do and that was sort of a turn-on."

"Well, turn it off." So much for fantasizing about him ending my virgin state.

We'd finished one lap around the mall, which meant six-tenths of a mile. I moved to take the escalator upstairs and walked the second level to avoid passing by the cinnamon-roll place again. I can only muster so much willpower.

"How about the mother murder?" Garnett asked. "That happened just a couple of weeks ago. Where were you then?"

I parodied Macaulay Culkin with my mouth wide open and one hand on each side of my face. No sound effects, though.

"Home alone?" Garnett said. "You've *got* to be kidding me. That's the best you can do? Better tell them you were with me that night, too."

"I'm actually not too worried, Nick." I tried sounding not too worried while saying that. "Because I know I'm not the killer. And I have no motive."

He closed his eyes and seemed to be counting to ten. As he opened them, he sighed deeply. "As an experienced homicide investigator, let me be frank, Riley. You knowing you're not the killer doesn't count. It's what the cops know that matters. And if your alibi stinks, they won't care so much about motive. Lots of psychopaths kill for no rational reason. Maybe the detective's right. Maybe you did do it

277

for ratings. A prosecutor would love arguing that and a jury would love deliberating that."

That's when I explained to him that the best way to prove I wasn't the killer was to find the real killer. A little extra incentive beyond ratings.

"Doesn't seem like that technique's been terribly successful for you," he observed.

He didn't name names, but I figured he was referring to the Chad and Sigourney episodes. "As much as you newsies like to talk about solving crimes, that doesn't happen real often."

There was some truth in what he said. Channel 3's career cop reporter has profiled twenty-two cold homicide cases—all still cold. But that doesn't mean she stops trying. And that doesn't mean we never succeed.

"If you recall," I said, referring again to my psychopathic adversary, "last fall I did find the real killer."

"No." Garnett shook his head. "Last fall the real killer found you."

Okay, he had me there. And not a subtle distinction, either. The difference between me finding the killer and the killer finding me could be the difference between life and death. Mine.

So I told him about the brooch.

And he told me to stay away from Madeline Post and let the cops do their job. Which was excellent advice, except nobody told Madeline Post to stay away from me.

CHAPTER 39

I was curled up at home on my couch, reading the melancholy "Fall of the House of Usher," when Madeline knocked on my door. I was at the part where the narrator begins to feel that he, too, is going mad. She could see me through the window, so while it was too late for me to pretend not to be home, I was determined not to let her cross my threshold.

I greeted her with some pleasantries about always being delighted to see her. "Let's go for a walk, Madeline. The weather's gorgeous."

Actually the sky was cloudy, the air damp.

"No, I'm cold," she said. "Let's stay in."

"I'll grab you a coat." I also grabbed Gracie to join us. By then I'd cleaned off Chad's blood and hair.

"What's that?" Madeline pointed to the award clutched in my hand.

"It's a weight I like to use when I'm out walking. I switch it from hand to hand to build muscle." I demonstrated for her.

279

"It's very unusual. May I see it?" She reached for my Gracie. By then we were on the path by the lake and other people were out and about, raking their yards and clearing the shoreline. With an abundance of witnesses, I handed my trophy over, but made sure not to turn my back on my walking companion.

"How striking," she said. "It's shaped in the abstract form of a woman." She swung it back and forth like I'd shown her. "Where did you get it? I'd like to buy two, one for each arm."

I mumbled something about it being a gift and switched the topic back to the weather. We walked for about a quarter of a mile before she asked if I thought the police would ever solve Mark's murder.

"I don't know, Madeline. Each case is different."

Before I always figured she was seeking reassurance that her case was important; now I wondered if she was really seeking information that she was reluctant to ask the police herself. I watched her face as I spoke, looking for clues. I couldn't come right out and ask to borrow her opal brooch, knowing she'd lost it. That would give everything away. Besides, she was still holding Gracie and I was unarmed.

"That the same gun was used in both murders makes some elements simpler and others more complicated," I said.

"What kinds of steps do you think authorities are taking in the investigation?" she asked. A natural enough question unless what she really meant was, How best can I continue to cover my tracks?

Evasion would only make her suspicious. So I reviewed Detective Bradshaw's drug money theory with her. I expected Madeline to embrace that idea enthusiastically to divert attention from herself; instead she nixed it.

"But, Madeline, you didn't know Mark all that long or

all that well. There's lots you might not know about him."

"I knew him well enough." Well, maybe she did. Maybe that's why she killed him. Maybe she knew he was a heel.

"Did you know he had a baby?" I wasn't going to tell her about baby Sven, but it just sort of slipped out because she sounded so smug about knowing her man.

Madeline stopped walking; Gracie slipped from her fingers and fell to the ground. Her thud left a depression in the dirt. I picked her up and wiped her off, glad to have her back in my hands.

"Tell me about this baby," Madeline said.

I kept the details sketchy. I didn't want to put Sigourney or her son in any danger. Jean Lefevre's murder still bothered me.

Madeline Post was steamed. She didn't say anything, but her gait was stiff and angry. We continued our walk past some boat slips to an old white gazebo in Matoska Park. She climbed up the steps, I followed, and we sat on a bench looking out over the lake. Madeline reached over, took Gracie from me, fidgeting nervously with her.

I found myself wondering if a sociopath could be created if she couldn't bond with anyone because everyone looked the same. I reminded myself to check back with Professor Vasilis for his take on that chilling hypothesis. From a layman's perspective, pulling a trigger might be easier, certainly less personal, if the victim was a blur instead of an individual. But if Mark's face was so very special to Madeline, that argument might make it even more difficult for her to kill him—unless she feared losing him anyway.

"Riley, do the police know about the child?" She startled me with her question.

"They investigated the mother as a possible suspect and appear to have eliminated her based on an alibi."

"That comedian had an alibi, too. Didn't he?"

"Alibis are the cornerstone of a homicide investigation. That and circumstantial evidence. Cops look at alibis for everyone connected to the victims."

Just then I got an idea of where to take this conversation for answers without making it confrontational.

"They might even ask you for an alibi, Madeline. I remember when we first met we talked about where you were after the rehearsal dinner, but run me through it again. How would you account for your whereabouts that night for the police?"

She paused before answering, as if thinking back to the night before her almost-wedding. "You mean my last normal night."

Madeline, Mark, her mother, and brother all had separate vehicles at the rehearsal dinner because they were coming from different directions and because three out of the four were too rich to worry about gas pushing four bucks a gallon.

I stopped her just then to clarify that Mark's car had never been found. Minneapolis police told me there'd been no traffic stops since his disappearance. And I figured Detective Bradshaw would have mentioned if the black Jeep had surfaced.

Madeline practiced her alibi by explaining that Vivian wanted her daughter to spend her last unmarried night back home at the Peninsula House. Her designer wedding gown was already there, waiting for her to slip it on the next morning.

But Madeline didn't go straight to the Post estate after the rehearsal dinner. She stopped at her condo first to water some plants and pack a few things, before driving out to the Peninsula House an hour or so later.

I swallowed as I did the math in my mind.

Madeline explained that Libby Melrose, her maid of honor, came over afterward and they giggled over old yearbooks for an hour or so. Then Libby left and Madeline fell asleep in her old bedroom. She woke up around seven, had a light breakfast with her mother while Roderick slept in. Then she began a flurry of appointments with a hairdresser, makeup artist, and other wedding professionals hired to come to the house.

She stopped talking and looked up as if daring me to challenge her litany.

"Sounds good to me," I said. But what I was really thinking was, Yep, Madeline had time to kill.

Something in my countenance must have given me away. Unfortunately, despite being profoundly face blind, Madeline could read body language and voice inflection, because suddenly she blurted out, "You don't believe me, do you?"

"I never said that," I replied.

"But you were thinking it, weren't you? You think it's me. You think I killed Mark."

First she looked shocked, then angry. And if looks were enough to kill, I'd be dead.

Then Madeline rushed down the gazebo steps without glancing back, like she never wanted to see me again. Which was fine on my end. Except she still had my trophy clutched in her hand.

I watched from the gazebo until a few minutes later when her trim figure disappeared from sight.

When I walked home, her Mercedes was gone from the street where I live, but one of my front windows was busted. And in the middle of my living room, in a pile of broken glass, lay Gracie.

283

CHAPTER 40

I didn't want to speak with Detective Bradshaw, so instead of calling the cops, I called my landlord who promised to fix the broken window the next day. I also didn't want to be alone that night, with just cardboard and duct tape between me and darkness, so I crashed on the couch in Channel 3's greenroom lest I become the victim in one last cover-up murder.

The greenroom is where news guests wait for their television appearance. It's a busy place an hour before each newscast; the rest of the time squatters from various station departments hang out for snacks, naps, and gossip. I slept fitfully because a couple of the overnight techies kept sticking their heads in to see if the couch was clear yet.

Just the day before, passing by the greenroom, I'd heard one of the assignment editors tittering that Noreen had left the station right after the six o'clock news to meet a mystery date. That was the first rumor I'd heard of our news director having a romantic life. Whether love made her easier or harder for the rest of the newsroom to endure remained an unknown. But unless I spotted Noreen blatantly flashing a ring on her finger, I wasn't about to utter the L word to her.

I also wasn't going to say a word to Madeline about our clash. Or my broken window. In fact, I wasn't going to say a word to Madeline about anything. But then I started to dream about the dead. Mark. His mother. And whatever Madeline's game was, I decided I had to play. For their sake.

So I left a message on her phone, saying something about journalists always playing devil's advocate and hoping she didn't take our conversation the other day seriously.

She didn't call me back, but her mother did.

"Madeline's not available." Vivian's voice sounded frosty. "She's out of town."

The Posts had several vacation homes. Madeline could be in Florida, New York, or on the West Coast, just for starters. The Caribbean and Europe were also possibilities. She might have figured it prudent to leave the country for a while.

"Do you know when she'll be back?"

"If she wanted you to know, I think she would have told you herself. It's probably best Madeline take a break from the media. She has a personal writing project she wants to pursue. A short story about heartbreak and betrayal."

I wondered if her story had a twist ending, perhaps involving the narrator as killer. Write what you know, they say. I tried gauging just how much Vivian knew about our fight. Plenty seemed a safe guess, considering their tight mother-daughter relationship.

"I think Madeline and I had a misunderstanding," I said.

"Madeline explained what happened," Vivian said. "She found it quite disconcerting that you would think her a murderer."

"Again, Madeline and I had a misunderstanding."

I wondered if Vivian had her own private suspicions about what happened to Mark. If I had a daughter, would I protect her at all costs, if I thought her capable of murder? Maybe.

So I didn't go into the details about why Madeline was about the only spoke left on my suspect wheel. If Vivian knew her daughter's opal brooch was missing, she might commission a new one to cloud the evidence.

Then it occurred to me that, under the process of elimination, Vivian showing me her brooch might be just as good as Madeline being unable to show me hers. Of course, I'd have to get it on tape.

"I want to return her wedding gown," I said. "I know how much it means to her and I'm not comfortable keeping it any longer."

I could hear Vivian breathing on the other end. She seemed to buy my ruse. "Why don't you bring the dress out to the Peninsula House and leave it with me. I'll see she gets it."

"I had hoped Madeline might do one last camera interview with me. Very short. Just to wrap things up."

"Thanks to you, we have a long list of reporters who want to interview my daughter. I'm afraid she's declining everyone."

I explained that in the media world, sometimes the best way to make a pack of journalists go away is to do one interview. The rest generally give up then, and move on to a new story.

"What if you just gave a statement, Vivian, about the toll this whole ordeal has taken on your family. That would be enough to wrap this story. You'd never hear from me again."

Sometimes journalists offer that option as a compromise if an interview subject is an amateur who doesn't want to be questioned, but we'd still like to hear from them anyway. I'd need to disclose that in the story, by saying something like "Vivian Post made the following statement . . ."

She didn't say no, but she didn't say yes, either. So I pressed a little harder. If she hung, she hung up. But somehow, during the next few minutes, Mrs. Post and I reached a deal. I'd stay clear of Madeline. And Vivian agreed to make an on-camera statement asking the public to allow their family privacy to grieve.

So before she could change her mind, Malik and I headed out to the Peninsula House in stop-and-go rush-hour traffic. On the way, I briefed him on what to expect.

"Best-case scenario, Malik, she shows us the opal brooch. That's the money shot." Or in our case, the murder shot.

Later, we could argue that because Vivian's brooch was accounted for, the brooch the police had in evidence must belong to Madeline. I'd already scripted a rough draft in my mind.

COULD A PIECE OF JEWELRY BE THE KEY TO SOLVING A MURDER? BURIED IN THE SAME GRAVE AS THE MISSING GROOM, POLICE FOUND A CUSTOM-MADE OPAL BROOCH . . . LIKE THIS ONE . . . WHICH BELONGS TO THE MOTHER OF THE BRIDE . . . THE ONLY OTHER ONE IN EXISTENCE . . . BELONGED TO THE BRIDE

HERSELF . . . WHO WAS
WEARING IT THE NIGHT
HER FIANCÉ DISAPPEARED.

"Okay, get shot of opal brooch," Malik said. "Got it."

"So after she makes her statement, while the camera's still rolling, I'll ask Vivian if she's aware police found an identical brooch buried with Mark."

Malik nodded that he understood the plan. "Got it."

"Now Vivian knows the only other such brooch is owned by her daughter. So there might be some fireworks when she realizes where we're going with this. But whatever happens, keep the camera rolling unless I tell you to stop."

Story subjects sometimes think they can order the camera stopped and started at whim during an interview. They can choose not to answer a question. They can choose to take off their microphone and stomp away. But they can't tell us when to turn off the camera. Sometimes they try, and those confrontations are virtually guaranteed to make air.

Normally I try to schedule interviews that might end with tension during the day so we can use natural light. That leads to a faster getaway. Otherwise we have to wait for our portable lights to cool down before packing up all the gear. That can get awkward.

But it was dark when we arrived at the Post estate, so we didn't have much choice. I hoped we could slip away after the interview while Vivian was on the phone screaming at her attorney to raise hell with my attorney.

The Post matriarch watched us pull up in our news cruiser. Her silhouette moved past the window as she disappeared briefly before opening the mansion door.

"It's Riley Spartz," I called. "Thanks for letting us come out, Vivian."

I introduced her to Malik as he pushed a cart of equipment into the house while I carried the tripod in one hand and Madeline's voluminous wedding dress in the other.

I expected her to be more excited when I handed over the gown, but she simply placed it over the back of a chair while we discussed where to videotape her statement. Then Vivian went upstairs while Malik set up the camera gear and tweaked the settings. She wanted to bring down a few jackets so we could decide which would look better on camera.

Meanwhile, I wandered over to the family photo corner to admire previous generations. One of their ancestors, who resembled Roderick, held an old revolver I recognized as similar to the one found at the scene of Jean Lefevre's death.

I didn't see the gun in the weapon display case, and couldn't recall if it had been there the last time I visited. Casually, I coaxed Malik over to videotape the old photograph. Just then Vivian came downstairs and noticed me pointing at the picture.

"I'll shoot it later," he whispered to me.

"There's not going to be any later," I whispered back. "As soon as this interview's over, we'll be asked to leave."

"Are we ready to begin?" Vivian's voice had enough of an edge that Malik and I moved back to the interview spot.

"Certainly." I tried distracting her. "Let's see those jackets of yours." I eliminated one immediately because it had a dark herringbone pattern and those sometimes strobe on camera.

Malik mounted the camera back on the tripod. Vivian went to the kitchen area, returned with a large glass of water, and took her seat. I'd picked a simple, straight-back chair for her interview so she wouldn't slouch, rock, or twist. Then Malik clipped a wireless microphone on Vivian's collar and hid the transmitter in an inside pocket of her blazer. She decided on black instead of navy or gray, all projecting classy images of grief.

Pinned to her lapel was the same emerald brooch she wore at the charity benefit the other night. I forced myself not to stare at it.

"Try to ignore the camera, Vivian, and just look at me. That way you'll appear more natural."

She took a sip from her glass, then delivered her line. "My family feels such sorrow for the loss of my daughter's fiancé. We just hope justice will bring us closure and that with privacy we can grieve."

A sincere enough sentiment, but her delivery seemed stilted. She must have realized that, because she repeated it. To try to elicit a more relaxed sound bite I asked if she ever imagined her family would be caught up in something so horrible.

"Never," she replied. "It just shows no family is safe from crime."

"And how is your daughter doing?"

"She's devastated. We feel such sorrow for the loss of her fiancé. We only hope justice will bring closure and that with privacy, we can grieve."

We both knew she nailed it.

Then I admired her emerald brooch. "Madeline tells me you two have quite the mother-daughter collection. I'd love to see it while we wait for the lights to cool."

Vivian looked uncomfortable. Like she was thinking, Damn it, I gave them their statement, why won't they leave?

"Please, Vivian. I'm an October birthday myself, how about just bringing out the opal? Please?"

Vivian did not seem flattered by my interest, but gave a

sigh of resignation. "All right, I'll just be a minute." She went back upstairs.

Malik and I looked at each other. "Money shot here we come," he whispered, giving me a thumbs-up.

"Quick, Malik, get some tape of that old revolver picture while she's gone. All we need is one shot we can freeze."

He pulled the camera off the tripod and moved to the corner of the room while I stood guard at the steps. Twenty seconds later he had it, and was back in position at the interview site.

Another minute passed when he suddenly yanked the camera off the tripod, grabbed my arm, and told me to run.

"What are you talking about?" I said. "We're not leaving until we get the good stuff."

"We're leaving while we still can, Riley. Hush."

He said the words in an urgent whisper that frightened me more than if he'd shouted them. So I played along as he pushed me to the front door where we watched Roderick driving our van into the garage.

I wasted a few seconds berating Malik for always leaving the keys in the ignition, before realizing I'd left my purse— and cell phone—back by the interview chairs.

"Hush. This way." Malik turned and we ducked down a hall in the opposite direction and found a small, cramped cubby in the kitchen. We crawled inside and shut the door. A dumbwaiter. Just like in the movies. Crouched, with the camera lodged between us, we rode up a floor because we didn't know what else to do.

Malik took his audio earpiece out of his ear and held it up to mine. We could both hear Vivian on the wireless microphone screaming for Roderick to "grab some weapons. They've figured it out and we can't let them escape."

I looked at Malik and he summarized her earlier remarks. "She thinks we must know she lost her brooch after she killed Mark."

Vivian killed Mark? Vivian's brooch was the missing one?

I started to tell Malik how sorry I was for getting us into this mess. After all, he had a wife and kids and a perfectly fine life outside of work. Then we heard Vivian discover her microphone was live and realize we were listening. And probably rolling.

"Find them" was the last command we heard before the mic went dead.

"Let's split up," I said.

Malik turned off his camera, ejected the tape, and gave it to me. I put it in my pocket, then told him to stay in the dumbwaiter while I tried calling for help. I found a telephone down the hall, a land line, but it was useless. One of the Posts must have taken an extension off the hook. That meant I needed to retrieve my cell phone from my purse.

On the way, I ran into Vivian. She carried an old double-barreled shotgun from the display case downstairs. Not far behind her, Roderick brandished a large sword, likely a Civil War family heirloom. Unsheathed, the blade reflected the colors of the room like a glimmering mirror of death.

"Find her friend," his mother instructed him. "I'll guard her."

I would rather be guarded by Roderick, but that didn't seem up for negotiation. He had a don't-blame-me-I'm-just-following-orders look on his mama's-boy face, and didn't even have the nerve to look me in the eye. Probably harder to do if you're not face blind. He seemed relieved to leave his mother with me and hunt for Malik himself.

I was still absorbing Vivian as murderer and struggling

to understand her reasoning. Even if Madeline and Mark's marriage went south . . . with a prenup, how bad could things have gotten? She'd even made that point. Clearly, I wasn't seeing the big picture in this homicide.

Vivian's white-knuckle grip on her shotgun reminded me to keep my priorities in the present, not the past. Or I'd have no future. If Vivian was capable of killing Jean Lefevre to cover up one murder, she was certainly capable of killing Malik and me. I suspected I was still alive because pulling the trigger now would leave too much evidence too close to home, as well as ruining the priceless Persian rug under my feet.

Vivian's eyes looked impersonal. Blind to my face. Blind to my fate. At that moment, I had no trouble believing she'd turned sociopathic, unable to bond emotionally because everyone looked the same. But while we waited, I tried to connect with her anyway. Because I really wanted to understand the choices she made. And if I was going to die, it seemed only fair to know why.

"Couldn't you just boycott the wedding?" I asked. "Or refuse to pay for it? Why did you have to kill him?"

"He wasn't a good match for Madeline," she replied. "I need to protect my daughter from foolishness."

"But Madeline loved him. Shouldn't her wishes count for something?"

Vivian justified homicide with a shrug and I began to suspect there was more to her motive than protecting her daughter. Probably some twisted logic to protect the family image.

"Oh, I understood her attraction." Vivian wore a mysterious Mona Lisa smile on her face. "How she was able to *see* him. Pick him out of a crowded room. Recognize him on the street."

293

Vivian's empathy seemed right on, probably because besides sharing a mother-daughter relationship, she and Madeline shared a bond of face blindness. But if Vivian truly appreciated how much Mark meant to Madeline, how could she have killed him?

"Vivian." Softly, I called her by her name to try to create the impression she and I were friends. "Help me understand what happened."

"Mark was too old for her." That came out of nowhere. And a difference of ten years seemed a made-up excuse to me until she finished her explanation. "He was a better match for me."

"You?" I regretted the word as soon as it left my mouth, especially the tone I used. A tone like that could get me shot.

"Now you're the one who doesn't understand, Ms. Spartz." She called me by my last name, most likely to clarify that we weren't friends. "You see, I was also able to see him."

Now Vivian had a sensual manner about her. "The experience was, in my daughter's words, *intoxicating*."

CHAPTER 41

She desired her daughter's lover. And her eyes were wide open the entire time she seduced him. As she described their hasty affair, she looked homicidal. I wanted to say, You can't kill me, Vivian, we've had dinner together. But she'd killed Mark, and they'd had sex.

She described how she'd never been attracted to anyone like she was to him. Certainly not her dead husband. That's why she'd never remarried. She had money. She had standing. She had children. What use did she have for a man when they all looked interchangeable?

Her philosophy held until Madeline brought Mark home to meet the family.

"He shook my hand and said, 'Pleased to meet you, Mrs. Post.' " Vivian paused briefly, savoring the memory. "I didn't realize how extraordinary he was until I left the room, came back a few minutes later, and there he was. I recognized him. I felt weak. And for the first time, I envied my daughter. She had something I'd never even known existed."

Vivian didn't seem to notice she was the only one talking. And as she rambled on, rationalizing her behavior, I thought of celebrities, politicians, and CEOs who risked everything for wanton desire.

"The Heart Wants What It Wants"—Woody Allen said it best to *Time* magazine, explaining his disgraced relationship with Soon-Yi, his lover's daughter.

Vivian must have known no good would come from her affair with Mark. She'd alienate her family. She'd endure ridicule from her friends. But none of that mattered. Because the heart wants what it wants.

"I couldn't take my eyes off his face," she continued. "Not then. And not even later."

Her voice dropped to a whisper, like she was confiding a dreadful secret.

"Sometimes, with a new lover, you sneak a peek below to look at him. With Mark, I didn't bother. I only—"

I interrupted her, because Vivian talking dirty was enough to make me risk a bullet just to change the subject.

"Did you give him the cash?" I asked.

She nodded. "I paid him to call off the wedding. But he reneged."

Even though she stood before me, holding an antique shotgun pointed at my heart, I had a hard time imagining a mother with so little love for her daughter. But Vivian continued to spin her tale like a politician defending a bridge to nowhere.

"He insisted he loved Madeline and wanted to marry her. And even threatened to tell her about us unless I tore up the prenup."

"So he was blackmailing you?" I could play along; I was skilled at telling people what they wanted to hear. "You were the real victim."

"Exactly." She seemed pleased to have gotten that point across.

"But wouldn't Madeline leave him then?" I needed to keep the conversation going. And honestly, I was no longer sure whether Vivian seduced Mark or whether he seduced her. Was Vivian an opportunity to be grabbed? Or was it the cash?

"Perhaps, but she'd also leave me. She was an adult with her own trust fund. Then I'd lose him and her."

And face. She didn't say the word aloud, but I'd have bet my life she was thinking it. The concept of social prestige can be a burden. Neither of us said anything, and for a second I thought Vivian had forgotten all about me as she seemed to be reliving those desperate days.

But then she astounded me . . . describing how she kissed Mark in the parking lot after the rehearsal dinner and whispered for him to meet her at Tamarack to sort things out.

"*You* kissed Mark in the parking lot?" Another plot twist, this story was turning into a Shakespearean classic of mistaken identity. "You know Madeline saw that kiss."

"But she didn't realize I was the other woman. That's why Mark came to Tamarack. He wanted to get our story straight."

"And did you?"

"That became irrelevant. He told me he'd made a mistake. Both with me and with the money. Claimed he wanted neither. Then he joked about our relationship and said he just wanted to call me Mom."

Vivian's voice choked. "He made it clear that it was over between us. Those were his exact words. 'It's over between us.' I couldn't have agreed more. So I shot him."

Because I was looking at Vivian down the barrel of another gun, I kept my mouth shut. But something must have made her need to further justify pulling the trigger on Madeline's fiancé. Her next words felt rehearsed, like she'd told herself the same thing over and over to solidify her talking points.

"I did it to protect my daughter. He couldn't be trusted."

She explained how Mark dropped to his knees, clenching his hands against his chest, blood spurting through his fingers in the moonlight. The point I think she was trying to make with all that vivid detail was that she was an excellent shot and I was doomed.

Then she described burying him in the woods, saving his face for the last shovel of dirt.

"I still can't forget it." She shook her head. "His face was amazing."

I was about to ask her if she knew, or even cared, that Mark was still alive for that last ceremonial scoop of earth when we heard a loud noise outside, and she motioned me to move over by the fireplace. I pretended not to notice my purse lying on the couch because I didn't want Vivian to notice my cell phone clipped to the strap.

"You're the only one I've ever told this to," she said. Great, I thought, a murderous gal pal. But the longer I kept her talking, the longer I stayed alive. Just call me Scheherazade—storyteller by exigency.

"But what about Roderick?" I asked. Clearly he was an accomplice tonight. How about back then?

"Yes, my sweet boy. I told Roderick that Mark tried to rape me. He agreed it was best to keep such unpleasantness from his sister."

So Roderick helped his mother dispose of Mark's Jeep. First by hiding it in a storage locker. Then, when the ice started freezing, they rigged the accelerator to drive onto a rural lake and watched the vehicle crash through and sink.

"So who killed Jean Lefevre? You or him?"

"Actually you did," Vivian answered.

My stomach cramped slightly because I knew where she was going with this.

"You gave me the idea," she said. "I couldn't risk that Mark hadn't left some clue in those boxes betraying our relationship."

Maybe I had some culpability, but now was not the time to beat myself up. I needed to concentrate on the danger before me.

"He initially broke up with me in a note," Vivian continued. "Imagine that. It read, 'It's over. This is the end.' I thought it only fitting I leave that note by his mother's body."

That explained the blue "suicide" note in Mark's handwriting. As I'd suspected, the second homicide was a cover-up murder. Just as mine and Malik's would probably be. This was the part of her confession where Vivian seemed most proud and crazed. By making Mark a suspect, she explained, she ensured no one would consider him a victim.

"They could put his picture out on TV all they wanted," she said. "They'd never catch him."

"How are you going to stage it for me and Malik?" I whispered. "Make it look like an accident or a murder-suicide? Or are we both just going to disappear?"

Unexpectedly, Roderick entered at the far side of the room. Unarmed. I hoped that didn't mean he'd used the sword on Malik. I was reminded of the similarity of their physical features. They were even wearing comparable dark jackets. But from the look on Roderick's face, it was clear that this heir to the family fortune would never be an ally to me. And that represented an important difference.

An idea flashed in my mind and before Roderick could speak, I did.

"Malik, look out!" I shouted, purposely calling Roderick by the wrong name. "She has a gun!"

Confused, as well as face blind, Vivian pointed the shotgun and pulled the trigger. The blast hit Roderick full in the face and he collapsed. He could only moan and bleed and thrash around on the floor.

Vivian resisted firing the second chamber into the body of her wounded son. Not because she realized she'd shot the wrong man but more likely because she was saving that final round for me.

Amazingly, Roderick was still alive, but barely. If the shot had been fired any closer, he'd be dead. "He won't die if we call for help." I tried to explain who she'd actually wounded. But she wouldn't listen and screamed for me to stop talking.

She picked Madeline's wedding gown off a chair and shook it so angrily I thought the sparkles around the bodice might fall off. "This is what started all the trouble." She threw the dress in the fireplace and tried igniting it with a fancy long-handled butane lighter.

Besides trying an awkward maneuver while balancing a shotgun, Vivian was having other problems. I'd done enough consumer investigations to know that most fabrics these days are flame retardant, so I wasn't surprised when the dress stubbornly refused to burn.

Vivian grabbed a bottle of booze from a built-in liquor cabinet and doused the gown with alcohol. A flick of the lighter. Flames. She waved the gun and burning dress in my face like the scene in *The Wizard of Oz* when the Wicked Witch asked, "How about a little fire, Scarecrow?"

She laughed when I backed up a couple of steps to escape the satin heat. I grabbed the glass of water she'd left on the table during the interview and threw it on the dress and on

Vivian, hoping to douse the blaze. But the glass must have contained vodka, because the gown exploded, along with the shotgun and the mother of the bride.

While Vivian didn't cry out "I'm melting," her dying screams were horrible to hear.

Like Dorothy regarding the Witch, I didn't mean to kill her. But I had no time for pangs of guilt. Though the wedding dress had been slow to burn, the old house was not. The velvet drapes, lace tablecloths, polar bear skin, and dry timber ignited like priceless treasures in many a gothic mansion.

Flames blocked my escape route and smoke filled the stately room. I hoisted a fancy antique chair and threw it out a floor-to-ceiling window overlooking the lake. The good news, the glass shattered; the bad news, the sudden influx of oxygen fueled the fire.

I dropped to the floor because it's easier to breathe down low. I know because I once did a fire-safety story called "Getting Out Alive." But this was no staged drill. My left hand felt sticky and I realized the window glass had cut my palm; my face felt sticky and I realized I'd also been hit by scattered shotgun pellets. I ignored the blood. As I stretched my arm around on the seat of the couch, I found my purse and unclipped my cell phone.

I speed-dialed Garnett and reached . . . his voice mail.

"Help!" I cried. "The Peninsula House is burning! And I think I love you." Then I started coughing, so I crawled back to the window, stood, and jumped.

The water was cold and dark and deep.

My muscles contracted as I fought to break the surface. When I finally crashed through, I gasped for air as debris from the fire hit the water around me. A figure appeared at the window, crouching, seemingly burning alive, before falling forward like a human torch. Roderick or Malik? I couldn't be sure. They were the only ones inside still alive.

Please God, let Roderick have had enough life left to meet his death by fire and water instead of a mere gunshot wound. Please, I prayed, don't let the flaming silhouette be my cameraman coming back to look for me.

I dove under and swam toward the center of the lake as far as one breath would take me. Then another. And another. Treading water, I watched the Peninsula House burn. And listened. I heard no other splashing, no sound of anyone else in the water.

My clothes started dragging me down. So I kicked off my shoes. Then unbuckled my belt and wrestled out of my jeans, leaving bikini briefs.

My sweater, a pricey cashmere, not an ugly wool, was harder to let go. Luckily, I wore a bra, so even if I didn't survive, at least my nude body wouldn't wash up on White Bear Beach or be discovered by one of my TV competitors during the bass fishing contest tomorrow.

I was also thankful sharks were not native to White Bear Lake because my hand was still bleeding. I floated on my back and tried to calculate the temperature of the water and how long before hypothermia might claim me. Flames shot through the roof of the crumbling mansion. The fire lit up the entire shoreline—like Manderley along the horizon in Daphne du Maurier's *Rebecca*.

In my mind, Mrs. Post became the infamous, villainous Mrs. Danvers. But then the housekeeper seemed a simple pawn and the narcissistic title character a better match.

The heart wants what it wants.

Still on my back, I started kicking in the direction of the conflagration when I heard the sound of emergency vehicles.

CHAPTER 42

As my kicks slowed, I started to sink and crashed my head on something hard beneath the surface—some kind of metal box with a pole attached. Clinging to the pole, I braced my feet on top of the box, like a platform. My chin barely stuck out of the water, but the relief of rest felt good.

I recalled Russ Nesbett saying the water was around sixty-five degrees, of course that was with the sun shining. He also talked about losing body heat faster by swimming or treading water. My odds of making it back to shore were lessening, though as long as I hung on to the box, I might last another hour. But my fingers were numb. And rescue unlikely.

For courage, I closed my eyes and tried conjuring up my dead husband's face. But I couldn't see him. It was like *I* was face blind. Instead, I saw Jean Lefevre and wondered if her face was a sign that I deserved to die. And I pondered what it would be like to touch the face of God.

So with one hand, I let go of the pole to contemplate

my future. Swim or stay. My life didn't flash before my eyes, but my regrets did. One of them was my husband. And suddenly I remembered what Hugh looked like and I *could* see his face and I sensed now was not my time.

My eyes opened and I reminded myself of a lesson learned months earlier: you are not responsible for the actions of a psychopath.

So I clenched the pole with both hands, even though my thumb and forefinger didn't want to stay curled, and reevaluated my options for survival. A light reflected across the water. I figured the moon was fighting its way through the smoke. Go, moon, I rooted. I heard a hum that turned into the sound of motor, and then saw the outline of a boat.

"Help!" I called for help, but the cold garbled my words. Waves splashed over my face. I tried raising my arms and fell off the platform. I kept kicking. Splashing. Yelling. Even though much of it was unintelligible. A search light reached for me, followed by officers from the Ramsey County Water Patrol. They fished me out, wrapped me in a tarp, and poured me a steaming cup of coffee.

My teeth chattered, and I couldn't talk. I couldn't hold the cup, so coffee spilled on my thigh but didn't even hurt, though a blister formed.

Then I saw Malik on board and I knew his was not the burning body at the window. I wanted to cry but my eyes were too cold for hot tears.

"You're a mess," he said.

He rubbed his hands against mine while explaining that, just one step ahead of Roderick, he spotted a canoe on the shore and raced for it. He and his pursuer dueled briefly, sword against camera. Sword had the advantage, but Malik, like most television news photographers, had strong shoulders and quite good reflexes.

"I knocked the sword out of his hand and whacked him good with the camera." Then Malik pushed the canoe into the lake, climbing aboard when the water reached his waist. "Roderick threw the sword at me, but I ducked."

With a splash, it sank.

And without a paddle, Malik floated in the canoe until the water patrol found him.

"So I out-escaped you."

ENDS UP, NICK Garnett summoned the fire department and water patrol after just missing my phone call, listening to his voice mail, and hearing a splash at the end of my message about the Peninsula House burning.

Splash.

The last sound my new cell phone made as it hit the water and died. Splash saved my life.

My water rescuers wanted to transport me to Regions Hospital in St. Paul because my skin was sort of bluish, but I insisted they just take me home.

First under a hot shower, now huddled beneath a down comforter, dressed in flannel pajamas with the thermostat cranked, I listened to the phone messages on my land line.

The first, from Channel 3, calling about a big fire in White Bear Lake and wanting me to do a live shot. "We'll catch you on your cell," the assignment desk concluded the call.

Lotsa luck, I thought to myself.

The second call, also from the station, wanted to know where the hell I was and why I wasn't answering my cell phone.

"Because it's on the bottom of White Bear Lake." This time I said the words out loud, a sign that my body was thawing.

The third call came from a steamed Noreen. "It is unacceptable for you to be out of reach, particularly when a major spot news story is breaking in your backyard." The slam following her message said plenty.

"Oh, Noreen, you have no idea just how major."

My voice had a smug tone now, a sign that my mind was thawing.

I wrapped the comforter tight around me, heading for the kitchen to reward myself with hot milk. I caught the big smile on my face in a wall mirror, anticipating the exclusive I was poised to break.

Nothing sells a news story like murder, mansions, and money.

My smile broadened.

That's when I realized the videotape evidence of Vivian confessing to killing Mark and plotting to kill Malik and me was at the bottom of White Bear Lake.

"COULD ALWAYS BE worse." As soon as I opened the door Garnett wrapped his warm body around my cold one. "Could be your body down there, too."

"I suppose I should thank you for my life." I murmured the words in his ear, a sign that perhaps my heart was thawing.

"No need for verbal thanks," he said. "You were my catch of the day. But if you're in a chatty mood, let's talk about what you said in that message."

"You mean, 'help'?" I asked.

"No," he said, leading me over to the couch. "The other part."

"You mean about the fire?"

"No. The part about the L word."

The L word. Love. Coming back to haunt me. "I was

306

hysterical," I explained, "and didn't know what I was saying."

"Because you thought you were going to die?" he pressed.

"Yes! That's it," I agreed. "I thought I was going to die."

"Good. Because dying declarations are considered truth and can be used as evidence in a court of law if the utterer believes she won't survive."

Before I could appeal his legal interpretation, he kissed me hard, and I kissed back. And I didn't mind him touching me.

BUT THE NEXT morning, when I rolled over and found Nick Garnett asleep beside me, I realized that the night before had not been a dream and might very well have been a mistake.

Again, I was no longer a virgin, but that didn't bother me; that actually seemed a positive development. But did last night redeem me or imprison me?

What if Garnett rolled over and asked me to marry him? If the L word nettled me, the M word might wreck me. So I picked my flannel pjs up off the floor, and walked to the kitchen so I'd be out of reach and earshot when he woke up.

307

EPILOGUE

Turns out, what I clung to in the frigid water while the Peninsula House burned was a metal cage containing a state-record largemouth bass. Authorities marked the fish with a small V clip in one fin, put it back, and kept it under visual surveillance from the shore.

The next morning, they observed two men reel the cage into their boat and throw it back overboard. Hours later, the men turned in a record size largemouth bass to the fishing contest to claim fame and a half million dollars.

The fish had a V clip in one fin.

Besides disqualifying the men from the competition, authorities arrested them for fraud. The Animal Liberation Front staged a giant protest at the fishnappers' first court appearance. Toby and Husky were guests on the *Today* show, talking about animal rights.

One of the fish culprits was Tom McHale, which helped explain why our station received the phony fishnapper letter. The general manager fired Tom for violating the morals clause in his contract, which actually worked out well because our network owners were poised to slash newsroom staff as soon as May sweeps ended. Cutting Tom's salary meant saving jobs.

Because no definitive proof existed that the recovered fish was actually Big Mouth Billy, authorities were unable to charge him with theft and vandalism. But because it is currently the largest largemouth bass ever caught in Minnesota, Underwater Adventures displays the fish proudly and huge crowds form to watch as it swims around the aquarium.

But that fish tale wasn't even the lead news story of the day. The body of Roderick Post was found floating in White Bear Lake by one of the other fishing contestants. His mother's charred remains were discovered in the ruins of the historic manor.

The death of her mother and brother made Madeline Post the wealthiest woman in the state.

When I tried to explain what happened in the Peninsula House on that fateful night, Madeline didn't believe me and accused me of making it all up for ratings.

An ironic twist, because Miles refused to let me broadcast the story of the murderous Post matriarch since I had no proof. All the evidence was underwater or in ashes. And this libel lawsuit was one Miles and Noreen didn't want to risk.

I argued, unsuccessfully, that you can't libel the dead. And while that's generally true, Channel 3 didn't want to gamble a drawn-out, expensive legal fight with the estate. And Madeline Post made it clear she'd see us in court forever if we besmirched her family's reputation. And right then, in the middle of a media financial meltdown, she had deeper pockets than the station.

The local authorities weren't about to take the word of

a brassy TV reporter over that of an influential heiress. So the Peninsula House blaze was dismissed as a tragic electrical fire.

Noreen didn't care. I'd found Big Mouth Billy.

That should have been the stuff legends (and ratings) are made of. But Channel 3 finished a distant second in the May sweeps. And in the world of television news, you're only as good as your last story. And a station is only as good as its last ratings book.

So to bolster a warm and fuzzy public image, Channel 3 gave the $10,000 reward to a nonprofit group that teaches inner-city kids to fish.

Despite, or perhaps because of, its now lurid watery reputation, the town of White Bear Lake landed the Governor's Fishing Opener for the following walleye season.

LITTLE SVEN NELSON'S DNA matched that of Mark Lefevre. So his mother collected the $98,000 found in the safe-deposit box as well as Jean Lefevre's modest estate. Soon after, Sigourney received a note that an anonymous benefactor had set up a college fund for her son.

THE RULE OF Chekhov's gun came into play. If a writer shows a gun in the first act, the weapon must go off in the third. The same appears true of wedding gowns.

No, I wasn't the bride.

Not even a bridesmaid.

I was cast as a dogsmaid at Noreen and Toby's wedding. The happy couple picked their favorite pets as best dog and dog of honor. I escorted Freckles, Noreen's dalmatian, down the aisle, followed by Noreen.

At the reception, instead of a bouquet, Noreen threw a steak bone with a white ribbon to the drooling canine attendants. Channel 3 ran a clip on the late news that went viral on YouTube. Because if there's anything viewers love, it's animals and weddings.

FROM NICK GARNETT, I got a reprieve instead of a proposal.

After our close encounter, he cornered me in the kitchen, insisting we needed to talk. Then Nick proceeded to tell me he'd accepted a strategy job with Homeland Security in Washington, D.C., and was due to start within a week. He felt the people currently fighting terror couldn't fight marshmallows, and that protecting a shopping mall was unfulfilling compared to protecting our country.

Days later, I drove him to the airport where he kissed me goodbye like Bogart kissed Bergman in *Casablanca*, 1942.

Except, instead of embracing on the tarmac with propeller engines as exotic background noise, we bid farewell in front of a line of travelers zipping their liquids into plastic bags and hoisting their purses and briefcases onto the X-ray machine belt.

His lips lingered, so I urged him to get on that plane or he'd regret it. Then I assured him we'd always have White Bear Lake. And he assured me he had plenty of frequent-flier miles.

MADELINE POST NEVER married, but wrote a bestselling memoir, *Faceless in a Crowded World*. I went to one of her book signings, but she didn't recognize me.

ACKNOWLEDGMENTS

My closest readers are dear friends. While not novelists, they know what makes a good story. Sometimes I think Kevyn Burger understands my protagonist better than I do. And I'm not sure how it happened, but while talking with Trish Van Pilsum, I suddenly realized the key motivation for *Missing Mark*. As usual, Caroline Lowe, Alan Cox, and Michele Cook all offered valuable feedback on cops, craft, and character for my sequel.

The folks at Doubleday are a fabulous bunch. I thank my editor, Stacy Creamer, for her initial skepticism, which improved my plot, and her steady support thereafter; Laura Swerdloff for her customary attention to detail, editing oversight, and intuitive ability to calm me; production editor Mark Birkey; Lauren Panepinto for cover design; Karla Eoff for copyediting; Lauren Lavelle for publicity; Jillian Wohlfarth and Adrienne Sparks for marketing; Karen Ninnis for proofreading; and the rest of the Doubleday team. It takes a village to launch a book.

My agent, Elaine Koster, a literary beast, and her associate, Stephanie Lehmann, made things happen for me on lots of levels.

Practical Homicide Investigation by Vernon Geberth, and *Forensics for Dummies* by Dr. D. P. Lyle provided valuable research. Texas K-9 instructor Billy Smith; Clearwater, Kansas, Police Chief Kim Demars; and Lakeville, Minnesota, K-9 officer Beth Eilers shared knowledge about dogs and their noses.

Special thanks to Catherine Nicholson for her generous use of the Bigelow House as a crime scene, and to the residents of White Bear Lake for being good sports.

International Thriller Writers, Sisters in Crime, and Mystery Writers of America offered me reassuring author camaraderie. My friends from the desperate world of TV news offered inspiration.

As far as family goes, some members earned their way into the acknowledgments by their special skills: Galen Neuzil shared his knowledge of bass fishing; Michael Kramer first alerted me to the existence of the corpse flower.

But all deserve deep thanks because they demonstrated their own personal popularity by spreading the word of *Stalking Susan* and bringing friends to book signings: Ruth Kramer and her red-hat ladies; George and Shirley Kimball and their church gang; Rosemary and Don Spartz and their Lake Summerset neighbors; Mae Klug and my entourage of cousins; Jerry and Elaine Kramer; Joe and Delores Spartz; Tom and Rena Fitzpatrick; Jerry and June Kimball; and Lorraine Kehl.

Thanks also to Bonnie and Roy Brang; Teresa and Galen Neuzil, with Rachel; Richard and Oti Kramer; Mary Agnes Kramer; Steve and Mary Kramer, with Matthew and Elizabeth; Kathy and Jim Loecher, with Adriana and Zack; Mike Kramer; Christina Kramer; Jenny and Kile Nadeau, with Daniel; Rebecca Nadeau; David Nadeau; Jessica and Richie Miehe; George Kimball and Shen Fei, with Shi Shenyu (Huan); Nick Kimball; Mary and David Benson, with Davin; Steve and Moira Kimball, with Craig; Paul Kimball; James Kimball; Vicky Blom (the first person I knew to have a Kindle); and friends in the Adams, Minnesota, area going back 130 years.

Much deserved hugs to my terrific kids, Alex and Andrew, of whom I'm so proud in so many ways; Katie and Jake Kimball, who make such a great couple; and Joey and David Kimdon, with Aria and Arbor in tow.

And always, Joe.